The critics love *Rich in Love!*

"To read Josephine Humphreys is to anticipate with pleasure each new page. Hardly a paragraph goes by without a surprising image, a memorable turn of phrase, an arresting insight."
—*The Detroit News*

"Both breathtaking and heartbreaking . . . A perfect tale of the effect of time, place, and the family on the fate of the individual"   —Carolyn See

"Engaging, bright, and resonant"
—*Kirkus Reviews*

"A fine and moving work . . . Will have you laughing out loud at times while at other times feeling a lump form in your throat."   —Gloria Naylor

"As perfect as an egg . . . Its first-person narrator, 17-year-old Lucille Odom, is so vivid and endearing that she belongs up there with Holden Caulfield. . . ."
—*New Woman*

"An astonishing and delightful little miracle of a book!"
—Robb Forman Dew

"Josephine Humphreys's qualities as a writer are not at all top secret. Sly humor, a flair for evocative scene-setting, and deeply felt compassion are certainly among them. But her ability to turn storytelling into an absorbing celebration of thinking and caring—and the myriad ways of loving and remembering—is certainly the most obvious of them all."
—*San Jose Mercury News*

"It is not often that a good first novel is followed by an even better second one, but that is the happy case in *Rich in Love*."
—*USA Today*

"Grains of startling truth are scattered across the pages, and the sense of discovery—the joy—one feels at finding them is reason enough for reading *Rich in Love*."
—*Kansas City Star*

"An excellent novel about all that messy pain and accumulating joy we experience in loving other people"
—*Houston Chronicle*

"From beginning to end . . . Lucille is a terrific narrator. . . . This is Josephine Humphreys's doing, of course, though it's all so very well done that Lucille seems to have a mind of her own and it's hard to remember there's a novelist at work behind it all. Humphreys's story is absorbing; her prose is engaging, risky, and virtually without false steps."
—*St. Louis Post-Dispatch*

"Even if *Rich in Love* did not possess its strong characters, entrancing story line, and vigorous outlook, it would still be interesting because its author is a dazzling stylist."
—*The New York Times Book Review*

CONTEMPORARY AMERICAN FICTION

RICH IN LOVE

Josephine Humphreys's first novel, *Dreams of Sleep* (available from Penguin), won the 1985 Ernest Hemingway Foundation Award from PEN for a first work of fiction. A graduate of Duke University, she lives in Charleston, South Carolina, with her husband and children.

Rich in Love

Josephine Humphreys

PENGUIN BOOKS

PENGUIN BOOKS
Published by the Penguin Group
Viking Penguin Inc., 40 West 23rd Street,
New York, New York 10010, U.S.A.
Penguin Books Ltd, 27 Wrights Lane,
London W8 5TZ, England
Penguin Books Australia Ltd, Ringwood,
Victoria, Australia
Penguin Books Canada Ltd, 2801 John Street,
Markham, Ontario, Canada L3R 1B4
Penguin Books (N.Z.) Ltd, 182–190 Wairau Road,
Auckland 10, New Zealand

Penguin Books Ltd, Registered Offices:
Harmondsworth, Middlesex, England

First published in the United States of America by
Viking Penguin Inc. 1987
Published in Penguin Books 1988

LIBRARY OF CONGRESS CATALOGING IN PUBLICATION DATA
Humphreys, Josephine.
Rich in love.
I. Title.
[PS3558.U4656R5   1988b]   813'.54   88-5852
ISBN 0 14 01.0283 3

Printed in the United States of America by
R. R. Donnelley & Sons Company, Harrisonburg, Virginia
Set in Stempel Garamond
Designed by Ann Gold

FOR HARRIET

With thanks to the

John Simon Guggenheim Foundation,

and to my family and friends.

C H A P T E R

1

On an afternoon two years ago my life veered from its day-in day-out course and became for a short while the kind of life that can be told as a story—that is, one in which events appear to have meaning. Before, there had been nothing worth telling the world. We had our irregularities; but every family has something or other out of whack. We had my mother's absent-mindedness, my sister's abnormal beauty, my father's innocence; and I was not without oddities of my own. We were characters, my friend Wayne said. But nothing about us was story material.

Until the day, May 10, when one of us betrayed the rest and set off a series of events worth telling.

I rode my bicycle home from school. All looked normal. I sniffed: high spring, Carolina, health and prosperity. People were shopping like crazy in stores along the highway. Plants were growing in the median, big sturdy weeds that looked a lot like carrots and celery, with thick stalks and ferny leaves dense enough to hide the underlying road trash. Traffic was a carefree stream of cars. The afternoon was average and happy, to the eye of a casual observer.

Supposedly your hair stands on end in the instant before you get struck by lightning. I had a similar sensation that

afternoon on the highway. I recognized the tingle as a premonition but a useless one: no specific details, only the feeling. Feelings were a problem to me at the time. I was prey to
them, and yet I could never tell exactly what they meant.
They seemed uselessly vague. For example, what good is a
premonition (*advance warning*, by the Latin root) if it doesn't
say what you are being warned against? I looked around me.
I rubbed my upper lip, a habit of nervousness.

Seventeen years old and in possession of a valid driver's
license, I could have been driving my mother's VW camper—
she didn't drive it much—or my father's Buick—his license
had been temporarily suspended for speeding. But I preferred
the open air and the way the afternoon spread out around me
with its sounds and smells. I could form a good idea of where
I was, whereas in a car I couldn't quite get the feel of a place
except as a sort of television show sliding flat past the window, dull as advertising. My sister Rae felt like I did on the
subject, only she didn't ride a bike anymore. She had a
twenty-year-old Impala convertible, a car as huge and smooth
as a parade float. Because it opened up, you could ride in it
and still feel the scenery. She had driven herself to Sweet Briar
College in that car four years in a row, and then to Washington, D.C., where she worked for a U.S. senator. When
the car malfunctioned, she cussed it up and down. "The salesman said this car runs like a dream, Lucille," she said in her
joke Southern voice, easygoing and high. "But I swear he
must have been thinking of those dreams adolescent boys
have. The engine overheats and the thing revs up and then
sputters and spits and cuts off." But she loved the car. She
had never had a pet or a doll in her life, and when the Impala
came along, I guess it filled a void.

I liked Rae's car fine, but the bicycle was better for me
because it was quiet. I liked to travel silently.

Where I rode, the old zones of country, town, and city had

run together. Originally we had the city of Charleston, the town of Mount Pleasant, and then the country, but now they were jumbled, haphazard as a frontier settlement. This new section of highway had been laid out with no regard to pre-existing roads, and some of the old roads came up to the highway and dead-ended in striped barricades. Wild animals, to judge by the carcasses, had not yet adjusted to the new system. Out in the developments, some of the new roads curved back upon themselves, and I sometimes lost my sense of direction trying to get somewhere; or I might be riding along and all of a sudden the smooth asphalt turns to soft dirt and I'm in the country, with wooden houses balanced on concrete blocks, and the tragic crowing of roosters, and the black people on porches, innocent as natives.

It was as if new places had been slapped down over the old ones, but some of the old was still showing through. I tried not to lose myself in those pockets. It could sometimes be too much for me, a house at the edge of a field, the rim of pines, the smoke. It wrenched my heart. There was too much emo-tion for me in the country.

Every so often I'd run across what I called a dream house, one that somebody had started but never finished. They were scattered through the woods like ruins of a defunct civiliza-tion, but they were only the ruins of defunct families. Some-body had wanted a house, and had gotten as far as slab and walls; but then the money had run out, or the wife had run out, and all that was left was a cinderblock shell, the house a dream of itself, square-eyed and black-mouthed. Soon weeds would hide it, snakes and raccoons find shelter in it. When-ever I saw one, I stopped by the side of the road and stood leaning on my bicycle to look.

Sometimes out there I would get the hollow feeling. I called it loneliness, though I knew it wasn't exactly loneliness be-cause I was the type of person that likes solitude. But maybe it was pre-loneliness, or loneliness anticipated. Whatever it was, it was hollow and sad. Had I known someone who had died? I couldn't think of anybody. My grandparents had died before I knew them well enough to grieve their loss.

Rae was never lonely.

In high school she had been friends with all the boys and more than friends with more than a few, but she had never paired up with one. She had never acted in love like most girls do, and thank goodness. Rae was on her own. She was well-known as wild, although she was actually conservative when it came to drinking, drugs, and sex. But she had an unpredict-ability of the sort that distinguishes an untamed creature from a domestic one. People were in awe of her because she was so brave. She sang with a black band and had a black best friend. She laughed whenever she wanted to. She was Miss Wando High and had left a trail of stammering boys behind her. Her looks were unnerving, brown eyes and blond hair.

But I knew her better than anyone did, and I knew the little shiver that now and then came across her mouth. Recently her postcards from Washington had worried me; the hand-writing had changed, loosened, and risen off the horizontal like a child's. I was pretty good at analyzing handwriting, and I could discern three things in Rae's: kindness, strength, and future disappointment. Women like Rae sooner or later run into disappointment because beauty has given them a height-ened awareness of themselves. It isn't vanity. It is high hopes and optimism. Think of starlets, how they begin and how they end.

From Wando High to Mount Pleasant was straight unin-terrupted shopping with no letup, a hive of purchasing activ-ity that was reassuring. I was a poor shopper myself, too easily baffled by the array of goods. In malls I became overstimulated and wound up taking a seat in the community service area watching cloggers or the kids' poster contest. So if I really wanted something I tried to buy it out of a catalog or at a yard sale, and once I even stole a lipstick rather than go through the process of legitimate purchase. Kleptomania did not strike me as a weird disorder: I could imagine ethics outweighed by desire. But methodical shopping as a daily activity was beyond me, and I was always impressed on this highway by the hordes of people stocking up on new shoes, blue jeans, groceries, hamsters, mini-vans, tomato plants, sheets of plywood, ice-cream cones. The level of shopping was an indicator, in my opinion, of human trust in the future. I myself sometimes woke up in the middle of the night scared to death. When I tried to pinpoint the fear, nothing logical came to mind. All I could come up with was the end of the world, but nobody else feared that. Look at them swarming into the Garden Centre, coming out with flats of two-tone petunias and soaker-hoses!

But I had that tingling. Maybe ordinary life can continue only so long before the extraordinary will pop into it. I didn't know where it might come from, but I was prepared. I admired the Boy Scouts (though I didn't know one personally) for their "Be Prepared" motto. Good advice. I kept my head down. The most immediate danger I could think of was from trash. If I hit a bottle or a shoe I might swerve into traffic, most of which was people my age heading for the beach.

People my age were murder. Sometimes they tossed stuff out of cars. I could tell when something was coming at me, even though I never gave them the satisfaction of a glance over my shoulder. Their car would slow down and let out a puff of music as the window opened. Then the beer can or whatever would hit my arm, and the car was already so far past I couldn't see who it was. Possibly the people in the car did not know what harm they could do me. Possibly they did know.

But if I had one personality trait it was vigilance. My personality *in toto* was a mystery to me; for some time now I had been trying to figure it out but could not seem to get a good look at it. I kept a diary by my bed so that if I thought of an attribute I had, I could write it down. But the list was short. One I was sure of was "vigilance." Let the world do its worst, Lucille Odom was ready.

I sensed that I was on a verge. A large block of time was due to crack open in front of me, the future that up till then had been impenetrable.

I stuck to the highway. Even though I had traveled it that morning, I saw new things. I noticed for the first time a new TV tower in the distance, making a string of six now in the long stretch of marsh up the Intracoastal Waterway. And then I saw that the small swamp between Seagull Shores and Oakview had turned into dry land, and a sign had gone up saying, "Gator Pond Estates." I noticed that the names chosen for these places were memorials to what had been bulldozed into oblivion.

A car went by. Something pinged against my helmet. A jelly bean could do me in, I realized.

I wore a safety helmet and did not care how it looked. When other seniors were screeching out of the Wando parking lot in their Cherokees and Broncos, I strapped on my helmet and backpack in plain sight and let them have a laugh if they needed one so desperately. If I had been a normal teenage girl I might have cared, but I wasn't and didn't.

When I say I was not normal, I don't just mean I had the usual adolescent delusions of being different from everyone else. My upper lip had failed to fuse during a critical embryonic stage, and I had been born with a split there. Not a full-fledged harelip, but a small, neat slice not quite all the way through. When I was three, the lip had been repaired, and now, they said, it was hardly noticeable.

Well: Does "hardly noticeable" mean "noticeable" or "not noticeable"?

But I wasn't one to set store by looks. In fact, my scar had taught me a thing or two. It had put me into a different sphere. I sometimes felt as if I were a member of a third gender or secret species. On occasion, I saw people in the street who for one reason or another struck a chord in me— a man with a rocking limp, a boy with one side of his face stained red—and I would say to myself, "There's one."

Of course, I never spoke this thought.

For a long time I felt guilty about my lip, and I had an urge to apologize to my mother for it. Imagine, expecting another wonder baby and getting one with a flapping lip. However, I later found out that I had no need to apologize. It was more likely that she needed to apologize to me. I accepted the seam, ran my finger over its shiny ridge whenever I was in deep thought, and went on with my life. I had no time for guilt or resentment; I had interests that required all my attention, interests unlike those of most teenagers. I was studying certain things.

Not that I counted myself superior. Gladly I'd have given up my pursuits in exchange for an afternoon in the hair stylist's chair getting my hair flipped over one eye, or lying on the beach slathered in Bain de Soleil, or trying on lingerie at Sweet Nothings in the shopping plaza. I'd have enjoyed those things as much as the next girl. But I wasn't free.

Something had come over me. Recently, like within the past few weeks. I could not tell at first whether it was an affliction or a gift. It was primarily a feeling, but different from the others in that it was constant, it didn't ebb and flow. I called it "invision" because it was almost as if I could see into things. I could not take my eyes off physical objects— plants, dogs, faces, birds, all the world of nature—but also manufactured items such as cars, mailboxes, chain-link fencing. Things glittered at me as I rode past. They had started glittering after I read in the paper about a study done by Clemson University scientists concerning the greenhouse effect. The level of the ocean, they had learned, was on the rise. Their computer had generated a map of the coastline of South Carolina as it would appear fifty years from now. I studied this map carefully. *We were not on it.* Our house, town, most of the city of Charleston, were shown in blue, i.e., covered by water.

Inundation would be gradual, inches per year, but inevitable, unless everyone in the world immediately stopped burning coal, using fertilizer, and spraying aerosol deodorant. Fat chance, I said to myself. So every time I looked at my own yard, every time I rode the bicycle, I saw not the good old world I had known forever, but a world it was nearly time to say good-bye to. Beauty doubled and tripled around me. The place was doomed.

"Invision," I decided, was a gift, and I received it the way a child receives something that may very well not have been meant for him. I hid it.

One time I mentioned it to Wayne, who was just nuts enough himself to sometimes know what I was talking about. We were at a Dixie Youth League baseball game; Wayne was coaching a team of twelve-year-olds. He sat on the bench with the team, and I sat behind the fence in the bleachers. Our team, which was quasi-integrated (a pale brown rightfielder whose parents were lawyers) was up against a black team. We didn't have a chance, even though some of the opponents had no gloves and caught with their caps.

I saw the red infield, the parched yellow outfield, the white lime baseline. The playground was a new one in the middle of nowhere: you could still smell pine resin from leaking stumps. I saw the little boys, ours tough and foul-mouthed out of fear, theirs wiry and friendly out of fear. I saw an aluminum bat flash in the sun, which was heading down behind a stand of long-leaf pine. Seagulls passed over with their disjointed flappy style of flying, and I heard thin radio music. Radio music out-of-doors has always been hard on me. I experienced a sort of heart flutter and called out to Wayne.

He motioned time out to the umpire and came up to the fence. "Yeah?" he said.

"Um," I said. "Is there something funny here?"

"We're getting our butts knocked in the dirt. I can't get another pitcher in there until the next inning, goddammit."

"No, I mean here." I waved to include the world. "Is there something about this whole design?"

"Design?"

"Well, the scene. I thought . . . the trees looked like they turned black. Our uniforms turned pink. I heard this song."

"Lucille?" he said, cocking his head at me. "Did you smoke something before you got here?"

"Of course not."

"Where'd you get it?"

"I didn't. I don't."

"That's what I thought, but now you're making me wonder."

So I said, "It must be the sun going down."

If Wayne didn't see what I meant, who would? I gave up. I don't recall the score of that game, but I know how the slow sun moved and the pines loomed and everything—*everything out there*—sank through a million changes before night fell onto it.

Pop had lost his license after a number of speeding offenses. He was a good driver, had never had a wreck, but he couldn't help driving fast due to his faith in the world. Caution is an attribute of the suspicious mind. When Pop got on the Interstate, he just naturally let the speedometer ease right up to seventy, eighty miles an hour. When last arrested he was doing eighty-three between Charleston and Columbia and didn't even realize the siren and light coming up behind were aimed at him. He apologized to the arresting officer, and they had a chat about the scarcity of black ducks this season, but the incident turned out to be the last straw in the opinion of the highway department computer, which suspended his right to operate a motor vehicle for six months.

A man without a car is a miserable creature, especially a businessman, especially a Southern businessman. What was he supposed to do, he said, ride the bus? Mother said the bus was quite nice, in fact. But she ended up driving him everywhere he wanted to go. He was embarrassed to the bone and sat with his head lowered. Sitting on the passenger side made him feel like a pansy, he'd said yesterday.

"Oh, Warren," Mother said. She was interested in homosexuals and protective of them, ideologically. I was riding in the back seat, listening. I loved their discussions and listened whenever I could.

"I can't help it," he said. "I'm not passing judgment, I'm just saying . . . I feel light. I feel passive. I feel like . . . like I'm not in the driver's seat."

"That's very interesting," she said, smiling faintly. She always seemed mildly amused by the world. "You feel threatened by my driving."

"Not at all, not at all. You are a fine driver, an excellent driver. I love your driving. Drive me to Builderama for shingles and nails."

"I think you should go to the hardware store," she said. "I don't like ramas and thons. Dioramas, telethons. Cineramas, walkathons. Let's just buy the shingles at Mr. Powell's store. He has them, doesn't he?"

"He does. Drive me to Mr. Powell's."

She hated the driving. She liked to have days to herself

instead of being at his beck and call. "How long till you get your license back?" she asked.

"Six months," he said. "Not long." He reached over and touched her hand on the wheel. They loved each other in their comfortable, easy way; I had been a constant witness to it ever since I could remember. They were what you could call devoted to each other.

"Six months," she said.

From my bike I could see over the stores to where the sky was clear. A few big pines still stood in the woods behind the shopping strip, tall enough to make that design against the bare sky that I liked, a black silhouette showing the essence of the tree, i.e., loneliness and heartbreak. *Pines.* I loved them.

I loved the weeds as well, their vast greenery and indifference to surroundings, their anonymity, their humility. Some bloomed and bore fruit even between the lanes of Highway 17. They were common varieties easily found in any patch of dirt, but they had no names that I knew of. So I named them. Spanish Thistle, Heart-of-the-Moon, Beanweed. That way I could think about them better.

In the distance the highway appeared to flare suddenly into the air; that was the bridge into Charleston. But before the bridge, just beyond the television station, was an opening in the shopping strip and a nondescript road that cut back behind the import repair shop. That was my road. It led to my town, Mount Pleasant, which huddled secretly behind all this new development. In Latin class (the only useful course I had at Wando High) I had studied the town of Herculaneum, buried by hot mud in the year 79 A.D. My town had been similarly engulfed, not by mud but by overflow from the city of Charleston, which had erupted and settled all around, leaving Mount Pleasant embedded in the middle. You might never suspect, if you were a traveler on the main route, that just down this unmarked road lay a real town.

I made the turn at Channel Three and then down behind the repair shop, where all the doctors brought their Mercedes-Benzes for tuning. Doctors were one of my interests, because of their unique vantage point both in and above the world. They know so much they could be priests, and yet they love the material world and participate in it fully. This was an attractive area for them: good hospitals, good boat ramps. The Mercedes mechanic had studied in Frankfurt. While he worked on their cars, the doctors often leaned over the hood observing, as if what they really wanted to be was mechanics. Sometimes Wayne's father was in there; his new 280 SL was regularly screwing up. He usually waved to me, knowing he had seen me somewhere before. But he wasn't there now, and I was disappointed. I had not seen Wayne in a month, I didn't *want* to see him, but seeing his father's car or his father's girlfriend or her car gave me a sort of thrill.

The simple truth about me and Wayne was that I could no longer keep up the sexual pace of our relationship. I had pretty much lost interest in it. Wayne's idea about sex was that it was still a healthy, fun thing for people in love to do, especially us because we were new at it. He said so whenever I held back. His argument was "gather ye rosebuds," slightly modified from the original. Sex, he said, was dying out, and we ought to take advantage of it while it was still available. He envisioned the whole world of pleasure eventually shutting down around us. "There's no doubt about it," he said. "Five, ten years, and you won't be able to drink anything or smoke anything or rub up against anything. I'm serious, Lucille. Nobody will be *moving*. We're looking at a classic case of now or never."

This philosophy seemed inadequate to me, but I had trouble discussing it with him, because in spite of his messed-up parents he was a good, caring person, and I didn't want to confuse him. I had nothing against sex. But with Wayne I never felt the feeling I call "desire." In "desire" there is darkness and some fear. You would never call it a fun thing to do. I had felt it only a couple of times, but its memory did not fade. The first time was at a black-and-white French movie in which a girl hiked up her skirt in front of a man, a stranger; and the second time was in a dream about Wayne in which he so differed from his real self in every detail that he was the contradiction of himself, and drew me like an undertow. After that, sex with the real Wayne was difficult. I thought maybe something was askew with me, and I didn't want to add to his troubles. I advised him to start seeing Laura Migo, who I thought most likely shared his sense of urgency in the matter. Besides, her father was a cardiologist; surely doctors pass on to their children a scientific and healthy attitude towards sex.

On the other hand, you never can tell about doctors. Wayne had told me about a big fight between his parents which indicated a non-scientific attitude. This fight was his earliest memory. His mother had taught him the word "penis." His father objected. "He will call it the tee-tee," Dr. Frobiness said.

"And what about the female anatomy? What will he call that?" said Mrs. Frobiness, hands on her hips.

"That's the woo-woo."

"Are you crazy?" she said. "You're a physician, and you want your son to say tee-tee and woo-woo? I cannot believe this."

This quarrel and other differences of opinion had escalated over a fifteen-year period to culminate in divorce. The Frobinesses were currently living out the one-year separation required under South Carolina law. Wayne believed they had detectives watching each other.

. . .

Past the repair shop I made one more turn and was on an actual street with sidewalks and a one-block downtown with a hardware store and a drugstore, neither of which did much business because anything they sold could be bought down the highway at a deep discount. But they stayed open for the few remaining old people who were suspicious of discount merchandise. The sidewalks had the springtime smell of damp, warm concrete. Houses were close to the street; they had picket fences, birdbaths, plastic big-wheeled trikes in the yard. I loved, loved, loved the place I lived.

Nobody in my school loved where they lived. Most of the students were either black kids or doctors' kids. They lived in shacks or they lived in executive homes, but they all wanted one thing: to be someplace else. I traced their unhappiness and antisocial behavior down to that one central trouble, geographic restlessness. It was what caused them to smoke marijuana and throw trash from cars. Home was exactly the place where they did not want to be. Greyhound, I thought, could cure the drug abuse problem overnight by giving out passes.

Nancy Reagan was wrong to advise children that they can just say no. A hunger rises. It is not exactly for drugs but for refreshment on the highest level: a new personality, a new world. . . . Listen, Nancy (I might have said), would you tell a starving child to say no to food? I had staved the hunger off; I was regarded as an abstainer in every respect, a good girl. But I felt the pang now and again. People like me are sometimes hanging onto their so-called goodness by a thread. I didn't know how I was going to turn out.

Wayne was going to turn out okay, because he had taken control of his life. Originally he had lived in Green Farm Estates in a four-bedroom house with a cathedral ceiling and central vacuuming; and even though only Wayne and his mother lived in it, there was not enough room for both of them. He had moved out and was living in his Ram Charger.

"Little holes all over the house. The place *sucks itself out*, Lucille. I couldn't take it," he had said.

There were other reasons, of course, which I probably understood better than Wayne did. (It stymied me, that I could fail completely to see my own life, yet have a sixth sense about somebody else's.) A divorced mother with one son is a good combination up to a point—they are perfect for each other for about six months, and then they are disaster, each the last thing the other needs. Both of them could use a Greyhound pass. My heart went out to Mrs. Frobiness alone in her cul-de-sac; but it went out also to Wayne in his Charger, and to Dr. Frobiness in his tennis villa.

These families let themselves in for it. All around me I saw the American family blowing apart, as described in *Psychology Today*. The American family needed to hold itself more closely, I thought. Like mine. We were a hermit family. We had each other and we had our house, and nothing could touch us. Whereas Dr. Frobiness had run off with a lady who team-taught the Episcopal Young Churchmen with him at St. Anne's. The Frobinesses had been active in the community, members not only of the church, but also of a fitness center, a plastic surgeons' supper club, a book club (Mrs. Frobiness), and a wind-surfing group (Dr. Frobiness). No family can stick together under the strain of so many outside interests. The human heart needs to be confined, not royally entertained, was my theory.

In the old village my tires rolled noiselessly through a thick, golden dust of oak pollen that had collected along the street and now stirred into clouds as I passed. I coasted in and out of the shadows of trees, past yards dark with a century of camellia growth, the bushes tall and gangly. The town had a physical effect on me; I shivered with pleasure. It felt good, *bodily*, to be here. Some of these houses, with their tin roofs and wide verandahs, had been built more than a hundred years ago. A ferry had once come across from Charleston to Mount Pleasant. It was the remnant of a summer town, a place people had escaped to when the city got too hot.

My heart quickened when I made the last turn and saw my house at the end of the street, or, to be accurate, saw the trees and bushes that rose in a jungle where our lot began. From the street the house was not visible. I lived in a hidden house in a hidden town. But the best thing about the house was that on its other side, away from the road, it faced the water with a curving porch. On one side it was closed and protected, and on the other—wide open to possibilities. I liked that.

Down the last block I pedaled fast to gain momentum so the bike would make it through the grass-and-sand yard to the back steps. As I hit the yard and the tires bit sand, I noticed my mother's camper pulled up at an angle next to the cedar tree, not parked properly in the driveway. But so what? Mother was never careful about parking, or about anything else. I leaned the bike against the steps and went to close the open car door. Mother forgot to close doors. She was not scatterbrained, exactly. She was more . . . *nonchalant*. She was loved for her nonchalance.

On the front seat was a bag of groceries. The bottom had sogged out, and a slick of butter pecan ice cream was spreading across the seat and under Mother's macramé pocketbook. As a young woman she had gone through a hippie phase. She still liked certain styles of clothing that she'd worn in the sixties. She was forty-nine now, but she wore peasant blouses and blue jeans and drove an old Volkswagen pop-up. She always looked good. She had macraméed that pocketbook herself.

I was thinking about how she looked—tall, thin but wide-hipped, often in white-soled boating shoes, sometimes smoking a long cigarette—when I realized how unusual it was that her pocketbook was there, that the ice cream was melting, that the car door was open. Beyond the house, the harbor sparkled but was quiet. I picked up the pocketbook. A pair of blue dragonflies coupled at eye-level; a crow cawed. Wind ruffled the feathery leaves of the cedar. Here was the extraordinary, the thing I had sensed hovering over my afternoon. Here it was.

Something had happened to her. I knew it just from looking at the dragonflies and the cedar tree, the car, the ice cream, the very sky.

It is not hard to interpret the world. I had recently learned to do it. You watch people and events and objects as closely as possible, then you put two and two together. Before I even made it to the house to look for her, before I called her name upstairs and down, I knew she would not be there. There was only the fan whirring in the kitchen window. And though the possibility had never crossed my mind before, I knew she had left us. It made sense, now that it had happened. Standing in the cool, dark hallway, with its bare gray floorboards running the length of the house, I could see out to the bright front porch and the lawn and the short mud beach and the dock where my father stood now catching a fish.

He jerked the rod to set the hook. I knew the pleasure he felt at that instant. Nothing made him so happy as catching a fish. And just as he hooked it, panic started inside me. That fish was about to be yanked into air it could not breathe; and so was the fisherman.

I looked away and caught sight of a piece of paper on the hall desk. A note, folded, addressed to him. While he reeled in the fish, I read his note. It had been written on Mother's word processor.

Dear Warren,
I should have discussed this with you in person, but the bus is coming and I have to run, so I will call you

when I get settled. This is not just a sudden whim, I have thought it over very carefully. We can get together and talk about it later, but to make a long story short, it is time for me to start a second life. Please tell Lucille.

Helen

He was still standing on the dock, in old khakis and a long-billed cap. He took his fish off the line and put it on a stringer hanging from the dock, then rebaited his hooks. My only thought was how I could soften the blow I held in my hand. Mother's note was hard as a hatchet-chop. Where was the sorrow and the regret? You don't walk out of a twenty-seven-year marriage—*or catch a bus out*—without conveying some sort of emotion to the other person. This note had no feeling. I read the thing again just to make sure I understood it; except for a couple of phrases, it might have been a note saying she was stepping out for a yoga class or a camellia show. But there it said, "start a second life." It said, "when I get settled." There was no doubt about the message. But not a word of pain or guilt. Not a word of explanation. Just those starry gray words off her dot-matrix printer.

Pop had cleaned his hooks and was loading the tackle box. I got a pen and notepad from the desk drawer and wrote another note.

Warren dearest,

I am so confused, absolutely *adrift*, I don't know what to do with my life at this point. After all these years I suddenly discover an emptiness at the heart of things. Please do not blame yourself, Warren, my love. This is something that I have to work out alone. Please forgive me.

All my love
Helen

Years ago, Rae and I had mastered Mother's handwriting, because she often forgot to sign our report cards and excuses and field-trip permissions. I could forge her signature perfectly. I hid the original note in my shoe. It was not as if I was changing the essence of the message; I had only made it more polite. I put the new note where the old one had been.

I might not have done this if my father had been a different sort of man. But he was a man with a breakable heart. Not many businessmen have one. For all his worldly success, he was an innocent person who took the world as it appeared and never questioned motives or suspected ulterior designs. It surprised me that someone like Pop could have made so much money. His demolition company had expanded into other states, and though he was recently retired, his partner still called him for advice. He had the love for his fellow man that you sometimes see, surprisingly, in war veterans. He trusted everybody, picked up hitchhikers, hired convicts on the work-release program, lent money to unemployed black people. In fact he lent money to Sam Poole, who was not only black and unemployed, but crazy to boot. There was no one Pop didn't trust, and he had trusted his wife most of all. To him she was the good center of a good world.

I knew the secret of long-lasting marriage because I had seen this one at close range all my life. The two people have to keep on an even keel. They don't need great passion, for each other or for anything else in the world, passion being the great destroyer; and I'm not talking about sex, necessarily. Passion means suffering, if you go back to Latin, which I often do when I want to know what a word really means. Love needs passion, but marriage needs the opposite—steady comfort, which they had.

He hosed down the dock, then turned off the water and stood looking across the harbor. A container-ship was leaving port, stacked with unknown cargo. He used to keep track of the shipping schedules, and whenever a ship came in or went out he'd know what it carried; he'd stop us in the middle of breakfast to point out the arrival of bananas or the departure of soybeans. But when container-ships were invented, it became impossible to tell what was on board. The shipping schedule in the newspaper said only "containers." He speculated: Korean computers or Communist automobiles. But he felt out of the know. For him, imagination was a poor substitute for fact. For me, of course, the opposite was true.

Looking back, I can see that that moment was the last of a stage, the protected stage, of our lives. He was sixty and I was seventeen, but we were heading into the second stage together. At the moment he didn't know it. As far as he knew, his life was what he had always wanted it to be. The fish were biting; he had money in the bank, a clean chest X ray, two fine daughters, a lovely wife. I knew that he considered himself lucky. He thought of himself as having successfully reached the end of the road without mishap. Like many successful businessmen, he had a lot of fears—fear of poverty, fear of disgrace, fear of solitude. And he had beat them all back! He had *won*.

That is why anger built now in me for what my mother had done and the way she had done it. My blood boiled. But what could I do? I hated my own helplessness. This was a familiar feeling, one that other people may or may not have, but I had it frequently, and there was no common name for it. I can only describe it by saying it was like sitting in a movie theater when something is about to happen on screen that you object to, but there you sit in the dark, stupid, seventeen, powerless. Things happen that you can neither halt nor moderate. Physically, this feeling manifests itself as a stomachache. I had named it "girlhood" and hoped to death that I would one day soon burst out of it.

"Many fish, Lucille," he called from the porch, taking off

his sandy shoes. "Get out the frying pan." This was a joke between us. I didn't cook.

"There's a note here on the table for you," I said.

"Let me rinse off. I'm smelly."

"I think it's important."

"Read it to me," he said. He tramped through the hall to the kitchen and slung the stringer of fish into the sink. Some were still flopping.

"I believe it's personal," I said.

"How do you know?" he said with his laugh. "Women. Your mother opens every piece of mail that comes with my name on it. She considers if it is addressed to me, it is addressed to her. A study could be done of the female conscience."

"Please, take it." I handed him the note.

He squinted at it. "Sorry," he said. "The old eyes don't like to read anymore. They seem to prefer the long view now, the big picture. They say to heck with the written word."

"Where are your glasses?" I was frantic; I wanted this over with, the note read, the day done, the future rolling again. What if he wouldn't read it?

"Here," he said, reaching into the pocket of his baggy pants and pulling out the old glasses, spotted with salt water. "Can't even bait a hook with the naked eye."

I turned away and let him read in private.

"You read this?" he said finally.

"Yes."

"It doesn't make sense to me. Does it to you? What does she mean here? 'I don't know what to do with my life.' Do you understand?"

"Well, yes, she's saying—"

"And 'adrift,' where did she get that? 'An emptiness at the heart of things'?" He was growing agitated. He sat down at the kitchen table and reread the note. "Ah," he said, as if only now had the message sunk in. He looked up at me, his glasses low on his nose. "Did you, uh, see her off, then?"

"No, she was gone when I got home. Her car's still here. Her pocketbook's still here."

"Then how did she go?"

"Took the bus, doesn't it say?" I looked over his shoulder.

"No, it just says um, after all these years—"

"She probably took the bus."

He nodded, but looked unconvinced. "This is . . . this is a surprise to me, Lucille. That is, I had no warning. Did you?"

"None."

"She didn't mention any plans?" he said. "She didn't mention any . . . dissatisfaction?"

"Never."

"Nor to me," he said, picking up the note.

"Don't read it again, Pop. You've read it twice."

"I just want to make sure here—you see, somehow, the tone is wrong. It's not your mother's tone. The word 'dearest.' It almost reads like a note that *someone forced her to write.*" His voice thickened, and he looked at me with eyebrows raised.

"Oh, it's her tone, all right," I said quickly.

"You think so?"

"I know so," I said, taking the note out of his hand.

"But she sounds so distraught," he said.

"Of course she does! She ought to."

"We have to find her," he said, getting to his feet. "We'll drive where we think she might have gone. Where does the bus go from here?"

"But wait, Pop, she doesn't want us to find her."

"She does. I can tell by this note. She has never sounded so upset before. It's a cry for help, Lucille. I've read about this. I'm going to look for her."

"You can't drive," I said.

"I didn't say I was driving. You drive. I'll look."

I went with him, though I knew how hopeless it was. I knew his wife better than he did, and she was not the sort of person who lets herself be found. Long ago, when we played hide-and-seek—Rae and I and Rhody Poole, daughter of crazy Sam—Mother sometimes played with us, and she played to win. We never found her on our own. She would stay in her hiding place until we began to be bored, having searched the whole house and yard in vain. As soon as we gave signs of losing interest, we would hear a little *whoop* from somewhere, and we'd zero in on the whooping until we found her—in the laundry basket covered over with dirty sheets; or atop the armoire in her room, in plain view but so high we had not thought to look up; or once, in the trunk of the car, the lid not quite shut.

She claimed that she'd married too young and had not had time to get her fill of children's games. Halloween was her favorite time, and she would make her own elaborate costume and go out with us into the neighborhood, a gypsy or a vampire or some kind of animal. Once she was a Cheshire cat, in a suit sewed up from furry material, tail stiffened by a coat-hanger, a paper-bag head with eye-holes, whiskers, and that frightening cat-smile. We were a foursome for years, Mother in her thirties but looking in her twenties, Rae and Rhody teenagers, me a child sometimes unsure who the official mother was. Rhody had had a baby at age fourteen and given it to her mother; and that baby, Evelyn, called its grandmother "mama" and its mama "Rhody," and the Poole family lived together without confusion. So—could Rae be my mother? I had my suspicions for years, though she was only eight years older than me; I believed Rae capable of anything. I read a tabloid story about an eight-year-old mother in Brazil, who, they said, was a top-notch mother. And then, Mother was never quite as interested in me as Rae was. Mother's interest was downright grandmotherly. Kind, wrathless, dispassionate. She was never upset with me, never dissatisfied, never emotionally entangled. Later I found out why, but up until the age of ten I didn't quite understand.

Pop and I drove everywhere that evening and into the night. We covered the city of Charleston, the town of Mount Pleasant, the surrounding suburbs, and even some of the countryside. I drove until he was no longer looking out the window and had fallen silent. When we got home, the telephone was ringing. He ran for it.

"Helen," he said, "what is this all about? Let me come pick you up . . . yes, well, I mean let Lucille drive me. . . ." He put a hand to his eyebrow. "But that's crazy, and not true. How could we possibly be better off without you? I'm telling you now, we would not."

His voice wavered, and he looked at me. "Yes," he said into the receiver. "Certainly. You have the right. Of course I see. Very well. Wait, wait, where are you?" He frowned. "Now, for God's sake, Helen. Suppose we had an emergency and had to get in touch with you. . . . I don't know, say Lucille got sick—okay, okay. Okay. Then you'll call when, tomorrow? Yes. And, ah, you're sure you know what you're doing, you don't want me to come?"

She knew what she was doing.

I have never understood how events are linked in the world, and I don't know now whether the disappearance of my mother was like a trigger mechanism setting off the series of surprises that was to follow. There is no reason the one thing *had* to lead to the others. But a family without a mother is vulnerable. She left us sitting ducks.

If she had stayed, I believe we would have been all right.

CHAPTER 2

*H*ow long can a grown-up woman hide out in her own home town? Granted, it's a place where people lose themselves with some frequency, but that is because substance abuse or poverty or madness has rendered them invisible. They can sleep under the azaleas in Calhoun Square unnoticed by citizens. But my mother was by no means invisible. Even in blue jeans she was eye-catching, somebody's wife, somebody *important*'s wife. A woman like that can't freely roam a town any more than an A.K.C.-registered Lhasa apso can. Someone will take notice of her patrician jaw, her good bones.

Besides, she wasn't streetwise. Didn't have survival skills. Without her Visa card, how could she do anything? She would be home soon, I knew. She could not stay hidden another day.

But she did. After ten days I wanted to stop looking altogether, just so Pop could get her off his mind. Her telephone calls were upsetting him. Some nights he waited for the phone to ring the way I used to when I was seeing Wayne, and I knew the feeling of that. I watched him pretend to be thinking about something else or try to busy himself with the paper or TV, when all he had in his head was the possibly imminent ring of the telephone. He could almost hear it. But there was no schedule to her calling, which made it worse; he didn't know when hope was reasonable.

I tried to talk sense into her on the phone. I cajoled and threatened. "What you're doing is against the law," I said. "If you don't tell me where you are, I'll call the police."

"Darling, I'm in a safe place," she said. "Don't worry about me. I just don't want to see anybody for a while."

"Well, is this something feminist?" I said, desperate for an explanation, "or is it something real? Can't you just give me the reason?"

"I'll tell you everything. I was driving your father back from Powell's Hardware. He had a box of shingles on his lap and his hands folded on top of the box, and we came around the corner onto Bennett Street at the spot where you can see the water at the end of the street, down that little hill. And so I saw the water, the way it sparkles, and I thought to myself, I would like to live a completely different existence. It just hit me like that."

"But I was with you! I didn't notice you getting hit by anything."

"I didn't know what it was. Then at home I couldn't get it out of my head. Everything at home seemed foreign. Worse than foreign, it seemed . . . sickening. It wasn't mine, you see, it didn't feel like the place I belonged. I wanted to start a new life."

"So it's feminist."

"I don't know," she said. "I don't know what it is."

"Did you feel adrift?" I asked. "Did you suddenly discover an emptiness at the heart of things?"

"Well, I suppose . . . well, yes, that's a good way to put it. You've put it exactly the right way, Lulu. I had a feeling you'd understand. You have your quiet way of watching and knowing just what's going on. I'll give you a call tomorrow or the next day, okay?"

"What about your clothes?" I said. "Don't you want them?"

"My clothes . . . no. They'd be reminders. I'll call you, Lucille."

Every day I drove my father around in search of my mother. We asked at the grocery store and the dry cleaners, we checked the Charleston hotels and the homes of acquaintances. She didn't have friends the way most women do, no confidantes. There were a few ex-friends from the days of her youth, but they hadn't been close to her. Still we drove, hoping to see her by chance. I got to know streets I had never seen before, parts of Charleston County I didn't know existed. We filled the gas tank at the self-service Gulf station every morning. He pumped while I paid, to save time.

"What about detectives?" I said one morning as he watched the numbers light up on the unleaded premium pump. At first there had been something challenging about this search, starting out early like a deer hunt. But now I was tired of it.

"Excuse me?" he said.

"We could hire detectives to look for her."

"Oh, no. I don't think so. That's only on television."

"I happen to know there are detectives for hire around here. You have to have one if you're getting a divorce. He watches your wife because if she goes out with somebody during that time then you don't have to pay alimony or give up your children."

"How did you obtain this information?" he said.

"I keep my ears open."

"Detectives never occurred to me." He squinted into the morning sun, pink under a thick haze. "No, it wouldn't be right. I could never put a detective on the trail of my own wife. That would be spying."

"Just to search for her. That's not spying."

"We don't need outside help. We'll find her. Sooner or later, her path will cross ours."

If Mother had been an average person, yes, then her path might have been predictable. But she didn't fall into the pattern of the Charleston matron. Looking for one of those, you would haunt the clothing shops, the restaurants on Market Street, the antique stores. But Mother might just as easily be seen in a rowboat crossing the harbor. Indeed, when we drove over the bridge every morning, I looked down, scanning the Wando River for a small boat rowed by a woman. It would not have surprised me to see her down there. But I saw only the tugs, freighters at the docks, men fishing from dinghies, and now and then the submarines sneaking out to sea. We had had them for years; we had got used to the idea of them more or less, and nobody ever wrote letters to the paper or demonstrated. Still, I knew what was in them. I shuddered as we reached the very top of the bridge, and the black thing slid under us. Parts of the world were too crazy for a woman to go out into.

"Cold?" Pop said, reaching for the air-conditioner controls.

"No, it's fine."

"Say, Lucille, when is graduation?"

"It's been," I said. "Day before yesterday."

"That was the day we went to the banks." We had gone to see if she had made a withdrawal or opened a new account. "You missed graduation for that?"

"I would have missed it anyway, even if I had been there. I didn't graduate. I didn't take my exams," I said, looking straight ahead, both hands on the steering wheel.

"Didn't take your exams? What are you talking about, you didn't take your exams?"

"Well, they started that week, when we—when Mother was first gone, and I couldn't see taking *exams* at that time,

Pop. I'll take them sometime. I can make them up. Don't worry about it."

"I don't want anything to interfere with your schoolwork," he said.

I doubt that parents have an inkling of how deep a child's love goes. It is more thorough than adult love. I loved not only my parents: I loved their love. While divorce swept over Charleston in waves, like a contagious disease, I felt as safe as if I had been vaccinated. To tell the truth, something akin to pleasure zipped through me when yet another classmate said, "Yeah, my parents are separated." While I felt sorry for these people, still I figured that every divorce among neighboring families made my own family stronger. We were not just two parents with two children, we were *the Odoms*, something more mysteriously amalgamated than a regular couple-with-kids. Or so I thought. Evidently, Pop didn't see me as in on this. To him, the trouble was private, his own. I was the chauffeur, not a fellow victim. He assumed I would go on with my normal life, sit in a hot lunchroom and tick off multiple-choice answers while everything that counted was falling apart.

And Rae. She was not taking the situation seriously; she was not even coming home till June. I couldn't believe it. On the phone she had sighed and said, "Don't tell me this now. I do not need to hear this now."

"Well, you don't have any choice. It happened. Come home and help me. He's cracking up. All he wants to do is look for her. I hear him sometimes *talking* to himself, Rae, asking questions and then answering them. He's gaining weight, he's sleeping too much. When can you get here?" I said.

"Lucille, I can't come now. It's not possible. Things here are in a mess, I can't tell you. You can hang on a while, can't you?"

"Who cares about the mess in Washington? There's a mess here, and which is more important, the national debt or your own parents?"

"Lucille, you mean well, but you don't know what you're talking about. I will get there as soon as I can. That's all I can do, take my word for it. I'll get there as soon as I possibly can."

"When will that be?"

"June," she said.

"When in June?"

"Sixth."

"You better be here then. I'm taking this as a promise. Because, Rae, this is too much for me. I don't like it. I'm cooking three meals a day and doing laundry and driving him to the ends of the earth, and at night I feel like I'm going to drop dead."

"I'll be there June 6, Lucille." She sounded frazzled and worn out.

"If you're not—"

"I will be."

Rae was a woman of her word. If she said June 6, she'd be here June 6, sure as the sun. I knew that. And yet I also doubted it. I doubt, sometimes, the sun's return. Nothing is to be counted on one hundred percent.

The morning of the sixth, I tried to call her to find out what time she'd get here, but there was no answer at the apartment. She lived in Georgetown, near the canal. I had been to stay a week with her last summer. Washington was full of single girls from Charlotte and Atlanta and Raleigh, more Southern girls than in New York even, because Washington was more like home. But they did not stay long. They went there after college and stayed three years, maximum, and then went home. Rae called them the weak sisters. "They're scared," she said. "They go running back home to marry somebody, because they're afraid to be alone." My mother had raised Rae to be strong in character.

When she didn't answer her phone, I assumed that she had already left. The Impala was fast. If she took the Interstates all the way, if she left, say, around seven A.M. (which I knew was too early for Rae, but *maybe* this time she had gotten up early), then she might be home by five, if she didn't stop along the way, which I hoped she wouldn't; but I knew better. Still, five was the hour I set for starting to hope. In the afternoon Pop and I drove up to Porcher's Bluff, a place north of Mount Pleasant where Mother had liked to drive on Sundays. We walked around and had Cokes and Snickers bars on the bluff overlooking the Intracoastal Waterway. Knowing that Rae would be home that night put us both in a good mood. A breeze kept the mosquitoes away, and when big yachts went by we waved to them. We didn't mention Mother. It was almost as if we had gone out for the purpose of having a good time. At four I said I thought we ought to be getting home.

And on the way home, looking at his gentle face, I actually thought, *time heals all wounds.* I pay attention to clichés because they are likely to be true. Otherwise they wouldn't have achieved cliché status.

For a while at dusk the western sky stayed lit, a bright June afterlight that brought out nighthawks. I heard them buzz high over the house, doing nuptial dive-bombs. From the porch I had a panoramic view of water: the ocean, the harbor, two rivers, and the Waterway; not to mention creeks that snaked out of the marsh, rivulets, and finger-wide channels through shining dark mud. I could also see, when the time was right, night in the east and day in the west, stars and sunset both. It was my favorite view. A view like that is a privilege, I told myself, and I began to get back the old feeling that I had once had, the feeling that my place was special, my family was special, I myself was perhaps also, in some tiny way, special; and therefore my troubles would soon be over. The present discombobulation was temporary, maybe even a sort of test to see if we were the tough and virtuous family I had always said we were.

At the kitchen table, Pop fidgeted. "Maybe the car broke down," he said. "I ought to have tuned it when she was home for Christmas."

"She'll be here. She's okay."

"She probably never changes the oil."

"She does. She writes her car information in a little book, the oil, tuneups, filters, all that, because she said most women have to get married in order to keep their cars going. She reads up on automotive maintenance. She takes care of that car like a boy would."

I turned on the light that hung low over the kitchen table. Its cord was tipped with a little metal bell-shaped clamp. I worried about the wiring. Last year a squirrel had chewed through a wire behind the kitchen wall; the squirrel had fried, the fuse had blown, and all Pop's fish had thawed and gone bad in the freezer. At the time I had not worried about it except from the point of view of the squirrel. But now I found myself in a different position. I was the one saddled with the household worries, of which there were more than I had ever dreamed. There was not only laundry and food, but also wiring, bills, termite treatment, moths, Jehovah's Witnesses, telephone calls saying that the lady of the house had won a microwave if she and her at-least-twenty-thousand-dollar-a-year husband would come spend a weekend at Myrtle Beach and attend a seminar.

I was seventeen! I was unprepared to be the lady of a house. Sometimes I wished I were already an old maid. The old-maid way of life seemed like one that would suit me. I had it planned how to wear my chignon, I liked those shoes with wavy foam soles and stacked heels. In the library, where I worked on Friday afternoons, I had run into many spinsters. Actually, several of them were married, but they had kept their spinsterly ways. Librarians, nuns, ladies who write poetry, are all spinsterly; they like a quiet place, they like to think, they don't mind being alone. That's what appealed to me. I also liked the predictability of these lives; old maids don't want a change in schedule. No surprises, please. I wanted, like them, to know a year in advance what tour I was going to take the next August. I wanted to make my Christmas list in October, and buy certain groceries on certain days of the week. I wanted to be well-organized. *Semper parata.*

In my own family there was little preparedness, and no rhyme or reason to the daily schedule. The ragtag nature of the household was due to our mother's nonchalance. If we'd had a mother like the mothers in other homes, then maybe the laundry would always have been aromatic and fluffy and folded in the right dresser-drawer, and a station wagon would always have been waiting for me when band practice was over, and I might have gone to church like every other person, black and white, in my class. But Mother didn't believe in laundry or carpools or God. We did our own dirty clothes and got places under our own steam. I had patched together my own religious education by listening to TV preachers and radio gospel programs.

I didn't want full-scale religion. I just wanted a smattering, for the background. It was embarrassing to go to school with people who were religious if you were not. They had gotten saved at an early age; some had done speaking in tongues as young as thirteen. And I didn't even know the basic Bible stories.

Rae, of course, would never make it as a spinster. I laughed out loud thinking of it. In spite of her independence, she was the sort of woman bound to tangle with men. She was going to give some poor man a hard time. I laughed again imagining the kind of person it would take to manage Rae. It would have to be somebody unusual, an old senator maybe, or a tycoon, or a preacher. Somebody a little crazy and outside the normal walks of life.

The only person I'd ever met who, it had occurred to me, might be a match for Rae was Wayne Frobiness. The thought of those two together, the nervous, chain-smoking Wayne and the beautiful Rae, made me laugh again.

"What is so funny, Lucille?" my father said.

"I'm imagining Rae as a wife," I said.

"Sometimes I can't keep up with your thoughts," he said. "You're imagining what?"

"Rae, married."

"Marriage is a wonderful institution."

I tried to bite my tongue and couldn't do it in time. "What do you mean? How can you say that?"

"Pardon?"

"It hasn't been so wonderful to you," I said.

"Ah, but it has indeed."

This sentimentalism drove me up the wall. He wasn't seeing things clearly. He was romanticizing. On the subject of love or anything connected with it, even the mockingbirds feeding their greedy young on the lawn, he grew wistful, and he recalled certain events in a far sweeter light than they had happened in.

"I can only hope that both you girls someday find the happiness in marriage that your mother and I were lucky enough to have. When I think about it—"

"Don't," I said.

"When I think about the coincidence of it, that's what floors me. There are millions of people in the world. Millions or billions. What is the world population, Lucille?"

"I don't know."

"An enormous throng. And out of that huge number, two individuals are able to come together, to find each other as if by some uncanny radar, and—"

"I doubt it's anything like radar," I said. "I think it's the opposite. Blindness."

"It's what?"

"You love what you bump into."

"Oh, no," he said. "Oh, no. There's far more to it than that." He got a faraway look in his eyes.

At times like these, I could almost read my father's thoughts. He sat across the table, his hands laid in front of him like caught flounder. His chin was down, his head tilted, as if he might be watching the miniature television I had just bought him. It chatted to him in a low voice. But his mind was off on its own again, and I knew where.

I didn't have E.S.P., just common sense. A man in his circumstances is likely to think along certain lines. Over and over again he was thinking, Why did she go? He pondered not only his private trouble, but the wider world as it might pertain to him. He puzzled over miscellaneous things—birds' songs, the weather channel, the arrangement of his own food on a dinner plate—as if they could deliver an explanation. Yesterday, riding the mower I'd bought at a yard sale, he had run over a slim green snake; I caught him examining its innards like an augurer.

Sunset turned the kitchen orange. In one shaft the light shot through the screen door onto the wooden floor, the enamel table, the refrigerator. I looked to see if his eyes were closed. It was easy enough to fall asleep this time of day, this time of year. The slanting light had a hypnotic power. I could smell myrtles and cut grass. Under normal circumstances I might have dropped off myself, sitting in the spoke-backed chair in the old kitchen with my father.

I liked that silence we had. I was not much of a talker anyway, by nature wary of chatter. I had never learned how to talk like a girl, the way Rae could: Rae could make a conversation occur, as if it were the most natural thing in the world. But my natural language was all private. What came out when I spoke was only a hacked-up version of the thoughts that lay graceful and complete in my brain.

And Pop, who used to talk plenty, had clammed up. When he did speak, he might say something not precisely connected to the subject at hand. Then I had to try to figure out what he was getting at. I was worried sick about him. He napped and snacked, napped and snacked. He weighed two hundred and forty now. The sorrow of a big man is worse than that of a small man, rocks him deeper, lasts a longer time. In his grief he reminded me of the large mammals that are everywhere dying out faster than the wily little ones.

But I would never have called him a good source of information, even before his trouble. He was a businessman. I trusted him to pay taxes and patch the roof, but I had never thought he had any information I could use, no lessons or wisdom to pass on. His experience was limited. By "experience" I don't mean adventures. He'd had all those manly experiences of blowing up bridges in Korea, flying an airplane, making money. He had been poor and hungry; he had been in love. But the kind of experience I mean depends not on the event so much as the state of mind of the person undergoing the event. My father was simply not as awake to the world as my mother was. What I call experience occurs inside the brain. Most often it happens to people who are flops—people who have been disappointed, who have at least for a time lost control of their lives. Flops are the best sources of information. I loved my father. But he was an innocent. Even as he was dropping off to sleep in the kitchen, I felt his innocence trapping me. His head fell to one side, and I was helpless.

But Rae was due home. I waited for Rae like someone hoping for rescue at sea. Rae was a natural boss, she was going to know what to do.

Outside, darkness collected. The two-inch TV picture grew bright and appeared like a white square hole in mid-air above the table. I envisioned Rae speeding south in her convertible. Rae was a good driver, but she could be distracted. Roadside peaches or a towel outlet could lure her off the highway. I closed my eyes and tried to will her home. *Stay on the road*, I sent out. *Come straight home.*

Mental telepathy is a ridiculous idea. I didn't really expect Rae to receive a verbatim message from me forty miles away. But we were sisters. In the past we had sometimes been able to understand each other without using actual language. Despite the age difference, we were close, and I knew her through and through; I knew she would be driving fast now, with the sunset over her shoulder, watching how the roadbed darkened first while the sun still tipped the pines. She might be singing. She had the ability to accompany herself mentally, so she was never lonesome. I could conjure up the sound of Rae's voice singing an old Drifters song. "This Magic Moment."

Some girls sing, some don't. I accepted that. I had my own gifts.

Pop cleared his throat. He needed a haircut, I noticed, and a shave, and he needed to get the hair in his nostrils clipped. I didn't know whether men get that done by a barber or do it themselves. How was I supposed to know? Pop was letting himself go, paying no attention to personal grooming, and I couldn't do anything about it. His shirt was buttoned crooked, but I could not tell him so; it wasn't my place to tell him.

"I can't make out a damned thing on that screen," he said. "I believe you've been hoodwinked by the Japanese, Lucille. You've bought all these gizmos that are more trouble than they are worth. What exactly is the point of getting your television screen down to the size of a postage stamp? Tell me what *that* is." He pointed at the screen.

He was right, the picture was so tiny it was hard to identify. It might have been an athletic event, or it might have been a science close-up of rods and cones. I said, "I think it's *Nova,* inside an eyeball."

I had hoped he would like this TV. I had also bought some other things from a catalog—products that were not really useful but were so clever I thought they might distract and entertain him—a waterproof radio that would stick to the shower stall, a computerized bridge game for one-to-four players, an exercycle that measured your heart rate as you rode. None of these had really engaged his interest, but I myself had become attached to the little television. The ambiguity of the picture appealed to me. It was always open to interpretation. Sometimes I could tell the program by the sounds. Right now it was doing a gentle science voice-over, calmly omniscient, my favorite. I also liked, though, the cheery noise of the morning quiz shows and the melancholy drone of the soaps. These TV sounds had a calming effect on me, especially when I was low on patience.

The telephone rang. Pop leapt to his feet, but he bypassed the wall phone and answered it in the living room. I could hear only muffled sounds, so after a few minutes I moved to the doorway of the living room, staying far enough back so that he couldn't see me.

"Well, I don't know," he was saying. "I understand that they might have survived the first few seconds after the initial explosion. Wasn't there a statement on that? . . . Yes, that's certainly what one would hope. It's just a thing that we'll probably never know." Then he listened for a few minutes. He was sitting in a comfortable chair, but he looked ill-at-ease, bent forward toward the floor, one hand holding the phone and the other holding his head at the temple. His elbows were on his knees. Then he shifted and dropped his head onto the back of the chair and stared at the ceiling.

"I have to say I don't agree," he said. "You really want the truth? . . . Okay, my idea of it is, when you die you die, and there's nothing more to it than that. . . . No, but that's what I think."

He listened more, sometimes nodding. He sat up straight and said, "Yes. Thank *you*, for calling." After hanging up he sat another minute in the same position, but he folded his hands in mid-air between his legs.

"What was that?" I said finally.

"Your mother."

"Why don't you have the calls traced? Good grief." I paced the length of the room and back. "You could get them traced, couldn't you?"

"I inquired," he said. "They'll only trace obscene calls."

"What did she want?"

"Nothing in particular," he said.

"What were you talking about?"

"Oh," he said, standing up. "The Challenger crew. She's a sensitive woman. A thing like that will stick in the back of her mind and keep cropping up. It takes her a long time to shake things off. She feels things deeply. Whether they suffered or not—that was her question."

He restacked his magazines on the coffee table. *Wooden Boat, U.S. News and World Report, Birdwatcher's Digest.* Those magazines broke my heart.

"Your shirt is buttoned wrong, Pop," I said.

"Oh. Thank you."

Rae, Rae, Rae! I willed Rae home along the roads and down into the Santee swamp, to the dark green lowcountry again, her headlights on now and nothing to slow her down, nothing to keep her from getting here, no excuse or hindrance in the world. I lit the night around her with fireflies and stars, down the last stretch of straight, pine-lined road. She might make one more stop, to put the top up on the car, and she would keep her eyes open for sights; a deer might leap the road, or a raccoon trundle out of the woods onto the mown shoulder. Rae claimed to have seen a bear on that highway last spring, and another animal she thought could have been a panther. Rae had a good eye. She often saw rare animals. But I could see *her* now, her face in the cool night as the top came up from behind. She might be listening for owls. She might *whoo* for them, and they might answer, and when she cranked up the engine again there would be only a hum left of the Drifters.

This was not clairvoyance. It was years of observation grown into an understanding of what Rae was like, what she would do, and how she would look even out of my sight. It was also desperation, which sometimes helps you see things you need to see.

"I hear a car," he said.

I went to the door. "It is a car," I said. "It's turning in." Like a slow yacht, the car came into the yard.

But we stayed put. We didn't run out to meet her. Pop sat back down at the kitchen table; he even picked up the newspaper and opened it. I stood by the screen door, glancing out sideways. I saw the car's headlights light up the myrtle bushes, the cedar tree, the ruined cistern. Then the lights went out and the motor quit.

The door did not immediately open. I eased closer to the screen. The yard was black. Then I saw the car door swing open, and the map light came on, showing Rae and a man. She took a hard drag on her cigarette and passed it to him and he passed it back. They laughed. She put her hand up over his mouth.

"Is it Rae?" Pop said.

"It's her."

"Why isn't she coming in?"

After a second I said, "She has somebody with her."

Above the spot where the sun had earlier sunk, I saw flat, dull lightning. There was a storm miles away.

Rae laughed again. She had a very unusual voice, its tone high but sweet, not only when she sang but also when she talked and laughed. It often caught people's attention. I likened it to honey butter.

The man opened the door wider and got out, and she slid over to get out behind him. With his hands on her waist he lifted her out of the car, and I flinched a little because, although that way a man has of lifting a girl is very pretty, it hurts a girl's ribs. He let her down next to him. Rae was not tall, not as tall as me. She came to the man's shoulder. A height difference like that always makes you think a match is wrong. The man and woman appear to be a poor fit.

Rae and the man tried again to stop laughing. They held onto each other and kissed, then Rae smoothed her hair and straightened her skirt, opened the back door of the car and hauled a cardboard box out of the back seat. She had on a scoopneck knit shirt and black flat shoes, and she looked not quite herself. She looked a little tawdry with her flyaway blond hair, her jangly earrings.

"There's Lucille," she said, coming up the stairs with the large box against her stomach. "Lucille, we're home," she called.

Who is *we*, I wondered in a panic.

Carrying the box through the door, Rae said, "This is my husband."

For an instant I imagined a tiny husband curled in the box like a kitten. I stepped aside as Rae came through with the box. She held the door open behind her with a toe to let the man in.

"Your what?" Pop said.

"Pop, this is Billy McQueen. Lucille, Billy. Billy and I got married on the way down, in Myrtle Beach. I should have let you know, but—we didn't have a whole lot of advance warning ourselves."

"Married?" Pop said.

"Yes, sir," Billy said, reaching out to shake Pop's hand, which he had to pick up from where it hung straight down. "Yes, sir, married." He pushed his hair back from his eyes. His blue shirtsleeves were rolled up to the elbow, and he was nervous.

"Don't gawk, Lucille, you're embarrassing him," Rae said.

"Was it an accident?" I said. "You accidentally got married?"

"I need a gin drink," Rae said. She set her box down on the floor. It was, I saw, full of men's clothes. On top was a pair of white undershorts. "And I want to call Mother," Rae said.

"Well," Pop said, blinking, "you see, that might not be exactly possible—"

"We don't have her number," I said.

"You said you talked to her all the time on the phone," Rae said.

Pop cleared his throat. "Yes, she calls us," he said.

"Well, okay. It's nothing earth-shaking. I'll talk to her when she calls."

Sudden marriage to a stranger is not earth-shaking? The last man Rae had mentioned was named Eric; and before that, Mark and Gary. I never liked their names. Billy was an improvement in that respect, at least.

"How did it happen?" I said. "You said, let's stop for a hamburger, and before you knew it you'd been struck by marriage?"

"That's about it," Rae said.

"Actually," Billy said, "we'd been planning it for some

time." He had the disarming politeness that coaches drum into athletes. But I knew athletes, and he didn't have the loose sockets of a ballplayer. Cross-country, maybe, or swimming, some lonely sport. He had a degree of broodiness.

"How long?" I said.

"Let's not rehash the whole story in detail, not right now," Rae said, twisting the ice tray to make the cubes pop out. "Now is not the time."

"I just wanted to picture it," I said.

"Not much to picture. A magistrate's office is all it was." She drank half of what was in the glass, and I hoped she had mixed it weak. She looked at Billy and then said, "I mean, I liked it fine, Billy, but it wasn't *Lucille's* idea of a wedding. Lucille is thinking of a church and stephanotis."

"I am not." But I was. I had always loved weddings, their strange ceremony, with the cheerful groom, the dumbly hopeful bride in her complicated get-up, the commingling of religion and sex. The idea of a wedding in a magistrate's office shocked me.

"Well, we saved Pop about five thousand bucks," she said.

"I certainly wouldn't have minded spending the money if you had wanted a wedding," Pop said. "I hope you didn't think you had to—"

"No, no," Billy said. "We weren't trying to save money."

Rae stood with her back to the sink. She looked at me and smiled, and she looked at Pop. "Oh, hell," she said. "Let's not beat around the bush. We're expecting a baby. We decided against abortion. We got married. It's a story everybody's heard before, I guess." She turned and rinsed out her glass.

Pop turned white.

"You're kidding," I said.

She wheeled around and to my surprise had hard anger in her eyes. "I'm not kidding, Lucille. I want you to do me a favor now and leave me alone, okay?"

"I only meant I didn't think it was . . . *possible*. Nowadays. With all the—the technology."

She stared at me. "It is possible."

"Okay, that's all I was asking." My voice tapered off. Rae did not have a quick temper, but when she did get angry, she was not someone you wanted to mess with.

In a flat voice she said, as if it were an announcement, "We need a place to live until after the baby is born."

I said, "Well, that's no problem. There are condos and apartments all over the place. I read in the paper that the area is overbuilt, and the rents are reduced fifty percent; some places give you a free VCR just to move in."

"Your old room is available," Pop said.

"Are you sure?" she said. "You wouldn't mind?"

"There's only the single bed," I said.

"We'll get a new one," Rae said. "Right now we don't have a dime. But we'll buy a bed as soon as we get jobs."

"What are you?" I said to Billy.

He seemed to draw a blank.

"He's a historian," she said. She lit a cigarette.

Rae was different. I noticed hundreds of tiny changes in her posture and gestures, new words in her vocabulary, an unfamiliar flush on her skin, a more desperate style of smoking. But at the same time she seemed stronger than usual, with a new way of moving her shoulders that could almost be called a swagger. I couldn't figure out what these changes meant. She spoke in a voice more ragged than the original, a voice that alerted me to possible hidden trouble.

We should never have let her go to Washington. I don't know why so many women do not foresee the future. They just do not see it coming. Then it hits them, and they say, Oh! a baby! Oh! a divorce! They have no foresight whatsoever, and get into situations they could easily have avoided with a little thought, a little observation, a little contraception.

"Lucille," Rae said, leaning past me to crush a cigarette in my saucer, "you live in your own little world."

I didn't respond. She was half right: it was my own. But it was not little.

We followed her into the hall. She opened the door to her room and said, "There's a bicycle or something in here."

"Exercycle," I said.

"Who rides?"

"I bought it for Pop," I said. "But he hasn't used it yet."

"I tried it out," he said. "Frankly, Lucille, I felt ridiculous sitting on a bike that has no wheels and goes no place. I appreciate the thought, of course."

"Can we just move it onto the porch?" Rae said.

"Feel free," I said.

After everyone had gone to bed, I sat by myself on the back porch. All around I could smell the myrtle bushes, and it struck me as strange that you can smell in the dark. Behind St. Anne's down the road was a fragrance garden: the Episcopalians brought blind people to it on Sunday afternoons. The blind must experience this same eerie sensation I had now, smelling the unseen myrtles, the shivery feeling of "something out there." In the grass, fireflies were blinking love signals to one another. Higher, the stars twinkled. It occurred to me that a firefly could easily be fooled into latching onto that signal from outer space and falling into eternally unrequited love. From where I sat, I could hardly see a difference between the bug and the fiery star. Indication, I thought, of just how far off my judgment could be.

My sister was going to be no help to me.

C H A P T E R
3

*I*t was significant to me that Billy McQueen was a historian by trade. I liked history. Not the kind in the textbooks, the treaties and political parties and government shenanigans, all of which gave me a headache. There was more to history than that. There were things hidden in it, mysteries worth going after. I didn't want to know about the Mugwumps or the industries of Japan or fifteen steps in the unification of Germany. I wanted to know, to put it bluntly, the secrets of life. I believed they were to be found in the dusty corners of human history. *Human* history.

The textbook I had, for example, went into some detail on the subject of John C. Calhoun's theory of nullification, holding that the southern states ought to be allowed to reject any federal law not to their liking. "A state shall not be bound by any law deemed injurious to the interest of the state . . ." blah, blah, blah. I knew what *that* was about. As a red herring, it was of some mild interest to me, showing how men can dress greed as philosophy. But of consuming interest to me was the statue of John C. himself in the city, so high on his fluted column that oak trees obscured him. To get a look at him you had to stand in a certain spot on Calhoun Street below and crane your neck. He was green, black-green from the boots up to the collar of the flowing cape, where he

lightened to blue-green. He glowered. Even from sixty feet
below you could see the deep brow, the wild mane. I loved
Calhoun's looks and sometimes believed the rumor that he
was the true father of Abraham Lincoln. Documents are said
to exist proving that Nancy Hanks had been the barmaid at an
upstate tavern frequented by Calhoun, just months before she
journeyed to Kentucky by wagon and delivered her fatherless
child in the famous log cabin. It is said that Calhoun made
several unexplained trips to that area at a later date, and it is
known that after the assassination, Tad Lincoln was caught
burning certain mysterious documents said to cast light on
Lincoln's parentage. If this is not proof enough, all you have
to do is look at pictures. The two men had the same face. I
liked this theory for its behind-the-scenes passion. I enjoyed
a glimpse of blood and gristle at the otherwise dry heart of
politics.

History should give you goose bumps. There's a thrill in it.
I wondered whether McQueen shared my view, or whether
he was a textbook man.

I also felt strongly that history was a category comprising
not only famous men of bygone eras, but *me, yesterday.*
Wasn't I as mysterious as John C. Calhoun, and my own
history worth investigating? I had spent some time doing so.

Parts of it I pieced together from the overheard remarks of
my mother and father at various times in my life. When they
said something that had to do with my childhood, my ears
pricked up. I tried not to act too interested, because I felt they
would say more if they were unaware of my interest. I listened. Other portions I reconstructed from the direct reports
of my best source of information—my sister. She was eight
years older than I was and had been an eyewitness to most of
my life's events. Of course, so had I, but I couldn't remember
them. I plied Rae for facts. Now and then I found out things
that gave me an initial shock, certain surprises I'd never sus-

pected; but nothing in your own history ever seems too disturbing, after it sinks in, as long as you are currently alive and well.

From what I'd heard of our two childhoods, it almost sounded as if we had been raised by different mothers.

Rae's was young, twenty-four. Married only two years, she was still optimistic. She wore the baby possum-style, strapped to her front for ease of conversation, and slept with it despite Pop's citation of a paragraph from Dr. Spock saying never sleep with your baby. Mother called Dr. Spock a bad name and pulled herself around Rae in the bed as if Pop were going to snatch her away. She claimed to be able to communicate with the baby long before it could talk, and maybe she really could. She said the baby understood things and had its own thoughts, but just could not yet make English words with its tongue and lips. Its own language of coos and burbles was one you could understand if you gave it half a try.

Then when Rae started talking, Mother went about inculcating ideas. She considered herself the sole influence on Rae; how Rae turned out would depend on what Mother taught her. So at every available opportunity she spoke seriously to Rae about major issues. In the grocery store, Rae sat with her dimpled legs dangling out the front of the grocery cart while Mother, nonchalantly loading the cart with groceries the family did not need, talked about nuclear waste, Supreme Court decisions, Indian health care, etc. There were so many things that had to be *passed down.*

This upbringing, of course, is what landed Rae in Washington, D.C. Ralph Nader had a mother like Rae's.

She never intended to have a second child.

Rae remembered a trip she took with Mother to the hot inland city of Columbia, driving the hundred miles in hundred-degree weather and sitting so close that Rae's head fit into the curve of Mother's armpit. Rae wrinkled her nose at

the smell of Arid cream deodorant but didn't move away.
Mother explained that she was pregnant and was going to get
the egg vacuumed out. They sang along with the car radio.
Mother was beautiful in her Mexican embroidered blouse,
and talked up a storm, Rae recalled. Your body is your own,
she said. One child is enough, given overpopulation, war
raging on and on, ecologies collapsing.

The highway was a straight hundred-mile leg of new Interstate without billboards or rest stops, and halfway there,
Rae had to go to the bathroom. Mother stopped the car, and
Rae squatted in the grass behind the open car, sure that every
passing motorist saw her bare behind. That shame kept the
whole trip in her memory, until she told it to me years later,
when I was ten and she was eighteen.

She remembered the city of Columbia as flashing with heat,
spread out on hills like an encampment, with no ocean. In the
doctor's office, a nurse said children could not be in the waiting room, so Rae sat for two hours by herself in the car, all
the windows down to prevent death. When Mother got back,
she grabbed Rae in her arms and held her even closer than
before, and they drove home. Once they stopped and Mother
leaned back to relax for a while, and then drove the rest of the
way.

"Honey," Mother said, "say we went to Columbia shopping, if anybody asks. To the mill outlets, I guess, for a
bedspread and—what else?"

"Towels?"

"Yes, towels."

"But we don't have any packages."

"He won't notice."

For weeks Rae watched Mother to make sure she was all
right, because she didn't seem the same. One morning at the
breakfast table, Mother turned white in the face and said
"Oh!" She touched her stomach.

"What is it?" Pop said. "Are you all right?"

She sucked in her breath and said, "I left the damned iron on upstairs." She ran from the room, dropping a piece of toast on the floor. It was not unusual for her to leave the iron on.

But after Pop had gone to work, Mother and Rae drove to the doctor's office in Charleston. This time Rae sat in a waiting room, and from her child-sized rocking chair she could see one lady's thighs, so thick and pink they seemed like two sleeping pigs. Rae was frightened by so much pregnancy; the room was full of it.

The doctor and Mother and Rae went down the hall to another office where there was machinery. When they came out, Mother looked calmer. The doctor asked Rae whether she'd rather have a little sister or a little brother, and Rae said, "Sister."

"And that's what I got," she told me.

"Wait," I said. "You're making this up."

"No, I swear to God."

"I don't understand."

"It's very rare. But it happens," Rae said.

"I survived an abortion? The suction thing?"

"Yes."

"It just—missed me?"

"Well," she said, "there were two. Twins. It got one. You were the other one. They didn't know you were in there."

At first, I admit, I reeled from this news. It was a complicated matter. I felt suddenly lucky, the way you feel when your heart is still pounding after a near wreck on the Interstate. I had survived. But then that simple feeling of luckiness flowered into horror, and fear, and something like loneliness, and then anger, all these feelings shooting out like an exploded bottle rocket. Why hadn't I been told this before? I had lived a full ten years of my life without crucial information about my own origin. I felt so many different feelings that I couldn't say any of them out loud to Rae, and she thought I felt none.

But after a while, I settled down to one primary feeling. It was the feeling, "Ah-yes-so-that-explains-it."

There were two. You were the other one. No wonder, then, that sometimes I had the strange sensation of incompleteness and loneliness and, now that I thought about it, bereavement. No wonder my mother seemed aloof.

And yet, I wasn't sure that there was any connection at all between that history and my current condition. I couldn't tell whether I was unique because of certain events, or whether the events actually had very little bearing on how I would turn out. That searching nozzle, though it missed me, might have disturbed the process of cellular growth and prevented parts of me, physical and emotional both, from developing correctly. I'm not saying it was necessarily so. In the long run, I was alive and well, and I knew some true things about my past. That was all I could say.

But I was a little nervous about the fallibility of history in general, after finding out my crucial facts from Rae. So much gets lost! Historians better buckle down, I thought, and individuals keep closer track of their own private history. It can be forgotten so easily, especially if a person's memory isn't efficient. My own memory was full of holes. I was a young person, but big chunks of experience had already gone into thin air. Even some wild and action-packed events had faded like invisible ink, such as the time Rae saved a burning man, and the time Pop went after an alligator that was eating his dog. I knew these events only from family reports, even though I had *been* there. Goodness, I thought, if your memory cannot hold onto a man afire or your father in the embrace of a reptile, what can it be trusted to hold? A brain like that isn't worth a dern.

Mother had lectured me on the importance of memory. She said that when she was pregnant with Rae, doctors in the labor room had given her "Twilight Sleep," an *ex-post-facto* anaesthetic. Instead of eliminating pain, it eliminated the memory of pain. "Pain is inconsequential if it's not remembered," the doctors had told her. She would hurt, but later she would not remember the hurt, so it would be as if she had never felt it. She went along. It worked the way they said it would: she had no memory of pain. But in its place was a queer sensation of having misplaced something important. "It was how a collie must feel after labor," she said. "I had been tricked. I mean, why not give that drug to everyone who's been hurt or unhappy or ashamed? Memory is all we've got over collies." Giving birth to me, she took only a whiff of gas; she wanted to remember the pain this time. "Nothing hurts as bad as they say it does, Lucille," she told me later. "And clear, pure memory doesn't hurt at all. What hurts is forgetting. They buried the pain of Rae so deep inside me there is no conscious record of it, but it makes its presence known. It moves at night, or at unexpected moments on an otherwise unclouded day, and I shiver and say, *what was that?* Remember everything," she advised me.

I was trying. I did memory exercises such as "I went to my grandmother's house and I took with me an aardvark; I went to my grandmother's house and I took with me an aardvark and a buttonhook; I went to my grandmother's house and I took with me an aardvark, a buttonhook, and a communist," etc. I also kept a diary in order to record my events in case the brain cells failed to do so. What good is a life if you can't remember its milestones and themes? That is the aim of history, to *get it down on paper,* to be the official human memory.

So, I was wondering, was Billy McQueen a genuine historian? I lay in bed the next morning thinking about what sorts of jobs for historians might be found around Charleston. The place was full of history. There must be plenty of historian work. The military history alone could keep a historian's hands full for years. Everywhere you looked there was fortification. You wandered in the woods and came across ditches and mounds; people with metal detectors regularly unearthed grapeshot and cannonballs and even cannons. We had Fort Moultrie from the Revolution and Fort Sumter from the Civil War, to say nothing of the installations up the river dedicated to current wars and wars to come. We were well-fortified. Some people said the water level, which appeared to be rising from the greenhouse effect, was not rising at all: instead, the city was sinking, under the weight of the Naval Weapons Station and the Army Depot, the Air Force Base, and the Navy Yard. There was a rumor that the highest concentration of nuclear warheads in the world was just up the river. That was something worth the historian's attention, it seemed to me. History was in the making all around us.

Outside my window doves landed. Soon they would wake Pop with their whirring love notes. They slept elsewhere but came to our windows for the day. When I took him his cup of coffee he was lying in bed on his side, staring at the doves on his sill. He kept a tray filled with millet out there.

"Ferocious animals," he said. "They drive off every other bird."

"They look kind and gentle to me."

"Your mother's face is like that. I try to think of something else, but it keeps coming to me, crowding out the rest."

Two fat ones strutted and dosidoed. Farther in the distance, small catamarans crossed the harbor, readying for a race.

"Do you want this coffee or not?" I said.

"The only trick I have against her is to go back before her time. To deeper memories. You'd be surprised how far back they go. I can remember 1936. The day my family walked to a new town. Daddy had heard rumors of a job in Winnsboro. I was so afraid of being poor then. Well, we *were* poor, and it was not so bad—I myself was happy—but I was afraid of getting poorer, because I could tell Daddy was afraid of it. We slept beside the road that night in a new-cut ditch. The smell of the dirt was sharp as plants. White roots stuck out of it, like worms. In the morning we followed that hot blank road again, the cars kept passing. Am I boring you, Lucille? What do you see?"

I was bending to get the whole view from his window. A fleet of small sails fluttered far to the western side of the harbor, putting out from the yacht club in the city. "Hobie cats," I said.

"There was some kind of grass, tall grass like wheat, blowing on the side of the road," he went on. "Daddy walked so much faster than we did. Every time a car went by, the grass lay down in waves, and—"

"I'm putting this coffee on the table," I said. It disturbed me to hear him say the word "daddy," and I didn't like the poetic tone I detected in this account.

"Wait, it's so clear. If I lie still, right after I wake up, it happens every morning. I get these scenes." He closed his eyes. "Now Daddy is out in front, then my mother, and then me, way behind. Then a car comes too close, whirls me around, one tire off the pavement and spraying dirt, and when it passes my mother it blows her hair and skirt and nearly knocks her down. I am so far back she can't even hear my voice over the car's horn, and Daddy is so far ahead he is lost in a roadbend." He hesitated, and opened his eyes. "I was thinking only one thing, that whole time. I was thinking, *if we had money, we would be safe.*"

"Okay, Pop, I'm going. Look: coffee." I pointed to the cup. "I've got to fix breakfast for Rae and Billy."

"Billy?'

I stared at him. "Rae's husband."

"Oh, yes," he said. "I'll come down. You know what I think? I think that was the formative moment. If you believe there's an incident that sets your pattern for life, that was mine. I never thought about it before."

When I left he was still stretched out on his side, looking at the window. It is disconcerting to see a man lying on his side, which is somehow a very feminine position. An odalisque. His arms and back had a slack look, as if all the muscles in them had been cut. He raised himself up on an elbow.

Uh-oh, I thought: Can a man become effeminate as the result of the loss of his wife? As far as I knew, nobody understood the causes. I'd heard a radio preacher say, "Bring these babies forward now, even the babies in their mothers' wombs, and let me touch them. No boy-child I touch will ever become a homosexual pervert." Even via radio you could hear them running down the aisles. I personally had been thinking the question over carefully for quite a while: it had been the hottest topic of conversation at school from the first grade on. "You're gay," the boys yelled at each other; "That shirt is so gay"; "Your wristwatch is gay"; "You're so gay, you can't walk," they were saying in the fourth grade. I hated the boys who talked like that, for their fear. On the other hand, everywhere I looked I saw homosexuals.

Wayne said I was unfairly judging people on a superficial basis. "Tell me that's not one," I said at a Dixie Youth game. I nodded in the direction of the visitors' dugout.

"Who, the *coach*?"

"Look at his pants. Watch that jiggle in his shoulders. Ho, what about that, he patted his pitcher on the butt!"

"Lucille. They all do that."

"I noticed that! That's what I mean."

In the stores, along the highway, at the movies, I saw them by the dozen. I doubted if they even knew it themselves. Lots of them had girls with them. I saw them all over TV: politicians, preachers, newscasters. The Dallas Cowboys, in their padded suits on their oh-so-clean grass; the Miami Vice guys in their special colors.

"Lucille, I'm afraid this reveals something about the observer rather than the observee," Wayne said. "Only sixteen percent of the male population is gay. You're seeing it at about 50 percent."

"Higher," I said.

"Why do you think that is?" he said.

"I don't know. Food additives? The species under stress?"

"I meant, why do *you* see homosexuals where no one else does? What does that say about your concept of masculinity?"

"I see lots of things no one else sees."

Downstairs, the air seemed stale. I opened all the French doors in the living room, and the combined smell of mud and salt air and marine fuel came in, one of my favorite smells. The pilot boat was going out. Its engine was louder than any other boat, and I could usually identify it without looking. It groaned through the water as if its trips were a particular chore. This was my hour. It was my habit to get up early and take a measure of the coming day, check the harbor and the sky, the wind, the activity of birds and men, and make a prediction for the day as a whole, not its weather necessarily but its atmosphere. Its spirit. This looked like a good one.

But something said no. Something said, *New man in the house. New man in the house.* I felt a cold stone sink to the bottom of my stomach, as if I had married the man myself. A bride must feel this, waking on the first morning.

Oh, Rae, I said to myself: What have you gone and done? But I tried to snap out of it. In this day and age, marriage is not the big thing it once was. You can shake one off like a flu bug. So there was no reason to have this trapped sensation. But, *oh, Rae*. I put a finger to my lips to stop the moan from getting out. I passed by the closed door to her room.

The first question was, what would he eat? I stood in front of the open refrigerator and tried to figure out what to cook. He was from the state of Illinois, and Lord knows what they eat out there. Probably oats and steak. Pop had put yesterday's catch of croakers in a plastic bag. I would fry those. If the man couldn't eat a fried fish for breakfast, I'd know he was worthless.

I owned the house, this hour of the morning. If I wanted to I could burn it down and everything in it, or I could fix breakfast. It was a moment of power and charity every morning, when I made the decision to cook. After only one month of practice I had learned to fix some good things. Spaghetti, grits, guacamole, cheesecake. I had also learned to fry a respectable fish.

I ran the little fish through cornmeal and flour, and heated some oil in the skillet. The heads were off, the bodies slit and cleaned out, showing how elegantly simple their design was, the body a simple bag for the innards. You don't think of the human body as being designed in that way, but perhaps, I realized, it is. And what I think of as Lucille, the visible person, may be only a container—only a *bag*—for another girl. One nobody had ever seen, who maybe had a different name. "Ellicul," maybe.

I folded the paper napkins to look like swans. Rhody had taught me how. But that was as far as I went. It would be an ordinary breakfast. In my opinion there was too much hullabaloo over just-married couples: the rice and tin cans and soap, and honeymoon travel specials, not to mention the suites covered with pink shag and the heart-shaped tubs. Good grief. It all seemed just a bit cruel when you stopped to think about it. It was all meant to embarrass the couple by reminding everyone about the sex these people were doing. If I were on a honeymoon I would not want anyone to know. I certainly wouldn't want any special celebration the morning after.

Rae and I had always had the two downstairs bedrooms, mine in the front of the house with an ocean view, hers in the back with a view of the road; my parents had had the two upstairs bedrooms. Because of the way the house was laid out, with the kitchen jutting off the back, you could see Rae's window from the kitchen. It was open. Its curtains moved. It struck me as very beautiful, the white curtains just sort of lifting with the morning breeze, now and then drifting all the way outside, a white corner brushing the sill. I did not call anyone to breakfast. If necessary, I could keep the food warm in the oven.

The fish sizzled. Small bubbles of skin lifted from the flesh. The tails fanned out and turned gold.

I had modified the cookbook recipe by increasing the proportion of cornmeal to flour. The fish fried up crispier. I was proud of my discovery, but I vowed I would never tell it. You must keep these things to yourself, I figured. If forced to pass on a recipe, it is a good idea to sabotage it by calling for some ingredient that shouldn't be in there. Keep your recipes to yourself, as you keep every valuable bit of knowledge, I said. Above all, keep yourself to yourself.

I poked at the browning blisters with my spatula.

"I went to my grandmother's house and I took with me an apple. I went to my grandmother's house and took with me an apple and a basketball. I went to my grandmother's house and took with me. . . ." The fish fried while I worked on up to the letter K. "Apple, basketball, corkscrew, doorknob, easel, featherbed, garden hose, hamper, ice cube, jockstrap, keychain—"

"Jockstrap?" Billy stood in the doorway, his hands high

on the jambs. I have an acute sense of hearing, but I had not heard him come in.

I picked up the spatula, which had fallen into the pan. "It's a memory game," I said, wiping grease off the handle.

"I know it well. Don't let me interrupt." He sat down at the kitchen table, which I had set for four. A quick glance told me the napkins had been a mistake. They appeared to have been crumpled by previous eaters and tossed onto the table.

He was pushing one of them along with his finger. "It was meant to look like a swan," I said, picking it up and undoing it.

"Good swan," he said. "I see the neck here on this one. Where'd you learn to do that?"

"Rae's friend, Rhody. She went to hotel-motel management, to train for resort work."

"And they taught her how to fold napkins?"

"Well, the opening in management closed. She's a waitress until something else comes up."

"And what are you?" he said.

"Nothing," I said.

"Well, student."

"No. High-school dropout, part-time librarian. Cook."

"That's not nothing."

"Pretty close," I said. "How about a fried croaker?"

"A frog?"

"A fish." I tilted the pan so he could see the four fish in it, neatly arranged shoulder-by-tail like sardines. "They're a little greasy," I said. "And bony." I watched him.

"What else is there?" he said.

"Stale Cheerios."

"Stale Cheerios are my favorite food. Tell me where to find a bowl. Stay there, I can find it. You go on with your trip."

But I had forgotten everything on the list. What threw me

off was realizing that Billy was getting the wrong impression of me. He was thinking I was a teenage girl. One thing I cannot stand is if someone has an image of me that is not accurate. I don't mind whether people laugh at me or ignore me or love me, but I hate it when they think they have got me pegged, and they don't.

"Up there," I said. But when he opened the cabinet there were no bowls in sight. The shelves were crammed with plates, cups, ramekins, spring-form pans, colanders, and such one-of-a-kind items as a partitioned, rabbit-decorated baby dish, a cup that said "Greatest Mom in the World," a corn platter painted to resemble an ear of corn, a mold that would turn out fish salad in a fish shape.

"They're in there somewhere," I said. "Look behind those orange plates."

He found a wood-look plastic bowl that was actually a salad bowl, but it would certainly do for Cheerios.

Our whole house was like those shelves, packed with the gathered possessions of twenty-five years. Not so long before she left, Mother had sat in the kitchen and cried over what she called "this creeping clutter." Pop had come in to comfort her, saying, "But, Helen, then why don't we simply throw some of these things away and clean out the house?" She had said through tears, "Do you think we could? Do you really think so?"

But I had had to object. Because she wasn't thinking about it from my and Rae's point of view. So she was nearing fifty and tired of seeing the same old dishes and bric-a-brac, but look at me, I'm seventeen, I said. I could *use* this stuff some day. But the real reason that I wouldn't let her throw anything away was that for me everything in this house had historical value. Not just sentimental value, but real historical value. These were the objects that my family had lived their lives with. That baby plate had been mine and

Rae's, that cup was the one I had given my mother years ago on her birthday. When I looked at the closed kitchen cabinets, I didn't think, as my mother did, of stacks and stacks of useless, chipped, crackling, unmatched dinnerware. I thought of *artifacts.*

All our other closets were similarly packed: the hall closets with thin old blankets that had seen us through all the childhood diseases, worn soft sheets, towels fraying on the ends, heating pads that had lost their flannel covers and stiffened like dried meat, the dining room hutch with odd wine glasses, a set of Rumanian liqueur goblets from which the color could be picked with a fingernail, silver forks in patterns that came close to being the same but missed by the curl of a scallop, and the clothes closets with every dress Rae and I had worn, jammed so tight it was difficult to add another hanger, plus— and this was the best trove of all—my mother's clothes going back to the day of her wedding.

I said to Billy McQueen, "We are a pack-rat sort of family."

"Yes, I see that." He opened another cabinet. "Looking for spoons now," he said.

"In the first drawer."

"Ah. Corkscrew, peeler, screwdriver, garlic press, unidentified item—" He held up something in his hand.

"Fish scaler," I said. "I meant the first drawer on the other side of the sink."

He closed one drawer and opened the other. "Got it." He held up a bent spoon. "Looks like Uri Geller got hold of this one," he said.

I began to realize there are certain indignities to be suffered by a family when a new person is thrust into its midst. He will go rummaging through drawers and closets; he'll see all the private things of the family that ordinary guests don't see. I thought of the mildewed shower curtain, the roll of paper towels substituting for toilet paper, the sheet that I had once bled on which now circulated freely through the laundry and could end up on anyone's bed.

I looked at him as he poured cereal into the bowl, and I began to have certain suspicions about him. I am a good judge of character; everybody says so. Wayne used to count on me to help him decide the lineup for his team, because character, in a Dixie Youth game, is about the only thing that counts. Oh, there are one or two stars who'll get a double every time, and there are one or two hopeless cases, but generally the only factor is character. A boy of good character can hit the ball. I could tell the difference between a swaggerer and a hitter. I loved hitters. They were honest, kind, and sure of themselves. They would not stay that way. Something happened pretty soon after they left Dixie Youth; they lost their courage. Twelve years old is the age when a man is at his best.

But I was also a good judge of adults. I looked at McQueen and I was struck by a thought. Maybe this marriage was no accident. Maybe he had tricked her into it. It came to me like a revelation, a sudden light bulb the way scientists get their breakthrough ideas. But I put it away. I knew nothing about him, and because of his new relationship to us, I was obliged to give him the benefit of the doubt, at least for the time being.

A sea breeze whipped the loose screening on the front porch and whistled in the eaves, an unusually stiff breeze for morning. The screens ought to be replaced soon. I could hear the whap, whap, whap all the way in the kitchen. The house was acoustically unusual. Entirely open, with high ceilings and that long hall front-to-back, it did not shut out external noises. Built for a rich man's summers, it had not changed much over the century. It had aged some, settled and weathered, the tongue-and-groove pine rooms turned the color of red tea, the window glass permanently clouded by salt air. During the forties somebody had added bathrooms and updated the kitchen. Pop had installed a gas furnace and ducts. Still it was a house with integrity, not the kind of house you would want to modernize with skylights or a deck and hot tub. At one time Mother had gotten an architect in to ask him how she could "lighten up the rooms somehow," and he came back with sketches totally disfiguring the house, insulating and sheet-rocking, painting everything white, glassing in the porches, tiling the bathrooms. I had found her one afternoon in her upstairs room with the drawings unrolled on the floor by her bare feet; she was sitting in her chair with a color chart in her hand, a sheet with small rectangles of paint samples ordered from light to dark in all the hues. "Listen," she said, "how good these colors sound: sea biscuit, heather mist, tapioca."

I said it would be a crime to paint these walls. They were supposed to be dark, how could she think of painting them? "Besides," I said, "it isn't fair. You have lived other places, this is just another house to you. I have never lived anywhere else. This is my only place. If I lived somewhere else, I would be someone else."

"But it would be the same house, Lulu," she said, smoothing my hair, "only spruced up a bit."

I looked down at the drawings. "*That* is a completely different house," I said, pointing towards the floor. "I could never live in that house."

She realized that I was right, that remodeling would be a crime. She rolled the drawings up and smiled at me, snapped on a rubber band, and stashed the long white tube in the back of her closet.

"McQueen," I said, as he crunched his oats, "do you know how to replace porch screens? Or do you work exclusively with history?"

He took this as I meant it, a challenge. We raised our

eyebrows at each other, posing as enemies; but I had not yet decided whether I would be his enemy or not. I didn't know him well enough.

"I don't do screens," he said. He looked up at me with his bent spoon in his mouth.

There are only so many categories a man can fall into. I had an eagle eye for the clues, the little gestures that give them away. I could look at a man and tell you whether he was a hero or a weakling. Women were not so easy for me to categorize—I was still studying them—but men were an open book.

This one was giving me some trouble. At first he looked strong as they come, a hard worker, good-hearted, tough-minded. His shoulders and forehead were broad, two excellent signs. He had good eye contact, and the thing that is known as a "twinkle in the eye," though that is not precisely accurate; it is more a way of relaxing the eyelid and letting a smile not quite start. *But:* he let his shoulders slump. Sometimes the twinkle effect vanished, to be replaced by a brief hint of a frown, as if something were on his mind. I'd seen this look before somewhere, this quick shadow. I'd seen it on my father's face.

Billy poured another bowlful of Cheerios and added the milk, and I watched him. Definitely there was something amiss about him, something weak. It could be a disease, I thought, something that doesn't show externally. It could be an emotional injury. That was how close I was getting, I almost had it on my own, when Rae came into the kitchen, fuzzy-haired, wearing a man's blue bathrobe, rubbing her eyes; and from watching Billy McQueen's face it suddenly hit me what was wrong with him. I almost said "Hunh!" out loud when I realized what it was. The man was in love.

Her presence in the room changed him. He stood up awkwardly, spilling some of his milk onto the place mat. He acted altogether like a bumbling cowpoke smitten with love for the schoolteacher, and frankly I had to smile. I had never seen anything like this before except in *Gunsmoke* reruns.

Once I understood this fact, a lot of other things fell into place.

His clothing, for example. I had noticed that he had an unusually crisp look. His blue shirt was starched so heavily it looked like paper. The cuffs didn't touch his wrists, but stood away in rings. His jeans were creased. These details were evidence of professional laundering. A cowpoke wants to look his very best for the schoolteacher, who is not the sort of girl who'll offer to wash out a man's dirty things.

His eyes, when Rae came in, lost both their twinkle and their boldness. He looked not directly at Rae but about four inches off to the side of her head. Shy boys on the baseball team had looked at me that way. And when she spoke, his breathing pattern changed. I heard an intake of air from across the table where he sat.

"I don't feel good," Rae said. Her eyes were red and her hair was tangled.

"Morning sickness?" he said, looking as if his own stomach hurt.

"Please. Now is not the time. We'll discuss it later." She sat down at the table. "Do we have coffee?"

"A whole pot," I said. "This thing is great. You load it at night and tell it what time you want the coffee and if you want it strong or weak. You load it with *beans*, not ground stuff."

"I think you're probably just tired from the trip," Billy said. "You'll get better. Take it easy today. We don't have anything we have to do except sign up with an obstetrician."

"We don't have to do that today," she said.

"We do. It's already four months; you forgot that appointment I made for you last month."

"Okay, okay," she said. "God, I'm tired. I could drink a couple hundred cups of coffee."

"We decided you were going to cut down," he said. "On alcohol and smoking, too."

"What are you saying?" She frowned at him. "Don't talk to me about cutting out coffee or anything else. I feel bad enough as it is."

He sat back in his chair. But I could tell he was not giving up. He was not the kind of man who gives up.

I thought to myself that a new husband is like a squatter. You can't run him off your property, he is there for good. All you can do is try to get accustomed to him.

I heard Pop coming down the stairs. It had taken him half an hour to shave and dress. Sometimes he got his underwear and trousers on and then lay back down in bed. If he moved his head around too much, he said, his scenes would go away. I was anxious every morning until he actually appeared in the kitchen. Some morning soon, I was afraid, he was going to stay in bed.

When he came in and sat down, I was pleased by the symmetrical look of the breakfast table. For the first time since last Christmas, the number of places at the table was correct. Four is the perfect configuration for a family. "Family of four" is what all the government projections are based on.

"So, Lucille," Billy said. "Do you have a love interest?"

"Excuse me?"

"Have you got a boyfriend?"

"Are Yankees naturally rude or do they make an effort to be that way?" I said.

"She doesn't have one is what that means," Rae said.

"What about that young man, Wade, the one I met one night out in the driveway," Pop said.

"Wayne," I said.

"Yes, that one. He was in Gifted and Talented with you."

"He's gone," I said, getting up from the table to serve Pop his fish.

"I see. Aren't there others?" Pop said. The presence of Billy had put it into his head to be conversational. Pop and I had spent a month together without any substantial conversation at all, but now he thought he ought to have a discussion with me, right there in front of a stranger.

"No," I said abruptly.

"Isn't there some sort of teenage hangout where you all congregate? I seem to remember reading that all the young people were getting together. . . ."

"Not me, Pop. There is a place but I don't go there. The burnt bridge."

"That's right. There was an article about it in the paper. Neighbors complaining and so forth. I thought it sounded like the old days, when it was something of a lovers' lane. We used to shrimp at night from the old bridge, and on full-moon nights you could see well enough to dance. Music carried over the water from the dance hall on the island side."

"Well, it's no lovers' lane. People go there now to drink and buy dope," I said.

"Wayne, too?"

"He goes there, but he doesn't do anything. He just goes to go."

"You could go with him, then."

"Ah, Pop, no."

"Why not?"

"Just no." But he looked so friendly and interested, and it was the first time in a month that he had spoken in a jovial tone, I felt bad cutting off his inquiry. I said, "Wayne doesn't want to see me anymore. He's not calling me anymore." I talked low to indicate my remarks were addressed only to Pop. To no avail. This family never recognized a person's need for privacy.

"Call him," Rae said, chewing on a fish tail.

"Of course," Pop said. "Your mother called me on the telephone all the time. But she was an unusual girl. It was an unusual romance."

"This is no romance at all. It isn't even in that category," I said.

"So call him," Rae said. "If it isn't serious, what have you got to lose?"

"I don't know," Billy McQueen said. "I'm not sure about this. If the fellow wanted to talk to Lucille he would do the calling, wouldn't he? Can't we assume, then, that he doesn't want to talk? I think she's perfectly right, to lay low. Play hard to get."

"I'm not *playing hard to get.* I don't want to call him; I asked him not to call me. The relationship is over, period. Nobody's calling anybody."

"I say don't call him," Billy said. "How many vote with me?" He raised his hand. "Okay, how many say call him?"

"Forget it," I said. "We're not taking a vote."

"This is a democracy, isn't it?" Billy said.

"I don't know why everyone thinks my private life is such a joke," I said. "When it's you all who have screwed up your lives. Mine is still intact, but it seems to be the one everybody wants to laugh at. I mean, I don't care, go right ahead, but it just seems ironic. To me."

I left them. I lay down in my room on my white iron bed. On top of the bedposts were four brass balls that I had restored to the original brassy sheen. They shone like small suns at the corners of my universe.

I would not drive my father all over creation today. He could get them to drive him. I might, in fact, spend the day in my room, in my bed, with all my windows open on the water side. People have no respect for girls. People think girls are brainless. Even someone who has recently been one has no respect for girls, I thought, recalling how Rae had pooh-poohed the girls who couldn't tough it out in the nation's capital. But maybe they had not failed; maybe Washington, D.C., had failed them. I imagined them living alone or two to a room, catching buses down to the Senate Office Building, eating salads in cafeterias. These were girls as brave as they come! If in the end they gave up and went on home to Charlotte, it was because they were not only brave, but good. Rae didn't understand them the way I did. Rae had beauty and brains, but not a lot of human understanding. I believe that is the norm with good-looking people. Not that it is their fault, but they do tend to be somewhat blind to the troubles of others.

C H A P T E R
4

*I*n old cities there are always statues. Charleston had John C. Calhoun, Henry Timrod (Poet of the Confederacy), and a toga-clad woman who was meant to be Confederate Motherhood, sending her naked son into battle with the Yankees.

But my favorite was Osceola, the Seminole chief. Down the road from our house was Fort Moultrie, where his statue rose from the top of a hill, looking seaward. I imagined his view, over the brick fort and the housetops of red and silver, the dark cumulus trees, to the slice of white dunes, blue water, Fort Sumter, and finally in the distance a black, jagged, double line of rocks, jetties that held the channel for incoming ships. From his perch he watched for whatever would be coming over the horizon—freighters, shrimpboats, seabirds, the sun and moon.

Bees lived in him. They appeared to get in through a hole in his neck, which made me wonder if he was hollow. And if hollow, was he filled with honey? He never flinched, in that wild swarm. I had grown up under his watch, and he had come to be a landmark and something of a hero to me, my idea of what a man should be. A warrior, secretly filled with sweetness.

In life Osceola had been betrayed in Florida, captured under a flag of truce, and sent here as a prisoner, where he died under what I considered suspicious circumstances. Caught a cold and died, they said. Well—perhaps. But in the fort was a portrait that the government was careful to get painted of him just weeks before he caught the fatal cold. He knew something was afoot, you can tell from the portrait. The eyes have the gentle serenity of a man who sees fools and traitors all around him. When he died, the attending physician sawed off his head and took it home to Savannah, where he pickled it and hung it on his son's bedpost whenever the child misbehaved. I swear this is true. The headless body was buried at the fort. A ten-foot cypress representation of the head in profile can now be seen marking the entrance to Osceola Pointe, a bankrupt development on the bypass.

You won't find the whole Osceola story in the history books, of course. I discovered these facts in the South Carolina Room at the library, where I worked on Friday afternoons. The room was kept locked—they said, to keep out winos and children. But I made some discoveries in that room, and I think I know the real reason they locked it. There was a lot of history in there that they didn't want to let out.

Similarly, in the contemporary world, something was going on behind the scenes. It was quiet; too quiet. I got the feeling something was gathering. These submarines snuck out every few days like Mafia Cadillacs, long and dead silent. A tourist snapped a photo of one from the Fort Sumter tour boat one day, and the Navy descended on him, confiscating his film. I often woke up in the middle of the night, looking out my window to see if everything was okay out there. Sometimes I couldn't tell; the sky was yellowish black, and a pestilent odor hung over the yard. Wayne said both conditions were caused by the mosquito sprayer, which came around at night.

Maybe so, I thought, but it's bigger than that. It's widespread.

Riding my bicycle in the country, I could see that even one poor man is capable of plenty of destruction. He clears a hole in the woods for his house, and then he builds the house, say out of concrete block, and he parks his car next to it, and behind it he stacks his extra block and his firewood and his tools. Then he builds a chicken house. Then he gets another car because the first one won't run, and he leaves the first one there in the yard, alongside the sheets of galvanized and the junked washer and the rolls of leftover chicken wire.

Rhody lived in one such house. Rhody and her mother and her daughter tried to straighten up after Rhody's father, but it was hopeless. Mr. Poole believed sincerely that his things were valuable. And then after a while they seemed more than valuable—they were art. He liked how his wire looked, stacked on end in a tower design! He liked the way the galvanized was crimped, and so he bent it up some more till it took on an interesting shape, something like a thunderbolt, and he painted it with aluminum primer, as if a jagged silver piece of heaven had fallen into his yard. Rhody caught him hauling in junk from elsewhere to add to the collection. He welded the heads of three electric fans to the hood of the bad car, and in a wind the blades moved.

"What are those for?" Rhody asked him. He had been sitting on the porch for an hour watching the fans spin.

"For power," he said.

The exact nature of our relationship with the Pooles had never been clear to me. Long before Rae and Rhody became friends, there were links between the two families. Mr. Poole did some work for Pop at one time; Mother bought tomatoes from Mrs. Poole's stand. Almost every white family I knew had a black family they gave clothes to, but there was more between us and the Pooles. As a child, I thought of them as our shadow family. They *matched* us.

The truth was, my mother loved the Pooles. That's what

"Call him," Rae said, chewing on a fish tail.

"Of course," Pop said. "Your mother called me on the telephone all the time. But she was an unusual girl. It was an unusual romance."

"This is no romance at all. It isn't even in that category," I said.

"So call him," Rae said. "If it isn't serious, what have you got to lose?"

"I don't know," Billy McQueen said. "I'm not sure about this. If the fellow wanted to talk to Lucille he would do the calling, wouldn't he? Can't we assume, then, that he doesn't want to talk? I think she's perfectly right, to lay low. Play hard to get."

"I'm not *playing hard to get*. I don't want to call him; I asked him not to call me. The relationship is over, period. Nobody's calling anybody."

"I say don't call him," Billy said. "How many vote with me?" He raised his hand. "Okay, how many say call him?"

"Forget it," I said. "We're not taking a vote."

"This is a democracy, isn't it?" Billy said.

"I don't know why everyone thinks my private life is such a joke," I said. "When it's you all who have screwed up your lives. Mine is still intact, but it seems to be the one everybody wants to laugh at. I mean, I don't care, go right ahead, but it just seems ironic. To me."

I left them. I lay down in my room on my white iron bed. On top of the bedposts were four brass balls that I had restored to the original brassy sheen. They shone like small suns at the corners of my universe.

I would not drive my father all over creation today. He could get them to drive him. I might, in fact, spend the day in my room, in my bed, with all my windows open on the water side. People have no respect for girls. People think girls are brainless. Even someone who has recently been one has kept us hooked to them so long. It was an odd love, but I do not think it came from guilt or charity or envy; I think it was just plain love. I recognized it at an early age, one day when I witnessed an argument between Mother and Rhody in the kitchen. Rhody was pregnant.

"How could you have been so stupid?" Mother said, slapping a dishrag against the drainboard. Rae and I automatically drew back. Anger from Mother was rare. Ordinarily nothing had the power to move her to rage, but now her eyes showed it, the rims tensed and the pupils like black stones. My first thought was that she hated Rhody, who stood there without flinching.

"You could have done anything in the world you wanted to do," Mother said, bitterness causing her voice to quiver.

"That is what I did," Rhody said. "And still can." Her tone amazed me. She wasn't talking back; she stood there calm and even-voiced, *explaining.*

Mother shifted her weight and looked at Rhody in surprise. Rhody was not her daughter, so there was a distance between them. Mother said, "I don't know, Rhody."

"*I* know." Rhody was tall and bony and still had her hair plaited in rows. She did not look grown; but I realized she was. They stood there facing off, and then Rhody started to giggle. She stopped herself and then started again. She had never been able to win a staring contest with me or Rae, but always broke into laughter at the sight of our artificially lugubrious faces.

"Excuse me," Rhody said, trying to compose herself, not fully succeeding.

To my shock, Mother laughed. She turned herself in a circle and touched her knees and said, "You're probably right! You'll probably set the damn world on fire one way or another. You've sure got the wherewithal." They hugged. Rae and I watched. That's how I knew my mother loved the

Pooles, from the way she had gone from fury to embracing, so fast.

I loved them myself, but not without trepidation. The Pooles all scared me somewhat. At their house I felt uneasy. Even Rhody was formidable, because she understood human foibles and rose above them. "I know everything," she once told me in a confidential tone.

When Rhody's baby, Evelyn, turned ten last year, I went over with Rae to deliver our presents. Evelyn always wanted books. She was reading at the twelfth-grade level and her schoolbooks bored her. We selected our books for Evelyn with great care, as if we were feeding crucial information into a computer. I gave her Ovid in translation and Rae gave her Betty Friedan. The yard was so full that we could not use the front door, so we detoured through the junk around to the back of the house, where a path had been left to the back door.

Mr. Poole had put up a sign by the back door, "Root Man for God." But Rhody said that her father had not always been a root man. In fact he didn't know anything about the cures and spells that a real root man knows. He called himself a root man because there was no existing word for what he had become. He cured motor vehicles and small appliances.

Rhody had plans to move to Osceola Pointe. "I can't raise Evelyn here," she said.

Evelyn was sitting on the floor already several pages into the *Metamorphoses.*

"Evelyn is done *raised,* and you didn't barely have a hand in it," Rhody's mother said from the bedroom.

"I get real depressed here," Rhody said to us.

"I never knew no black women had time to get depressed," her mother called out. "You must be the first generation."

When her father welded parts of a lawn mower, a Tonka truck, an egg-beater, and a Smith-Corona typewriter to the hood of the old car, Rhody left home. She was employed by Palmetto Beach Resort and Villas. It was nothing more than a waitress job, but since she had an associate degree in hotel-motel management, she knew there was something in the future for her, and she didn't mind paying out more than half her salary to rent a one-bedroom in Osceola Pointe. She had her own balcony. It was the first time she and Evelyn had lived alone together, and it was like a honeymoon. They grilled hamburgers and sat out on the balcony at night.

I visited them. She gave me a Coke and we watched television. I just sat there not watching with all my attention, because it was relaxing to be in Rhody's apartment, so much cleaner and nicer and cooler than her old house. There was a dumpster outside, and the trash was carried away every day; it could not pile up. There were no cockroaches because pest control came twice a month, also taking measures against rats and termites. The grounds were stark since it was not a high-rent development—construction costs are lower if they cut down all the trees first—but Rhody stayed inside most of the time, anyway, so she didn't mind not having trees.

We were lounging in front of her TV when we heard a horn honking outside, not just taps but long blasts. When they didn't quit, Rhody went to the window.

"Oh, Lord." She slid open the glass door and stepped out on her balcony; Evelyn and I followed.

Mr. Poole had gotten the old car, the one that didn't run, running. On the hood was the completed work of art, composed of tools, utensils, toy-parts, and china figurines wired and welded and glued together. A growing philodendron cascaded over the grill. On top of the whole structure was a yellow toy chicken, the kind you get in an Easter basket, wearing a striped party hat.

"What is the chicken for, Daddy?" Rhody said, elbows on the railing.

"That is no chicken, Daughter, that is a fighting rooster, for courage."

"What is the plant for?"

"Hope." He leaned up against his car as if it were a brand new Mercedes. I guessed this car was a Plymouth, but it was hard to tell, so many sections of it were missing. Except for the yellow chick and the philodendron, the whole thing had been spray-painted silver, including the tires and side windows.

Rhody smiled and leaned far over the balcony. "You think it's going to work?" she said.

"That's what I'm here for, to show you, girl! The car's running, isn't it?"

"Looks like it," she said. "You want to come in?"

"No, thank you. I got appointments. Gentleman out by Awendaw has got a tractor that won't go, and a lady in Cain Hoy called me about her air conditioning."

He drove off, and for a long time Rhody stood leaning on the railing, staring down the road. It seemed sad to me that she had to let him go like that. The sight of my own father driving away had always made me feel sad. Rhody stared. No cars came. The road disappeared into trees.

Then in the fall a small hurricane hit at the time of a full-moon high tide, and water came up three feet in Rhody's complex, shorting out the electricity and weakening something in the foundation so that a crack appeared in the stucco-over-plywood exterior wall. The complex was discovered by building inspectors to be in violation of seventeen sections of the building code. The water had no place to drain out to, since Osceola Pointe was the lowest spot around already, having originally been a marsh. Everybody had to move out. Rhody moved back home.

The newspaper, which I had begun to read faithfully that year on the assumption that it would tell me what was going on in the world, described the Osceola Pointe development as a boondoggle. A fire had since damaged one section, bringing the builders a little more insurance money. The building stood empty, windows out, weeds coming up in the recreation court. Hawks nested in a third-floor apartment.

I concluded that the world can accommodate the mess that one private individual makes on his own. One man's mess may even acquire artistic merit, or religious significance. What we had to look out for was men in packs, making messes the world could not stomach. Building, spraying, burning. Something deep and ungovernable as hunger was driving those men. That was my personal opinion. I never voiced it. But damage was being done, and nobody seemed to notice.

Was my father one of them?

It was a question I did not like to face. I said no, he was not. I knew him so well. I knew *him*, his personality, or whatever is a man's essence. But I did not know, specifically, his history; I could not vouch for all the actions of his life. I did not even know the reasons my mother had for leaving him, and she must have had more than she was letting on. She must have had something against him.

Sometimes I felt a strong urge to quit loving my father. Just quit, the way you can go down to a bank and draw out your life's savings. It was a kind of love that tuckered me out while returning no great reward, and maybe that is how it's meant to be, so that sooner or later a child will realize love is more wisely invested elsewhere than in a parent.

But at the time I was still locked into a habit of deep devotion and could not have got out of it if I'd tried. Most love works that way: you can't get out until its natural term is up.

I did love him, no doubt about that. From a burning houseful of friends and relations I would have dragged him out first and never given a thought to the others until he was safe. But the love itself, the work of it, was debilitating, requiring me constantly to imagine the world from his point of view. Dragging him from a burning house would have been easier. I could not just relax and take things as they came. I had to think at every instant, what does this mean to him, this television show, this rainstorm, this new marriage? Sometimes his perspective came easily to me, and I could know instantly what he was thinking, but more and more often the effort became a strain. It was like looking through someone else's eyeglasses: you can do it if you squint down to the exact right point and tighten the tiny muscles behind your eyeballs, but it hurts, and when it's over you can't see with your own vision for some time.

This morning, when he took his coffee onto the porch and sat in the swing, I watched from the living room. The newspaper lay on his knee, still folded. He looked out over the yard to the water.

This was the view he had had for twenty years, out from under the cool brow of the porch onto green grass and then the sun-scorched myrtles, marsh reeds, dock, mud, water, sky. But he gazed as if it were new, as if he had not till this morning noticed the amount of empty space contained in the view. The land was a low strip, the water a blue bank, and everything else was air.

He closed his eyes. I closed mine. The smell of myrtles came in on waves of moving wind.

Suddenly he jumped up, so fast that the newspaper dropped from his lap, the coffee spilled across the floor. I thought to myself, goodness, he looks as if he's seen a—and then I thought, well, of course—that's what it is! But there was nothing I could do to help. If he was so obsessed with her that he saw her face in the empty air, no one could help. I hoped it was not a sign of craziness. Lots of people tend to see faces, like the man in the moon or the Savior on a grain silo. Seeing faces is not as crazy as hearing voices. I myself had seen faces on automobiles and on small houses. Do not panic, I said to myself.

He pulled a white cotton handkerchief out of his pocket and leaned down to wipe up the spilt coffee. I heard him mumble, "Roofing paper." Then, "Toolbox. Shingles. Mmm, shingles?"

He left his cup and the unread newspaper on the table and went out the screen door, down the steps that led to the water. But in the yard he turned and disappeared under the house. He had a little workshop down there, a one-window room where he stood at a carpenter's table to build small pieces of furniture for dollhouses. Not for us—we had always disdained dolls—but for adult hobby shows.

I followed him into the yard and looked back through the lattice panels to the workshop, in time to see the door close behind him.

He was the kind of man who should never have retired. We all knew that and had tried to talk him out of it, but something had convinced him that the time had come to step down. After he did, he was at a loss. Mother complained that he followed her around while she vacuumed. Without projects, he was subject to clouds of thought that only confused him. He was not made for rumination. Someone like me can think nonstop and never suffer damage from it, like those wizened little farmers who turn one hundred and claim to have smoked cigarettes for eighty years without effect on their lungs; but I was unusual. Pop, like most businessmen, was a man of action. He needed projects.

Years ago he had flown a Cessna. He liked to remember what it was like to fly, but he didn't want to fly now. He was earthborne now, he said. But he still talked about the Cessna. He had had the kind of license that requires you to keep the ground in sight. But once or twice, he confessed, he had gone into the edge of a cloud on purpose. A cautious man in every aspect of his life, he did this one thing that was as stupid as Russian roulette. He was shocked by his own foolhardiness, but he couldn't help it, that soft dazzle tempted him. Then once he got in, it was not so white and comfy as he had expected, but gray, and grayer the deeper he went. What if it was deeper than he had figured? But soon the light changed, the muck brightened, and he was headed out, towards clear sky and sun again. He said that was the best sight in the world: the world.

Which way was out now? He had endured two months' worth of gray fluff, since her departure.

I heard a *cullunk* against the side of the house. What was he doing? I couldn't see him from the window, but I heard the squeak and groan of aluminum and knew he was climbing his ladder to the roof. In a moment, the actual sun in the actual sky would be beaming down on him, and his cloud of thought would have vanished. He'd be suddenly happy, kneeling on his own roof, replacing shingles. He loved roofs. On a job he had always gone up to get a feel for how a building was going to come down. Parnell, his business partner, thought he was crazy. What could you tell from the roof, Parnell wanted to know. Parnell was the brains of the company, the one who studied the numbers. But Pop worked by the feel of it. Parnell had paid attention to him, too. Pop had been good.

You want them to go down straight, he told me, like a man shot in the knees, crumpling. You do not want them to swing or blow sideways. His last job was the old Wade Hampton Hotel in Columbia, eleven stories with clearance problems and no original structural drawings on hand. But standing on the roof, he had known the building would fall clean. He stayed up there awhile because there was a temple in the middle of the roof. Out of a landscape of roof junk—ventilators, condensers, antennas, a dilapidated louvered cooling tower—rose a small Greek temple, columns and all. He had not noticed it from the street. As a temple it was convincing, even though he knew it housed the elevator switch gear. He stood in its portico, looking out past the spread of Columbia towards the sandhills, and he felt queerly lifted from his own life into a clean and quiet myth.

He related this experience without self-consciousness. There was a lot of sky around, he said. Pigeons cooed in the pediment. The moment was still and bright, and wonderful in his memory for weeks after. But it hazed over, and he could never quite reconstruct it. He recalled the feeling, but he could not feel it again, and couldn't quite describe it. "A sort of airiness," he said. "In the world and in me, too. I've never been able to get it back."

The Wade Hampton had gone down the way he had foreseen: first, puffs of smoke out the lower windows, no noise, the afternoon still apparently innocent to bystanders; then the inward buckle at third-floor level, ruin assured. At first the temple hardly moved, as if it might hang in the sky alone. Then it shivered and dropped, intact, straight down. "It was beautiful," he told us, "in free fall like that above the collapsing base; and then it disappeared into the rising dust. Just right." The sound was right, too, a rumble that seemed to come up out of the earth to meet the falling building.

Brains were not enough in his business. Pop had succeeded even though he didn't have a Clemson degree like Parnell. He was maybe even better than Parnell. He was somewhat famous. Contractors all over the Southeast said Warren Odom was the man to get for a tough job.

And he had taken satisfaction in his work. He could claim partial credit for the new look of the cities he loved: Columbia, Charlotte, Atlanta, Charleston. He had helped clear the way for all their downtown Mariotts and Sheratons, office plazas and civic centers. Some of those hotels had indoor streams, and vines and trees genuinely growing in the lobby. Those buildings were proof that the Southeast had become nothing to be ashamed of. Meanwhile, he said, the Northeast was on the skids. It was good revenge, to have sucked out all their mills and then their light industry and now their banking and investment business.

He was not a waver of the Confederate flag, claimed he would not have fought for the Confederacy if he'd been alive at the time; but he did hate the North. He hated it for that century of hard scrabbling and fear and kowtowing that came after the war, and for the way his mother's dress had blown when the cars passed, showing how close danger could come and leave your heart a cripple.

In the Cessna he had flown city-to-city and watched the growth of his Southern cities. He had been one of the first to notice that the Southeast was coming back, slowly, starting in the sixties and gathering steam, until now the cities had all burst open with prosperity, new buildings, jobs, people moving in from all over the country. He had slept in those fantastic hotels.

But I knew that his favorite place was his own house, this old ramshackle house across the harbor from Charleston, where he had settled with his young wife years ago and raised his children. Buying this house had been a turning point in his life. He could hardly believe his luck at first. He owned this house! The woman in it was an even more stunning stroke of luck. He had never fully understood how he got her. While he had her, he had not wanted to wonder too much about it. He was superstitious, like everyone in a dangerous line of work. It was bad luck to question good luck.

But now, he had told me, his head was full of questions. "Why she left, of course; that's the one I ask myself most, Lucille. But then I come to the question of why she—what she *saw in me*, you know, in the first place. Not money. She was strange about money. Didn't like to fool with it."

I knew that she had always used a credit card in the grocery store. He paid the bills, but there was never anything on the charge except food and children's clothes and supplies for our household. He often bought clothes for her. When she opened a dress box and parted the tissue paper, I watched his face. I interpreted these purchases as true signs of love. A man who buys clothes for a woman must really love her.

"What are you doing up there?" I called. I stood in the sand next to the ladder, but I couldn't see him. There was no answer. It had crossed my mind that he was suffering a partial hearing loss, the lost part being the range that included my voice. I climbed the ladder. It leaned against the house just below the roof, but there was an overhang, and I couldn't maneuver myself over it. I wanted to get up there: I loved high places. I was acrophilic as well as claustrophilic and agoraphilic. I loved all the various kinds of places.

"Lucille!" he said. He was sitting on the ridge, looking out in the direction of the sea. "Come on up. Come look at what you can see."

"I don't believe I can," I said.

He got to his feet and walked to me, and with one hand lifted me over the overhang onto the roof itself. I crawled up to the ridge.

He said, "Don't knock the box of shingles."

The roof showed plainly a history of leak-stopping over the years, patches where the shingles were red instead of brown, or places where in desperation he had spread roofing tar over a trouble spot. Some day he meant to tin it, he always said, but I knew he would not. He was reluctant to make major changes. His reasons were different from mine though; they had to do with money. He was not a miser, in fact was probably at heart the opposite of a miser, but because he had grown up during the Depression, he did not like to spend money unnecessarily.

"It looks like a copperhead," he said.

"What does?"

"The pattern of the shingles, different reds and browns, like scales." He stretched out his hand with the palm and thumb forming a right angle. "Soaking up sun like a lazy snake."

It was unlike Pop to use similes. He was not a man who often saw likeness; he saw things as they were, straight.

"What a view, eh?" he said.

Next door, the Lawtons' Confederate flag snapped in the air, and farther down the street a mower mowed. On the curve of our small bay I could see six houses, clusters of empty lawn chairs, one drooping badminton net, and everybody's green grass stretching towards the water as far as it could go before giving way to wax myrtles and then marsh. Most houses had a two-plank dock on piers, widening to a small platform over deep water.

"Reminds me of what you see from the little plane," he said. "From above the world looks, well, *gorgeous*. The higher you go, the better it looks."

We heard the screen door slam. Rae in a bathing suit went down the front steps, carrying a towel and pillow. I made a mental note to buy her a maternity bathing suit.

"It's extraordinary," he whispered. "You get the feeling it's all a different world. She looks like a different person. Don't you get that feeling? She looks like some grown woman in another town."

"She is a grown woman."

"Well, I know that. But she looks more like someone who you didn't know as a child. I think I only just recently began to think of her, and you, as a true person."

"What did you think of us as before?"

"Oh, I don't know. Well, pets, to tell the truth. Your mother's pets. The way she talked to you in secret code, little tsks and chucks. Or behind closed doors. She had a way of keeping her children to herself. I never really got to talk to them except through her. I never talked to them in the way you should talk to people, as your real self to their real selves. I always talked like a cartoon character." He thought that over. "A bumbler. Mr. Magoo. When in fact, Lucille, I had a lot to say. I couldn't quite put it into words. I think if I'd had a son—oh, I'm not saying I wanted one—but if I'd had one, I might have—I might have—"

"Talked more."

"Yes, exactly. Your mother, you know, is smarter than I am. Sometimes I eavesdropped on her, when she was talking to you and Rae and Rhody. Her topics were intriguing! Walt Whitman, the search for the city of Troy, that fellow Oppenheimer. She had a way of seeming to know the world's secrets. It's difficult to speak up in the presence of such a woman."

"I know," I said.

He began hammering shingles. I watched his eyes as he placed the nail with one hand and simultaneously raised the hammer with the other, while I would have done one thing and then the next. His lips were closed tight over four long nails. She had not married him for his money, he was sure of that. Had it been to escape her family? He drove a nail into the glittering asphalt shingle. It went in soft, then hit wood and caught. Was it the money, after all? There was nothing else he had that she could have wanted.

I saw him frown as he raised his arm. He cracked a shingle down the middle with a mislaid blow and watched the two halves slide to the edge of the roof and go over, making no noise when they hit the sand.

Mother seemed to have slipped easily out of this marriage, as if she had only been visiting. But he was catapulted into a whole new world, and lost in it. The sky was different. A ham sandwich was different. His own shoes lined up in the closet this morning had looked so unusual, he said, that he could hardly reach for them. "They resembled animals, in pairs like that, Lucille, facing the same way like cows." He had stared at them. It was not a completely crazy idea. They had once *been* cows. Maybe still had cow DNA under the cordovan polish. He had closed the closet door and put on canvas sneakers.

From the roof we saw Rae again. She walked barefooted through the grass and realigned the wooden chairs so that they faced the water. Billy came up behind her and touched her back. She moved away. They stood six feet apart, both of them leaning on the damp chairs. There was not much of Mother in her looks, but she had Mother's I.Q. Maybe she was even too smart. Pop said he was glad she had married abruptly, because he had been afraid that she might try to make it on her own. And even Rae at heart did not have what it takes to barrel alone through the world. In his opinion she needed the protection of a husband, to keep her in one place and focus her energy. Rae had a diffusive aspect, Pop said, that could have been her ruin, unmarried.

But he had an anxious feeling about Rae and Billy McQueen. Looking down from the roof, he said, "I can look at those two and tell, there is too much sex there. Excess of desire can unbalance a marriage."

I stared at him. The most intimate subject he had ever mentioned to me before was toothbrushes.

"Your mother and I had a similar phase; everyone goes through that honeymoon stage. But this looks different. This looks possibly explosive."

I looked down. My goodness, he was right. I hadn't seen that, and he had. I watched Rae spread her white beach towel in the grass and let herself down on it to sunbathe. She was on her back. Billy came up behind her and stood a few inches from her shoulder. If she knew he was there, she didn't let on. She didn't move. Her eyes were shut. Billy's shoes looked like some kind of military boots, heavy-soled and old, stiff as wood. With one toe he nudged her side. Her arm was as fast as a sprung trap, grabbing the boot and twisting it as she rolled her body. Billy was off guard. Rae rolled into the grass with his foot in her hands, and he fell next to her.

Surely they knew we were up there. Rae would have seen us when she came up over the rise. Pop tried to announce our presence by hammering a nail, but the wind was blowing our way, and the neighbor's lawnmower had come closer, so we had not been heard. I looked again at Billy and Rae. They were squirming. I looked into the next yard, and down the road, and to the water. No one else could see them. They lay this side of the myrtles, where the ground dipped. A thick hedge of oleander protected them from the view of the neighbors. Pop and I crawled to the far side of the roof, careful not to let the toolbox slide. He looked at his watch. How long would we have to hide up here? Five minutes? Twenty minutes? Pop was ready to wait them out. He lay back against the sloping roof, his arms folded under the back of his head. "Young people!" he said. "Men and women!" He seemed not embarrassed, but thoughtful, mulling the subject of men and women. Now that he himself was a man without a woman, the mystery of it was deeper.

I lay back and looked at the sky.

After a while he fell asleep, face toward the sun. His jaw loosened and his head slipped from his chest. The sunlight beat down on us; it seemed to have a rhythm. Maybe he let an image into his head of Mother's strong jaw, and the face turned into a dream. His hand twitched and one foot kicked up; dogs and old men enact their dreams like that. I knew a dream of her would fill him till nothing in him was not the dream, and desire overwhelmed him to a degree he may never have felt in real life, a sad-hearted, musical desire.

But when he woke, it wasn't true. He sat up slowly, looked at me, looked at his watch. "We're on top of the house, by God," he said.

"Yes."

"My head is throbbing. I believe I have baked my brains like a meat pie." The skin on his forehead looked tight and red. "But I saw it, Lucille, just like on the top of the Wade Hampton hotel. I have seen past the rough-and-tumble, into the serene."

I nodded. "That's great, Pop."

He stood up and strode to the ladder, and didn't appear to hear me when I told him to be careful. Backing down the ladder, he was so full of thoughts he babbled as they came.

"I'm into a new phase. What was I thinking of, all those years? All that work and activity, all in the wrong direction. I'll have a new outlook. I'm in the age of wisdom now. I'll be the old philosopher! Lucille!"

"Yes?" I looked over the edge. The yard was empty except for the white towel in the green grass.

"I want to go to the bookstore. Can you drive me to one?"

I grew suspicious; I thought he had women on his mind and wanted to buy himself a magazine full of them. Well, I could hardly stop that. I tried to have an open mind. Sex is everywhere. I certainly couldn't keep him from reading those magazines but did I have to aid and abet him?

"Do you want a magazine?" I said.

"No, I'm tired of magazines. I want books. Heavy hard-back books."

"Paperbacks are a lot cheaper, Pop." I knew he hadn't been inside a bookstore in years, and he would never pay twenty dollars for a book.

"I don't care about that. I want the weight. I don't want to feel like I'm reading a paper napkin."

"What book are you looking for?"

"No one book. *Books,* Lucille. You can drop me off and come back for me later."

He didn't want me watching what he bought. "I don't mind waiting," I said.

"It may take some time," he said. "I may very well be making a sizeable purchase."

"Of what?"

"Well," he said, blushing. "I don't have much of a personal library. I thought I might, well, start a private collection."

"Of *what?*" I said, imagining so-called artistic photography books.

"Oh, reference books."

"I'm going with you," I said, scrambling down the ladder.

"One thing is sure. It's never too late. Am I right?"

"Right." But it is always too late, once you get to the point where you have occasion to say it is never too late.

I found the keys and we were on our way. I was getting good at this: started the engine with only the slightest motion of my thumb, a mere flick; backed out of the yard looking over my shoulder, my right hand behind the seatback; and shifted into forward while the car was still moving in reverse. I loved that little instant of hesitation before the gears engaged, a moment of grace between backward and forward; then we took off, fast. Even Pop commented on the speed. Those old jokes about women drivers were obsolete—women were the best. My models were the carpool mothers I had seen in enormous station wagons. Not even Richard Petty could outdrive them. I might see one rocket down the road at sixty-five, left elbow resting on the door, hand propping a tilted head, children tumbling in the car like laundry in a dryer. She's good, I'd think, and then I'd realize—on top of all that—*the woman is in a deep trance state!* It takes talent to move sixty-five miles per hour over the surface of the earth in a two-ton vehicle while your mind is on the dark side of the moon.

I could almost do it. Interestingly enough, I became a better driver as my mind drifted. It was Zen motoring: I could drift up to a stop sign and on through the intersection without effort, change lanes and merge as smoothly as if the car were driving itself. I didn't even watch the scenery. My interest in it was on the wane these days, anyhow.

Simultaneously, my father's interest in it was growing. Instead of sitting there helplessly as he used to, he was watchful. He had a comment to make on everything we passed—the waterslide, mini-warehouses, money machines, surf shop—as if he were seeing it all for the first time. Why a waterslide so close to the ocean, he wanted to know. Why the proliferation of mini-warehouses? Did people own so much junk that their own houses could no longer contain it? I let him ramble on. I was busy achieving a spiritual state.

On top of the bridge he said, "Look at that, would you," shaking his head in appreciation at some aspect of the landscape below, where the wide rivers came together and the city skyline rose abruptly from the water's edge. I was in the trance and didn't listen too closely to what he said.

"Marriage tells you what you are," he said.

From my fog I took note of that statement, but I didn't say anything.

He muttered on. "Then it's gone, and you're a blank page. I can honestly say I don't recognize myself." He lifted both hands and stared at them.

"What?" I said.

"I mean, who would you say I am, Lucille? Am I the same

as I was with her, or not the same? There's so much I never—the books, the ideas—I never sought the higher truths. I never delved. Here I am sixty years old and I haven't considered the basic questions."

"Like what?"

"Well, good versus evil. The nature of man."

"Oh. Those."

I had to interest him in a lighter topic. Philosophy was not up his alley, and too much thought along such lines could be bad for him. If you're practiced in it, if you're a preacher or a historian, then you can mess around all you want with man versus nature, God in the universe, etc. But for an amateur, it is more than the mental system can handle. You think you are progressing logically towards the great truth, when really you are stumbling in a maze. I had encountered several *bona fide* crazy people in my life, and all of them talked endlessly on these subjects. Metaphysical truth is beyond the scope of the human brain. It exists but it can't be known. I respected the limits of cerebral capability. I didn't want Pop to blow his fuses.

Still! I was filled with sudden wonder and stole a glance at his old dear face. Was this my father talking? Who never spoke of things weightier than the Federal Reserve?

As we neared the bottom of the bridge, he started talking again.

"The only books I own, I own by default," he said. "You know that little shelf in my room under the window? Those are all the books I own, every one. I've got several paperback novels that someone left out in the yard from time to time and I rescued. I read your *Cujo* and *The Thorn Birds.*"

"Oh, Pop!"

"I quite enjoyed them. Then, I got some books your mother was sending over to Evelyn. I admit I took two without her permission, stole them, two books by Judy Blume, and I read those. I have a Louis L'Amour, found that in a grocery cart. And I picked up some mysteries at the barber shop; they didn't have covers and the stylist suggested that I might like to take them home, a kind gesture, I thought. I enjoyed all those books. But now I'm thinking, they are not really permanent books, are they? I want some permanent books. You hear about geniuses when they were growing up, and they are said to have read widely in their father's library. I want the sort of library that a child can read widely in, and discover at an early age the joys of learning."

"But your children are grown," I said.

"Oh, not you," he said. "I didn't mean you. I'm thinking about your sister's child."

I had not thought about my sister's child, or certainly I'd never thought about it in terms of a genuine person who might eventually do something as complex as read a book. All I had thought of was Rae's belly, with of course something in there, but not a baby, just a—well, to be frank, a sort of a blob. To think of it reading a book was difficult.

"But mainly I want some books for myself," he said. "I have to admit, they are mainly for me. Will you help me make the selection?"

"Sure," I said. "Sure. It's a great idea." I looked at him and smiled. "But it's going to be expensive," I warned.

"We're rich, Lucille. We have money to burn."

I had never heard him say anything like that before. He had always said things more along the lines of "Save for a rainy day," and "Money doesn't grow on trees." He had often said how poor he had once been, as if poverty were a disease like rheumatic fever that struck during childhood but could return unexpectedly.

"You know, I was once very poor. Very poor," he said. Here we go, I thought.

"The worst memory I have is looking down Fountain Street,

1937 or so. That was our business street, but you've seen the same street in every Southern town. A straight and short street, Belk's on one side, beauty salon, First National—and on the other side the grocery store, Rexall Drugs, hardware store with green wheelbarrows out on the sidewalk. There are some people who remember their old main street fondly. All these movies now put you back in time, there's a lot of nostalgia these days, but I'll tell you: I hated that street, and I hate the memory of it. I tell myself it wasn't the place I hated so much as the time and situation. But when I think of it now—that particular block, hooded traffic light swinging, pickups parked diagonally—I still hate it. My one dream was to get out of it to a place where there was a future. But when I walked down Fountain Street I felt myself in its grip. My mother worked in the shoe department at Belk's, and I had to be there at three-thirty every day so she could see I had not been killed somehow at school. She was a tragic figure, a woman who had once been a beauty, kneeling in front of customers and touching their feet. I had to look at tragedy every afternoon at 3:30 P.M. I thought if we had money, she'd have stayed pretty, and happy, and sane. My father had quit trying to make money, but sat on the porch all day. I didn't like to go home. I hung around in Belk's until closing time, rode the painted buffalo in the children's shoe department, tried on men's hats, sneaked into the foundation garments alcove. My mother *needed* money, I thought. I believed the lack of money turned her eventually into a bitter and crazy woman."

"You think poverty drove her crazy?"

"I thought so for a long time."

"But it could have been something else," I said.

"That's exactly what I'm thinking! I'd always assumed that her bitterness resulted from not having the house she wanted, the clothes and so forth. But things have been coming back to me."

"In your scenes."

"Yes. After she got the job at Belk's my father treated her badly. I didn't understand at the time. He never did find permanent work, just did odd jobs around town. He drank, and he . . . mocked her."

"How?"

"He imitated her, fitting shoes."

I didn't say anything. We were in front of the bookstore; I parked and turned off the engine and we sat there a minute.

"I blamed the world," he said. "I blamed Herbert Hoover for my mother's mental breakdown! My major error, Lucille, has been faith in money. I should have given more attention to other things."

He wiped his hand over his mouth. "Well! We've certainly had a conversation, haven't we?"

It had been more of a monologue, but I said, "Yes. I liked it, Pop. I'd like to do it again sometime."

He patted my shoulder. "We will. Meanwhile—the father's library must be stocked." He reached for the door, then stopped with his fingers on the handle and said, without looking at me, "I think I'm going to do all right," and I knew what he meant. *Alone*, he meant.

"Of course you are," I said.

We walked arm in arm down East Bay Street, amid tourists and lawyers and children and waiters, a good miscellany of citizens. I felt happy being one of the throng there, in the summer afternoon. Pop had a new gait, a slower, almost uncertain step. He was looking at everything. He pointed out a building where he used to buy rope and marine paint; it had turned into a law firm. Across the street, where two years ago there had been a wholesale hosiery place, was the bookstore. As we went in, a string of little bells jingled on the door. A pretty girl behind the counter smiled at us. "Isn't she beautiful!" he said. He stared too hard at the girl, causing her to look away.

The store was self-service; he was expected to locate his own books. But he was not a man who could browse. He said he felt like Bigfoot, lumbering down the aisles and hoping that nobody would notice him. He pretended to browse, but he was really feeling his way cautiously down the shelves, as if all the books were balanced precariously and one false move from him would bring them down like the Wade Hampton Hotel.

He studied the categories.

"Fiction, no. At a younger age I might have been interested, but time is too short, Lucille. I want books you can learn out of. The same for Poetry, and, I'm sorry, for Inspiration, not my cup of tea. What about these —Food, Travel, Art? I don't think so." He stopped at the Juvenile shelf.

"Do they still have those books about mythical places— Camelot, Atlantis, Oz, Troy?" He looked down the spines, but all these books seemed to be about pregnant teenagers. We moved on.

At Nonfiction he cocked his head and read the titles. "We're getting close," he said. "The lives of famous men, accounts of war, studies of ethnic groups. Wisdom could probably be dug from books in this category. If you learned every battle of the Civil War, for example, as my partner Parnell has, or all the military strategies and the statistics, if you amassed in your head a large body of historical fact, wouldn't you gain some wisdom?"

"Parnell never did," I said. "It's only made him worse. He calls civil rights workers 'abolitionists.' "

Pop stopped in his tracks. "He said that to you? I told him I'd break his neck if I ever heard that talk—"

"No, I overheard him in the office once."

"I've got it," he said, looking at the shelf in front of him. "We search no further." I looked. Birds, rocks, fossils, butterflies, shells. Animal tracks. Animal droppings! All catalogued and illustrated by reliable authorities. "Scientists have been keeping this material to themselves," he said. "When I was young, you couldn't get access to this information." He picked out five different field guides. "We'll come back later for more," he said, "I don't want the girl to think I'm crazy." He watched her ring up the purchases.

"You did good," I said outside.

"Yes?"

As we waited at the curb to cross the street, a yellow Mazda passed. The driver tooted the horn and waved; she smiled. "That was Helen," he said in surprise.

"I don't think so," I said.

He was sure of it, in spite of the car, which was not hers and not the sort she was likely to drive. I knew it wasn't Mother, but there was no convincing him.

"Helen!" he called, but the car was already out of sight. "Let's go!" he said to me, dropping the bag of books. I picked them up and followed him to the car. "Get in, hurry!" he said.

At every intersection we stopped and looked both ways to see if she had turned there. No yellow Mazda. At the Market we had to wait for a gang of tourists crossing the street. "Where could she have been going?" he said. "Turn up, then take Calhoun to Meeting." There he couldn't decide whether to turn or go straight. On our right was the Baptist church and its daycare center, to the left the Holiday Inn, and ahead was the square where John C. Calhoun stood on his sixty-foot pedestal, looking south.

Cars honked behind us. We turned right from the left lane and almost got hit by a Jeep driven by a blond teenage girl who gave us the finger. I pulled into the lot next to the daycare center. "Let's just go home," I said.

He was breathing hard and sweating. "No, no. If I could just figure out where she might have been going—"

"Well, let's go sit on a park bench," I said. We got out of the car and crossed the street into the square. I chose a bench from which we could see John C.'s mean bronze-green bony face. Pop sat with his hands on his knees for some time; I set the shopping bag next to him on the bench.

"Why did she toot the horn?" he muttered. "What am I supposed to make of that?"

I understood why old men sit on park benches. It is because they have finally tired of chasing women. We gazed at the statue, the church, the Holiday Inn. Old men on benches probably notice details that never caught their attention before. Under Calhoun a black woman spread a tattered plastic raincoat and sat down. Pigeons puffed and twirled in pairs. In the yard of the daycare center were small horses on springs screwed into the ground. One bobbed, as if a child had recently dismounted.

I looked up pigeons in the new bird book. "Look," I said. "They are called rock doves, and they come from another land." We held the book between us and discussed the pigeons. Questions occurred to us that could not be answered by the book (do they know they are in a foreign land? do they long, in some dark birdly way, for their original home?), but we were satisfied, for the time being, with what we had learned.

It takes more than will power to stop thinking of someone you have loved and lost. I could see that in the slump of his shoulders and the way his feet were set close together. He had tried, in a burst of energetic resolve. But it would take more than that, to stop. Whatever new beauties he could discover in the world would still, for a long time and maybe for his whole life, not be quite enough to keep memories away.

"We need to move on, Lucille," he said.

*I*t is a good thing that human beings have hormones to drive them blind into marriage. Otherwise no one in his right mind would do it. There are too many pitfalls. What did Rae know, really *know*, about McQueen? Maybe he had some flaw that wasn't readily observable. What if he was tone deaf or lazy or in need of extensive dental care? He might go bald! I asked her if he had had braces, because his teeth were suspiciously straight. She didn't even know, and hadn't thought to ask. He might have an overbite passing invisibly via DNA to Rae's unborn child. No question: marriage is as risky as Las Vegas.

"What this family needs is a little nightlife," Rae said.

We were sitting around a pile of shrimp shells on a table covered with newspapers. I had overeaten. All the pink translucent shells, the juice soaking the papers, the four empty bottles next to my plate were evidence. Ordinarily I was not a big eater, but lately I found myself attracted to food. It wasn't an eating disorder; I wasn't binging and purging. But food had a new appeal to me, and I had that feeling in my abdomen that was similar to hunger, so it made sense to eat the food. Sometimes food made the feeling of hunger go away.

"I have never seen a girl drink four beers in twenty minutes," Billy said.

I shrugged.

"That's how we are down here," I said.

"You aren't even shaky," he said.

"We start on beer at age ten. We drink it for breakfast. Think I'll have another one right now. How about a guzzling contest?"

I got him a can of Miller Lite. He rocked back in his chair, eyed me, and popped the top. I unscrewed my bottle cap. "Ready?" I said.

"Oh, Lucille," Rae said, lowering her head into one hand.

"Go!" I tilted my head back and opened up the back of my throat, stopping twice before the bottle was empty. Billy wasn't half through.

"Jesus," he said. "You could kill yourself."

"Nah," I said.

"I'm serious. I don't want you to do that again, Lucille. Rae, how can you let her do that? It's her fifth damn beer."

"Don't worry about it," Rae said.

He shut his mouth and frowned. I felt guilty. "It's fake," I said, passing him the bottle.

He read the label. " 'Non-alcoholic malt beverage'? "

"Lucille doesn't drink," Rae said. "No liquor, no beer, no wine. She's a teetotaller."

"I think that's admirable," Pop said. "In this day and age. It takes real backbone to resist peer pressure."

"That's not the problem," I said. "It makes me sick. I think it has something to do with the inner ear. I throw up if I get dizzy, whether it's from beer or a joint or a ride at the fair. I don't even go on the merry-go-round. It's physiological. I'm not trying to be morally superior or anything."

"Morally superior people never try. They can't help it," Rae said. "Lucille is just plain good. She was born that way and the rest of us just look on in wonder."

"I believe you're right," Pop said.

"You're wrong," I said. "You have the wrong idea of me. I'm not like that at all."

Billy looked at me. I couldn't tell what he was thinking. He read the fake beer label again.

"So how about it," Rae said. "I'm feeling frisky. How about some nightlife?"

Rae could *get* frisky, I well knew. The surprise was that her urge for nightlife had not come on sooner. Maybe pregnancy hormones had calmed her down some. For weeks we had done nothing but eat, swim, fish, and sleep. Like unsupervised children, we spent whole days in our bathing suits. Rae had found an old maternity suit of Mother's shaped like a blue bubble. We lay on the warm wood of the dock until the heat drove us into the water, and then we dried in the sun again; we showered under the spray of the outside shower, which drew cold water from a deep well. At night, sunburnt and still in our suits, we cooked supper—shrimp, crabs, fish, tomatoes, corn, okra—and later played Monopoly or Scrabble or ghost or dictionary, the games that only happy families can play. Once I saw the Frobinesses, when they were still intact, sit down to a cutthroat game of Scrabble played entirely in silence until the end, when violence erupted; Mrs. Frobiness threw her rack and all her tiles into the trashmasher, and hissed at her husband, "You knew I had the Q, and you blocked that U on purpose!" But we left spaces for one another; Billy looked at my rack and rearranged BROWIAN so that I could see what was in it. RAINBOW. I got 72 points for that. I wanted this daily schedule to become permanent.

But Rae wanted nightlife.

"Let's *go* somewhere," she said.

"Fine with me," Billy said, but not in a whole-hearted voice.

Pop looked at his watch. I remembered that we had agreed to play honeymoon bridge every Wednesday night. The com-

puterized game I had ordered for him would set up the number of hands you wanted and play the extra hands; you didn't
even need cards. He loved bridge, but since we didn't always
have four players he sometimes had to play it solitaire or
honeymoon style.

"Let's go, Lucille," Billy said, slapping the table.

"Can't. I'm playing bridge with Pop."

Rae came over and slid her arms under mine from behind,
lifting me half out of the chair. "Come on," she said. "Live
a little."

"We made a date, didn't we, Pop?" I said, sitting down
with a thump.

"Pop can come, too."

"He doesn't want to and neither do I."

"Oh, Lucille, you are such an old lady. Do you realize
that? Isn't she, Billy?"

"Maybe she's just not a night person," he said.

I looked at him in surprise. How had he known that? I had
to give him some credit for perceiving that characteristic in
me. I was definitely diurnal. Evenings made me edgy, and full
night was downright scary. I still had a night light in my
room, one of the Flintstones that plugged directly into the
outlet. Recently I had tried to find a new one, something less
juvenile, but I was told by the K-mart lady that all night lights
are cartoon characters because they are all for children. That
was an insult and a falsehood, I thought, but I didn't say so.
Certainly many adults would like to have a small light in the
room to fend off the night-worries. Mine were identical in
subject matter to day-worries, but bigger and blown out of
proportion like parade balloons. Even after I managed to fall
asleep, they often kept coming on, fat and bobbly monsters.

As for going out at night, I had never seen the fun of it.
Daylight is the time for human beings. In prehistoric days the
earth was blanketed in darkness for eons and everybody was

scared of getting eaten, and then it lightened up and men had time off from fear, time to learn how to reason.

"I've been looking forward to this bridge game all day," I said. Actually I didn't like the game at all, or any card game, because my mind tended to wander from the cards, off to the popping of firecrackers on people's docks or cicadas in the myrtles, and then I would lose. But I played for Pop's sake. "Have you got the game?" I asked him.

"Er, Lucille," he said, pinching his nose. "I know we did agree to a couple of hands tonight, but why don't you run on with your sister. You don't want to sit home with me."

"Of course I do. Let's get started."

"The truth is, Lucille, that I have other plans. For the evening."

How could he have plans that excluded me? The buses didn't run at night. Once or twice he had asked me to drop him off at Cinema East, but I had talked him out of it because the theater was always full of rowdy teenagers who made it impossible to watch the movie.

"You're not going to the movies, are you?" I said.

"No, actually, I'm going over to watch the VCR with Mrs. Oxendine."

"Good for you," Rae said.

"You're what?" I said. "With who?"

"Mrs. Oxendine, who cuts my hair. She has a new video cassette recorder, and she invited me to come over and watch a movie. If you are going out, Billy, I could use a lift. She lives over behind the high school, too far for me to walk. Could you drop me off?"

"Sure," Billy said.

I turned to Rae for help, but she was doing her preoccupied act. Or maybe it was no act at all; maybe she was preoccupied. I couldn't tell. She poked around in her pile of empty shrimp shells and found an unopened shrimp; she put it in her

mouth whole with the little pink cleft tail sticking out. She shelled it with her tongue, the way a parrot hulls seeds. Still working on it, she got up and stood in the breeze by the door. I followed her.

"Rae," I whispered.

"What?" She spit the shell into her fist.

"Don't leave this up to me."

"Pardon?"

"Do you think you can just live your own life, just go off on your own and not pay any *attention* to this? Am I supposed to take care of everything?"

"Hey, I invited you to come with us, didn't I? What is the problem?"

"That isn't what I am talking about. We don't even know this woman. We don't know a thing about her! Why, she could be—she could be—"

"See, there's nothing bad she could be. Relax. I never saw you so neurotic, Lucille. Since when did you take on the cares of the world?"

"She could be a golddigger or a slut or a bimbo or—"

"What in the world has come over you?" She stared at me as if I had grown hair on my face. "You need to get out of this house," she said. "I mean it. You've lost your perspective."

"Never mind, then. If you won't help. If that's the way it' going to be."

"Sweetie, look, the man is only going to some woman house to watch TV."

"No. No, *not* TV. The VCR."

"So what's the difference?"

"Don't you know what VCR's are for? Don't you kno why people buy them? To watch X-rated movies, that's wh]

She laughed and shook her head. "Lucille, Lucille."

"Forget it," I said. I went back to the table, where Pop telling Billy that if he and Rae were about ready, they m

as well get a move on. "I'm already behind schedule," he said. "I said 'after supper' but she eats earlier than we do, and she may be wondering where I am—"

"Let's go," Billy said, pushing his chair back.

"Pop," I said. "I thought you went to the barber shop in the mall."

"I do. Mrs. Oxendine is the new stylist. She gave me this haircut I have now. She said I have unusually thick hair, and she thinned it across here so it doesn't stick up at the top of my ears like it used to. She is an excellent stylist. Vera Oxendine." The way he said her name raised my suspicions.

"And this is your first date?"

"As a matter of fact, no." He cast his eyes down at his plate. "I, ah, have seen her several times. Nothing serious. As you say, Lucille, not exactly in the romance category."

I noticed that his nose hairs had been clipped.

"We'll meet you at the car," Rae said. "Come on, Lulu, let's change." Then she said in a lower voice, "Ease up on the old man."

"What's wrong with what I have on?" I felt stubbornness creeping into my jaw and lower lip.

"Well, you want to get a little dolled up, to go out on the town."

"I don't have anything to doll up in."

"Let's see." She ushered me to my own room and turned on the light. "Don't slouch. Take these pins out of your hair and just kind of shake your head." She ruffled my hair with her hands. She tilted the lamp shade to throw more light on my face. "You're an Autumn," she said. When I looked puzzled, she said, "That's your season. It means you should wear reds and greens." She opened the door of my closet. "Uh-oh," she said.

"What?"

"What do you see there?" she said.

"My clothes."

"I see Drab City. Not one bright color. Look—brown, brown, tan, gray—"

"That's blue-gray," I said.

"Your entire wardrobe is earth tones. No, moon tones." She plucked at sleeves and hems. "Dull, dull, dull. That's not you in there. This is you." She raised her arms and took off her own red sweatshirt and draped it over my shoulders. She turned me in the direction of the mirror.

"No," I said, unwrapping the arms of her shirt from around me. I pulled my hair back behind my ears and anchored it with my metal barrettes.

She watched me. "You think you are virtuous, Lucille, but it is only a form of vanity."

"I know it," I said. I was experienced at avoiding arguments with Rae.

"You're too self-conscious. That's what vanity is, you know. Forget about what you look like. You'll have more fun."

"I know," I said. But what she didn't understand was that I was as tired of self-consciousness as I could be. I didn't tell her that what I really wanted to do was to never have another thought about myself; never again hear the sound of my own voice, outer or inner; never hear my name spoken.

If she'd told me *how* to avoid self-consciousness, I'd have jumped at the chance.

"Twelve-seventy-two Rookery Lane," Pop said from the back seat next to me, leaning forward to look out the front windshield between Rae and Billy. "It's on the left. The mailbox has a wooden goose on the top with rotating wings. There, that's it."

The goose's wings were going strong, making it resemble a swimmer backstroking like mad. The house was small, with siding of wavy mint-green shingle. Pop bounded out of the car and was on his way up the walk by the time I slid over and stuck my head out the window. "Wait," I called out. "What time do you want to be picked up?"

"Don't worry about me," he said. "You young folks go out and have a good time. I'll make my way home."

"It's too far to walk. You can't cross the bypass."

"Vera can bring me home."

Behind him the white stork on Mrs. Oxendine's storm door thinned to the side as the door opened. A woman came down the walk to our car, ducked her head, and waved in at us. "I'll run him home," she said. "Eleven-thirty or so, how's that?"

"Why, thank you," Rae said.

I rolled down my window all the way and stuck my head out. "If we aren't back by then, he can go on in. I left the kitchen light on, and there's a key under the—" I stopped cold. I didn't want this person to know where the key was!

"Under the first step," Vera said. "Hee-hee." She hooked her arm through Pop's. "I know more about this family than I do about my own," she said. "You're Rae." She pointed. "And you're Lucille, and there's Billy McQueen, newest addition to the clan." Vera was a square-shaped gray woman, with a blunt, mannish haircut. She wore white round earrings that struck me at first glance as deformed earlobes. Her small hand shot through the window at me and I recoiled before realizing that all it wanted was a handshake. I shook it. The fingers were stubby and damp.

"Night-night," Vera said as we drove off.

I could only conclude that a man is at his weakest in the barber's chair. Fine, so long as the barber is the old trustworthy variety, the pharmacist type. But with the advent of female "stylists," everything's different. All that clipping and shaving, the vacuuming of the neck and brushing of the shoulders—of course, it will foster intimacy. A bond will be forged. What all had he told her about us, sitting high in his chair while she moussed him? I felt betrayed.

Usually a man will replace a lost wife with someone similar. But if God had created a person to be the exact opposite of my mother, it had to be Vera Oxendine.

Rae chortled. "Now, Lucille, what did I say? You can't see any danger in *that*."

"Appearances can deceive," I said. "She's after him."

"Aw, you're taking the situation too seriously, Lulu."

"I take every situation seriously."

"Well, maybe you shouldn't. Maybe you should relax."

"And take everything as a joke?"

"Everything *is* a joke, sweetie. Isn't that right, Billy?"

He didn't say yes.

"That is your outlook, not mine or other people's," I told her. "Some people think nothing is a joke."

"That's the grim outlook. It means everything is deadly dull."

"Not at all," I said. "It means everything is important. That's what I think. Everything in the world is important."

"And what do you say, McQueen?" Rae said.

"I say neither one of you knows herself very well." He swung the wheel and put us on 17 North.

"What do you mean?" I said.

"You're the joker, Lucille. Rae's the one that takes things too seriously. Now one of you tell me where I'm going."

"Fishbone's," Rae said.

"Then take me home first," I said.

"What are you scared of?"

"I'm not at all scared, I just don't want to go there. We'll be the only white people."

Billy looked at Rae questioningly.

"True," she said.

Rae got along with black people. Starting with Rhody in grammar school, she had had a string of black friends. I couldn't talk to them the way Rae could. Of course, I was tongue-tied around white people, too, but with black people there was the additional problem of three hundred years of bad history. The history sat brooding over us like a thunderhead. Rhody and Evelyn were the only ones I felt halfway comfortable around. I was reasonably sure they were not going to stab me.

"Rhody will be there," Rae said. "She got laid off from Palmetto Dunes, so she's waitressing for Fishbone. I want to see her."

Rae had sung with the band at Fishbone's during her vacations from school. The band had no name, and its members came and went, like the Drifters. Only the piano man, Tick Willis, stayed; so people called the band Tick Willis's band, but the phrase was never understood as a name, only a description. Tick was cousin to Fishbone Johnson, owner of the club. Tick was also father to Evelyn, Rhody's little girl.

"Okay, I'll go," I said.

There are some white boys who like to prove they can get drunk with black people. Sometimes a crowd of them would come into Fishbone's and line up at the bar and try to talk black. They brought girls in sundresses who, when Rae sang, sang along with faraway looks in their eyes because they all wanted to be girl singers with a black band.

Every time I went to Fishbone's I was torn by conflicting emotions, because in spite of the cloud of history and the knife blade about to be slipped between my ribs, I loved the black people. I loved not only near-sighted Evelyn, lithe Rhody, and high-waisted Tick Willis, but the others, too. Fishbone, mum in the corner, scared me most, but also was the best. I'd never heard him speak a word. He took in money and watched everything and had a straight razor in his white fisherman boot.

. . .

"What's Evelyn doing now?" I asked Rae in the car.

Evelyn was a child prodigy. Nobody claimed credit for it. Rhody had taught her to read, but Evelyn was one of those children that learns things as if by magic, and once Rhody had given her the sounds of the letters, she was off and running.

"She just got back from Duke University," Rae said. "They have a special summer program for seventh-graders."

I had known many smart people, and I was interested in the question of smartness; what causes it, how it manifests itself. Ever since ninth grade when I got put in Gifted and Talented, I had tried to figure whether I was really gifted and talented, or whether the authorities had made an error. Certainly I was not like the smart people I knew: my mother, Rae, Wayne, Evelyn, all four of whom had fast thoughts. They were quick with answers, and their minds jumped from one subject to another. But I was slow-witted. In bridge I forgot trumps; in Scrabble I could see my letters only as they appeared on the rack. Rae said that because I was left-handed and right-brained, I could not be a rational, logical type person; instead of thinking step-by-step I would think holistically, in pictures. Mother laughed and said, "I call that day-dreaming."

But of all the smart people I knew, Evelyn was the smartest, so smart it almost made me think something was wrong with her. At birth they had said she would be a vegetable because her head-to-body proportions were wrong, and she didn't respond to lights in her eyes. At eight she was reading W. E. B. Dubois, and at ten she became a member of Mensa. Rhody said the X rays they did on Evelyn in the womb after nineteen hours of labor had mutated her brain. Otherwise there was no explanation. There was no heredity and certainly no environment to account for Evelyn turning out a genius.

Fishbone's used to be out in the country. You had to drive

miles up Highway 17 to the little settlement called Germantown. There had never been any people of German descent there; the town was named for Isaiah German, a preacher who in 1866 had moved his entire African-Metho-dist-Episcopal congregation of two hundred out of Charleston with the idea of starting a new city. But nothing came of it beyond the building of a miniature church, which over the generations had lost its congregation as people drifted back to Charleston for jobs. Fishbone's club was in the church.

The trip to Germantown seemed short now. We passed the lit-up quick markets and used-car lots still waving plastic orange pennants in hopes of a late customer. I was working on a theory that a person's sense of time is affected by scenery. A drive through trees and fields and nature lasts a long time. But the same distance through stores and signs is short. You don't get the feeling of progression. Germantown was no longer far from Charleston. It was nearly connected. Sooner or later it would get swallowed up.

There were cars pulled up around Fishbone's on all sides like creatures at a water hole. Under the light from one tall pole, the building looked as if it were about to collapse into a heap of scrap lumber. Supposedly it was built from cypress that would last forever, but over the years Fishbone had shored it up with what was available, and it had the look of a squatter's shack.

But inside you could see the original walls. Around the windows were the carved faces of angels, and at the end, where an altar had been, there was a bas-relief of odd animals, resembling real ones to the extent that animal crackers do: one was either a small wooly bear or a large sheep, and another was surely a goat with a lion's head.

"What is this place?" Billy said.

"A one-hundred-year-old church, and the best nightspot in the county," Rae said.

We were not immediately recognized. I thought that a

hush fell as we came in, but it might have been my imagination. I thought everybody was saying, "Lord, white people." Rae didn't mind a situation like this. She assumed she was welcome anywhere in the world, and probably she was. After a minute, Tick spotted her from across the room and started a new song. Rae smiled and nodded to him.

When the Wando kids were not in Fishbone's, it was a sedate place, even old-fashioned. It was the kind of place people dressed up to come to, where the dancing was slow and the talk polite. If white kids came in, Tick might play something lively, but generally he stuck to old songs. For Rae he went into "The Great Pretender."

We took a booth. I smelled cigarettes and beer and kerosene.

"Looks like a hard bunch," Billy said, looking back over his shoulder at the band.

"They're not college kids," Rae said.

He nodded. He drummed his fingers on the table, not quite in time with the music. I wanted to tell him to calm down. I knew exactly what he was thinking: that these were the last few moments of his life. But he couldn't say so. His own wife wasn't even on guard.

I saw Rhody and Evelyn at a table near the band. Rhody was still tall and thin, copper-colored. Evelyn was stocky and black like Tick, and she had on new eyeglasses. They had been watching the band but when they saw Tick wave, they turned toward us. Rhody broke out in a grin, and came over to our table. She pursed her lips and shook her head when Rae stood up and showed her belly.

"Do I see what I think I see?" Rhody said. "Do, girl. I thought I explained things to you better than this."

"Rhody, meet Billy McQueen, my husband."

"Oh, my," Rhody said, cocking her head to appraise him. "You the responsible party?"

Billy laughed nervously. Don't let her get to you, I wanted to say, knowing Rhody would sure try.

"Thought I taught you, two wrongs don't make a right," Rhody said to Rae. "Lord. Rae Odom, a married woman. Ain't that unique. Which came first, the chicken or the egg?"

Rhody was saying all this to Rae, but her eye was on Billy. I knew what she was up to. Evelyn put a hand on her mother's arm to hold her back. Rhody was a hard one to hold back.

"Did you have ultrasound?" Evelyn said to Rae.

"No."

Rhody said, "Evelyn's new idea is she's going to become an obstetrician. Can you feature that?" Rhody teased Evelyn, but she was proud of everything Evelyn did, from grades in school to her own personally invented hairdo, braids that started close to her head and then looped down like spaniel's ears on each side. Rhody worshipped Evelyn, but not so you could tell; she covered it with teasing.

"Who needs ultrasound?" Rhody said. "Come here." She laid her hands on each side of Rae's abdomen. "You got a boy baby there. By the way you're carrying it low." She rubbed her hands on Rae. "Big old boy."

"Oh, no," I said. "It's a girl."

"What you know about birthing babies, Miss Lucille?" Rhody said.

"Well, nothing," I said. "I just have a feeling about it."

"You ought to get ultrasound," Evelyn said. "Not just to find out the sex, but to see if it's twins."

"Oh, God," Rae said.

"It do look *large*," Rhody said.

"It's a giant," Billy said. "You know those pictures of the giant boy standing with his parents in their living room? I think it's one of those."

"So, Mr. McQueen speaks," Rhody said. She slipped into

the booth next to me. Evelyn stood with her hand on the table, keeping an eye on her mother. Evelyn sometimes kept Rhody out of trouble. "And she married you," Rhody said accusingly.

"She did," Billy said. "Hard as that seems for everyone to believe."

"I hope you know what you got hold of."

"What would that be?"

"Hah," Rhody laughed. "They never know! Grown, two-eyed men." She whistled and shook her head. She looked all of us over. "Well, I'm the waitress in this place," she said. "May I take y'all's orders?"

"Two beers and a Pepsi," Rae said.

Rhody snaked out of the booth. "Sit down, Evelyn. Tell these white people what you been up to."

Evelyn sat. She pushed her glasses up on her nose. Every time I saw her I was taken aback. Evelyn was the unattractive genius offspring of two handsome, average-brained people. Maybe she was invited to Duke University now, but I was worried about Evelyn's future. She was not normal enough to mix into the world. She dressed in out-of-style, little-girl clothes, limp dresses with sleeves and sashes. Rhody tried to get her into sweat shirts and cut-offs, but Evelyn had her own ideas on clothing. She asked her grandmother to sew her these dresses, because you couldn't buy anything like them anywhere, nowadays. She designed them; she *wanted* to look that way.

"Rhody said you went to Duke for a month," Rae said.

"Yes, ma'am." I frowned. Evelyn had never said "ma'am" to us before.

"And it was fun?"

Evelyn thought. "I wouldn't call it 'fun,' " she said. "The work was challenging. I studied Chinese."

"Wow," Rae said. "Chinese. That must have been tough, all those strange letters to learn."

"Yes, ma'am."

Rae looked at me.

"What about the other kids? Did you like them?"

"I liked them," Evelyn said. She stared into her lap. When Rhody came back with the drinks, she gave Evelyn a long look and then asked if she was tired. Evelyn said no.

I saw trouble in Evelyn's future. How could a child grow up normally in a place like the Poole house, with her mother in and out, absent father working on telephone poles by day and playing piano by night, grandfather the self-styled Root Man of God and burying his house under helicopter parts? No wonder Evelyn was strange.

Rhody was looking serious when she returned with the drinks. "You planning on a comeback?" she said to Rae.

"I don't think so," Rae said.

"Could, if you wanted to."

"Thanks, Rhody." Rae held her beer with both hands and looked Rhody in the eye. They had been friends for fifteen years. My mother had paid for Rhody to go to Camp Kanuga with Rae three summers in a row. Rhody claimed to be the only black girl in the state that knew how to shoot a bow and arrow. Later Pop had contributed to sending her to Parkers Business College, paying what wasn't covered by the Sojourners Scholarship. Rhody was a scrapper from the word go, always thinking of how to get ahead. Evelyn had no fight in her at all, but I hoped maybe she wouldn't need any, if places like Duke were already after her.

"Where are you from, Mr. McQueen?" Rhody said.

"Land of Lincoln," Billy said, lifting his bottle to her before taking a swig, watching her closely all the time.

"Thought so. A Yankee white boy will sit in this place all night and never crack a smile. I don't know what causes that, do you? I think they stick something up they—"

"Rhody," Evelyn said. "People at the tables want something."

"You're right, baby. I got my career to think about." She stood up and smoothed her skirt over her flat stomach and thin hips. "Listen," she said to Rae. "Go easy on him, honey. At first."

Rae shook her head and tried not to smile. "Okay," she said.

When Rhody was gone, Billy said, right in front of Evelyn, "I wouldn't want to run into that woman in a dark alley."

"Rhody is the kindest-hearted person I ever met," Rae said.

"I'd just as soon she didn't put her hands on you again," he said.

Rae straightened up in the booth, glancing at Evelyn. "You what?" she said.

"Forget it. I need another beer."

"I'll get you one," Evelyn said and left for the kitchen.

Tick Willis's band played the Platters, the Temptations, the Persuasions, and the Impressions. We sat there drinking and listening. It was as bad as all the dates I'd been on, not counting those with Wayne. Nobody talked. I tried to think of things to say, but each one was so lame I couldn't get it out. The things that were really on my mind were not topics I could safely bring up. Rae watched the band and sang the words. Billy did not watch the band and did not sing the words. He looked everywhere but where the band was, studied the angels in the window frames, moved the beer bottles around.

When the band took a break, Tick came over.

"Rae Odom. You done got married, I heard. Hard to believe. *Hard-to-be-lieve.*"

"For Christ's sake," Billy said.

"Harold Willis," Tick said, holding out his right hand. Billy nodded and took his hand. "Billy McQueen."

"See, I just never did *envision* it. Rae marrying anybody. You can't predict the future, though, it's going to go how it's going to go. And Lucille sitting there like usual, how come you didn't have a say in this? Lucille don't like monkey business," he explained to Billy. "Rhody tells me you come from Chicago, Illinois."

"No," Billy said. "Winnetka, Illinois."

"Well, I guess young people today they don't matter much where they comes from. I got a cousin married a Vietnam, another one married a dwarf."

"He's putting you on," I whispered.

"We different down here," Tick said. "We got a lot y'all don't got."

"Yeah?" Billy said. His thumb was digging at the label on the beer bottle.

"That's not his real way of talking," I whispered to Billy. "He's pulling something."

"Sure," Tick went on. "We got niggers. You got those in Winnetka, Illinois?"

Don't say yes, I prayed. *And don't say no.*

Billy said, "Winnetka is an Indian word. It means 'No Niggers.'"

Tick said, "You serious?"

"Swear to God."

"They don't let 'em in, huh?" Tick tapped his beer bottle. Sometimes men scared me, when they faced off like this.

"Not only that," Billy said. "One comes in by mistake, they enslave him. They kept a bunch of them at the Country Club, wiping wine glasses in a back room."

"Well," Tick said, "that ain't all that different from here."

"No," Billy said. "It ain't." He finished off another beer. Men also sometimes surprised me, the way they could convert animosity to friendliness without spelling out the deal.

Rae excused herself to go to the ladies' room. We all watched her walk across the room. Tick and Billy had their necks drooping. I was only drinking Pepsi, but when you are with drunk people, you feel bleary yourself. We stared at Rae's bony shoulders, her body thin everywhere except where she carried the baby and its milk.

Tick did a double take. "She *pregnant?*"

"Sure as shooting," Billy said.

Tick sat back as if he'd been whipped in a card game. He stared at the ladies' room door. "Does something to me," he said.

"Like what?" Billy said.

"Gets me right here." Tick thumped his chest. "Like when you kill a doe. You feel *bad.* No matter how much you wanted it, once you see it laying there you know you are no good, no better than a white man."

"Hey, you didn't do it. I did it."

"That's right, but all the same. You know what I'm saying, man. You heard her sing."

"Nope. Never heard her sing."

"You shitting me."

Billy didn't say anything. He drank more beer.

"Well, you got a pleasant surprise in store for you, Mr. McQueen. You went and married something and didn't know what you had. What did you marry her for if you never heard her sing? That's like somebody marries a millionairess without knowing about her millions."

"There were other attractions."

"Hell, I know about those, but me being a musician, the music overshadows the rest. Someone's a musical genius, you don't notice her tits. I say honestly I have never heard any live white woman sing like that one. What I came over to see was if you'd let me get her up on stage to do a couple of tunes."

"I don't think so."

"Everybody'd appreciate it."

"No," Billy said.

Tick said, "How long you been married to her?"

"Two months."

Tick nodded. "Makes sense," he said. "Don't blame you a bit. Keep that rein *tight.*" He jerked his fist toward his chest and clenched his teeth. "If she was mine, I wouldn't let her out the house."

"Not to sing in the band?"

"Hell, no. Let me give you a piece of advice it looks like you need. Don't trust a woman like that. Maybe she's true in her heart. But you have to realize, she don't *need* you. That's the bottom line."

"Thanks," Billy said.

Tick raised his bottle. "And if she don't need you, the only thing holding her is happenstance." He smiled. "Happenstance. You got nothing on her, am I right?"

"On her?"

"You got no leverage. Something she needs, she can't get any other place. Look at there." Rae was coming out of the bathroom. Sometimes if you saw Rae suddenly after a period of not seeing her, even a brief period, you could be stunned by the sight. Neither man spoke for a minute. Rae didn't come directly back to the booth. She detoured to the stage area and had a chat with Rhody and the drummer.

"There's not a thing in the world she couldn't get someplace else," Tick said, staring at her.

"You're right," Billy said.

"Course I am." Both of them looked as if they were going to cry. Billy looked into his bottle.

"So what do I do, Tick? If you were in my shoes, what would you do?" He was making a serious inquiry.

"You done the only thing, already. Knocked her up. Most

of the time that'll work, will hold her down at least as long as most men want one held. If it don't, God help you, you got something by the tail and it'll be a blessing if you can let it go and escape bodily injury yourself. I *know*," he said. "Got one like that myself."

Rae was stepping up onto the stage. The drummer and the guitar player took their places and Rae spoke into the microphone—she held it on the neck and squinted into the lights. "Where's Tick Willis?" she said. Her voice was sweet as a peach. I had not heard it amplified like that in so long, it went through me like electrotherapy.

"Tick, we need you up here," Rae said.

Tick looked at Billy. "What do you say? You're calling it."

"Why not." Billy shifted his weight and stretched an arm across the back of the booth. "Let's see what she's got."

"You sure?"

"Like you said, Tick, it's all happenstance. What can I do?" He spread his arms and smiled.

Tick left his beer on the table. When he got up there next to Rae, they were very business-like, adjusting mikes and wires. Tick didn't introduce her.

"Am I the only one that's never seen this show?" Billy said to me.

"I guess," I said.

"Pretty good?"

I nodded. I could see tight muscles in his face, around his eyes and his mouth. When Rae started, he put his fingers on his forehead.

She sang "I've Been Loving You Too Long."

"Christ," Billy said. I didn't know the song.

Rae didn't look at all like a singer, she looked like a teenager. The lighting was bad, bouncing off a silver backdrop behind her so you couldn't see her features clearly. She looked like a pregnant girl in a sundress, like somebody auditioning.

She didn't move like a singer, either, just stood still. No finger-snapping. There was really nothing to her act except the voice.

The first time I had heard Rae sing, I got the feeling of watching someone else. The girl singing was different from Rae: *better* than Rae. I realized that singing was not just singing. It was a way to let out something.

Probably, every woman has a singing self, I thought. Even me. That thought startled me, and I sat up quickly in the booth. My movement was so sudden that Billy gave me a look, and I pretended to be angling for a better view of Rae. But I was angling for a view of something else, a look inward. The silver stage disappeared, with its band and its singer. Billy's head, the curled knuckles against the eyebrow, faded too. I closed my eyes all the way and tried to see back towards the retina, the optic nerve, and beyond. I saw people. There was a singing girl, but even more astounding, there were other sorts as well, a gang of them in there. I opened my eyes fast, out of fright. Maybe people with multiple personalities got started just this way, by looking inside.

I tried to concentrate on watching Rae. Nobody else was having trouble doing that. Rae was like a sorceress. People had crowded near the low stage and were grinning like fools. The women were especially smitten. While in daily life women despise a stunner like Rae, they'll adore her on a stage or on television, even more fanatically than men will. At the end of the song, "I don't want to stop now" were the words over and over again, and Rae sang them like a slow-going rocket. There was dead silence when she quit. Then a girl in the crowd at her feet shrieked "Whoo," and everybody broke into shouting. There was no applause; the people could only yell.

Billy's hand had settled over his mouth.

Rae made her way back to the booth. She slipped in beside

me, smiling against her will and breathing hard. She kissed me on the shoulder.

"How long has it been since you sang with them?" Billy said.

"God, forever." She drank some beer. She was exhilarated, I could tell, but trying not to show it.

"It wasn't good," Billy said.

She looked up in surprise.

"It was so far beyond good you can't compare it to good," Billy said.

"Did you think so?"

"I'm reeling," Billy said. "Why didn't I know about this?" He put his hand on hers.

"Because it is minor. I've only had time to tell the major things."

"Well, it was beautiful."

"Thank you," she said.

"Come sit over here." He motioned to the space next to him where Tick had been. Rae moved around the end of the table and sat where Billy wanted her.

Slowly Rae's pink face faded back to white, and her mood swung down. "Oh, God," she said.

"What?" Billy said.

"I'm going to miss this."

"We'll come back," he said.

But she didn't mean the place. She meant the light, the songs, Tick's piano following her lead, the sense of her own presence: she'd miss her single self as she'd known it. She was married now. I understood her condition maybe even better than she did, because I could see its effects. She was *wed*. It wasn't just love, which she could have survived; it was something more pervasive and real.

"You can sing with them again," Billy said, leaning forward and trying to cheer her up. He touched her hand, and she drew it back.

"No, I can't. I'll be too big," she said. "And after that, I'll be too many. It's over, that's all there is to it. That life is over."

On the way home, I drove and Rae sat in the middle. He tried to get her to nestle against him, but she stiffened and sat like a child between us, her hands on her knees.

I cut off the highway and took the old beach road home, a roundabout way, but my favorite road. Along the left-hand side were fat humps of sand dunes, and along the right, beach-houses with porches. But because of the fog, the familiar features of the road were now disguised, and I could imagine myself on a road I had never traveled before. The dunes looked higher than I remembered, and closer to the pavement. The houses looked unguarded. Other people's houses at night always surprised me, the way they appear to be so vulnerable, inviting Peeping Toms. At the lit window you might see one figure pass, or two stand face-to-face, but they never look out. I could see how feeble each house was, with a lamp or two yellow in the window, and how dark the night was all around: how far darkness stretched, always exactly half the world. The two faces next to me were wide-eyed with despair.

I stayed up late, waiting for Pop to get in. At two-thirty Vera's Datsun dropped him off, and he made his way up to his room. From my window I saw her car go on to the end of the road where there was a turnaround. As the car came back toward the house, its headlights went off, and it slowed to a stop. For ten minutes she sat there, the way a lovesick teen-ager will watch the house of a loved one in pure fascination. Then she drove away, still without lights.

C H A P T E R

6

One morning a week later I climbed the stairs with Pop's coffee and heard him whistling in the bathroom as I passed. He was an expert whistler, but he had left off whistling; this was the first time in months that I'd heard him do it. I pushed open the door to his room, glad that he had found something to raise his spirits, and I saw Vera Oxendine in his bed.

"Oh, excuse me," I mumbled, backing out. She was sitting in the bed holding a makeup mirror framed in light bulbs.

"No, no, come on in," she said, adjusting the neck of her bed jacket. Her left eye was lively with mascara and eyeliner, and the right one looked faded out. "I should have been out of here by now, but we were up until three A.M., and instead of driving home at that late hour, I just stayed over. I hope you don't mind, Lucille."

"Not—not at all," I stammered. "Where'd you get the night clothes?"

"Ah, your father found a few things for me."

I focused my eyes on the bed jacket. "It's Mother's," I said.

"Is it? It's lovely. Real silk, it looks like."

"He bought it for her three Christmases ago." I hadn't recognized it at first because on Vera it lost all its splendor and hung like a dish rag.

She proceeded to beautify her right eye. "I'm new at this," she said. "I used to just let my eyes do my seeing for me, I never thought of putting all this stuff on. And my hair, I used to just cut it to keep it out of my eyes. Do you like my new style?"

"It's very becoming," I said. I had thought it was mussed from sleeping, but I could see now that it was meant to look like that.

"Gloria Steinem was on television yesterday, and she had on gobs of makeup, and her hair was beautiful, so I don't think it's a vain or frivolous thing to do, to fix up. I used to think it was vain and frivolous." She dropped her chin and put her eye up close to the mirror, brushed the lashes with her wand, then clamped an eyelash curler on them. "I could be doing this all wrong," she said. "What do you think?"

"You clamped too hard. There's a right angle in the lashes instead of a curl."

"Hah, you're right. I look like a clown!" She seemed delighted at the thought. She dabbed rouge onto her cheeks and smiled. "Oh, well," she said, smoothing the color in. "I'll get the hang of it sooner or later."

"This is Pop's coffee," I said.

"I'll take it," she said, reaching for the cup. She sipped some. "Ooh, no sugar," she said, making a face. "Put a little sugar in it for him next time. He likes a half teaspoon."

"I know that, but it's bad for him."

"Half a teaspoon of sugar? That's nine calories. Worth it." She smiled a genuine smile at me. Then she leaned forward and whispered, "I'm having such a good time!"

He was still showering when I went downstairs. I could have made a scene and demanded to know what was going on here, did they think they could carry on like that under my roof; but I didn't have the energy for it.

Nobody showed up for breakfast. I left the food on the

table, the grits congealing, fluffy omelette shriveling. Pop and Vera sneaked down the stairs and onto the front porch, where they settled into chairs and read the paper. Then I heard them talking, and I heard him say, "Of course, go right ahead," and then her hee-hee, and a high mechanical whine that I couldn't figure out. A fan? Curiosity got the better of me, and I went out there.

"Good morning, Lucille," Pop said.

Vera was pedaling her heart out over in one corner; if she'd been on a real bicycle she'd have been doing twenty miles per hour on a flat stretch, but she was up on the exercycle. Pop grinned his approval, and she waved. "Getting-into-shape," she said to me. "The-time-has-come."

"Isn't she something?" Pop said.

I nodded.

The telephone rang, and I snatched it off the wall. I didn't want Mother to know what was happening in this house.

"Lucille, goddammit." It was Wayne. "Why are you doing this?"

"Doing what?"

"Barricading yourself. I've been trying to get in touch with you. Don't any of those people deliver the messages I leave? Who is that guy, not your father, that answers the phone?"

"That's my new brother-in-law. Yes, they deliver the messages."

"Why didn't you call me back, then?"

"I don't know."

"What's it going to take, Lucille? I don't have time to go through the usual question-and-answer routine, where I have to figure out what's on your mind by eliminating everything that's not on your mind. Just tell me. Why won't you see me?"

"We already talked that over," I said.

"I told you I would give you all the time in the world. I'm

not pushing you. I don't care about any of that. I'll keep my distance, I'll stay five feet away from you at all times. Or two feet. I won't so much as touch you. Unless you say so."

"That wouldn't be fair."

"Fair? What are we talking about here? I'm the one that wants to see you. Under any conditions."

"You say that now, but it doesn't work. We tried it. You went crazy."

"I did, but that was because I didn't really understand. Now I understand."

I sighed. What I liked about Wayne was his tenacity. He was single-minded, and this single-mindedness caused him to be nervous, quick to panic, slow to yield. He wasn't like the other boys at school, whose minds were always on themselves; Wayne didn't think about himself.

The other white boys at Wando High had hair suspiciously blond in the forelock, pleated trousers, shirts as soft as babyclothes. I sensed something wrong with those boys, something *off*. They were overly careful about their clothes and their athletic equipment and their vehicles. A man's attention ought to be directed out upon the world, I thought, onto tasks and labors. The great heroes never *studied* themselves. They were busy seeking golden apples, routing suitors, founding Rome. I had noticed boys at school sneaking a glance at themselves in the plate glass window of the lunchroom. Their special watches and name-brand soccer shoes, their fat-tired four-wheel-drive cars with rear ends lifted in the air—weren't these things signs of something not quite right? Some of these boys carried combs. They had a smell that was not, to me, alluring—similar to the smell of peaches gone bad.

Wayne was different. His car was a mess, full of Whopper wrappers and parking tickets. A sleeping bag was half rolled in the back seat. His everyday outfit was an undershirt and blue jeans, and he never smelled like anything other than Dial soap. And always, his mind was on his labors. He was a volunteer worker at the Crisis Center, where he took phone calls from runaways, druggies, pregnant people, you name it; and his constant worry was how to solve their problems. He was not interested in any other career, even though Dr. Frobiness had explained to him that social work was not a good career choice.

"Look, Lucille," Wayne said, "I'll meet you at the picnic tables. I'll stop by Burger King on the way. Do you want tomato and onion?"

"I don't want anything," I said. "I'm not going to meet you there."

"I'm getting it all the way if you don't say."

"Wayne, I can't."

"Mustard, ketchup, pickles, onion, tomato. Fifteen minutes." He hung up.

He would have to eat it himself.

I was not going to go.

I wandered into the kitchen and opened the refrigerator. I got a fake beer and a cold Snickers and a piece of smoked Gouda and ate them standing there with the door open. I found a piece of cheesecake and ate that, too, but I was still hungry. It was not the taste of the food that I was after, but the comfort; though it didn't take deep thought to recognize that the comfort of food was false comfort. I didn't know where to find real comfort, which is more than satisfaction. Real comfort, as the Romans knew, is fortification. I slammed the refrigerator door and laid my index finger across my sealed lips.

Nothing by mouth, was the treatment I prescribed for myself. *Think*, I thought: *what do you really want?* The question was not a tough one, but I had never asked it before. I closed my eyes. What would be a true comfort? I saw it materialize before me.

"Rae! Billy!" I called down the hall towards their open door. "Hey, let's all go swimming. Your suits are dry." I stepped onto the back porch and grabbed her blue bubble suit and his black tank suit from the railing. The scene I had envisioned was the three of us diving off the dock, swimming and basking. The exercise would be good for Rae in her condition and me in mine. "Tide's high," I called to them. "We can dive without sticking our heads in the mud." I wished I'd thought of this sooner, before I'd opened the refrigerator door. Exercise, yes: at its origins the word meant driving the animals out of their pens. I was headed towards Rae's room with the suits when something stopped me, some sounds, and then Rae's muffled voice said, "Uh, don't come in, honey."

Automatically I said, "Oh," and turned in my tracks.

Even though I was alone in the hall, I felt my skin heat up. It was not a blush, exactly; it was a combination of things. It became suddenly clear to me that Rae was correct when she said I was right-brained, because I was definitely thinking in pictures. I went into the kitchen and then into the living room and then into the dining room. Vera's pocketbook was hanging on a doorknob with Pop's tie flung over it. Billy's shoes were on the floor, his beat-up old boots. Rae's shoes were next to them, sandals of thin leather straps designed to come up between the toes and circle the heel. My heart was going crazy, tumbling around like something alive inside my chest but not part of me.

The Episcopalians had a picnic area next to the fragrance garden. Nobody ever picnicked there except me and Wayne. We had found it one afternoon and started taking our lunch there, since seniors were allowed to leave the school during the lunch period. The tables were "redwood," i.e., not redwood, with benches attached. They had sunk into the dirt and were beginning to rot at the feet. Every time we went, more wood had gone soft and disintegrated, so that the tables had sunk just a little bit lower. A line of electric lights was strung overhead from a pine to a palmetto, and there was a sort of oyster-roast pit built of brick by somebody who had never laid bricks before.

When I got there, Wayne was asleep on top of a picnic table.

I stood over him and looked down. His shirt was on the bench; he must have taken it off to get some sun, and then fallen asleep. His chest was white and narrow; his nipples were the same color as his lips, pale brown. I thought he looked sick. His jeans stood away from his hips, showing the elastic of his shorts below his belly button. He wasn't getting the right foods. I had seen Mrs. Frobiness last week at the Piggly Wiggly, her cart loaded with Brie and kohlrabi and artichokes and smoked salmon. No wonder he had moved out.

I looked away. It was dangerous for me to start worrying about Wayne. I knew how it would go: I'd worry about his well-being, and then I'd think how I could go about straightening his life out for him, the same way I thought about Evelyn. But I had too many people within my own family, whose lives I was trying to straighten out. I couldn't afford to take on outsiders. And if he was such a great crisis counselor, he ought to be able to take care of himself.

I sat on the bench. The churchyard ran to the water's edge, a straight shore where the Army Corps of Engineers had channelized a yacht highway from Miami to New York, the Intracoastal Waterway. No doubt it had once served some military purpose, but the main traffic now was the parade of sparkling white, overpowered, heavily antennaed boats. When they passed, waves cut into the mudbank and undermined it; chunks of slick blue-black mud and marsh grass plopped into the water and bobbed away. Later, when the tide dropped to show a thin sandy beach, pieces of Indian pottery were left high and dry. I had a box full of the gray pocked clay shards, most of them barely big enough to show the curve of the original pot. I loved a number of things in this place. The wide sky above me, tables sinking into the earth, the string of lights, millionaires' boats, relics of ancient men.

A skinny arm snaked around my neck and held me in its crook.

"Don't move, lady. One little snap of my arm, and your head's off. I know karate. Or something like that, the one where one little snap of my arm can take your head off."

I nipped him with my front teeth.

"Hey!" he said. "Damn, teeth marks!" He sat up and examined his forearm.

I opened up my hamburger. It was fixed the way I like it, with lettuce and mustard only. I ate it in silence.

He reached for his shirt and took a pack of cigarettes from the pocket. "You were looking at my chest," he said, tapping out a Winston.

"I was not."

"I saw you. I wasn't really asleep. You came over and stood behind my right shoulder and you looked at me." He took a deep breath to make his chest expand, but he still had a frail look. Then he put his shirt on and lit a cigarette, and raised a finger. "Don't tell me not to smoke," he said. He took a drag. " 'Just quit.' I hear it every day. 'Why don't you just quit drinking,' they say to the old wino. 'Why don't you just quit screwing her,' the wife cries to the husband. Why don't people *just quit* these things? I'm glad you asked. I will now explain the Law of Increasing Reality. The older you get, the clearer you see. The clearer you see, the more you need to forget what you saw. So people smoke, drink, stuff things up their noses, eat, and screw. We *need* some of these pleasures. And the clock is ticking, Lucille. You need—"

"I need nothing."

He changed the subject. "Are you aware," he said, "of the various attempts I have made to get in touch with you? I left messages with that man in your house, not knowing who he was—"

"He is my new brother-in-law."

"I heard you say that, but I didn't know it then, did I? The last time I called I accused him of not delivering the messages. Yesterday I came over and beat on the door. I had the feeling you were right there behind it, listening to me slam that little lion's head up and down a hundred times. So I looked through the security peephole. You can see through those things, if there's good light. I saw you."

"You didn't. You can't see through that hole."

"Yes, you can, I swear to God. Try it. There was light behind you. You stood there looking at the door. Admit it! You had on something yellow."

"Okay. Yes. I didn't feel good. I didn't want to get into this with you."

Across the water was the burnt bridge that used to go to Charleston, its black piers now sticking up out of the waterway at angles. Cormorants sat on the stumps, spreading their wings.

"Look at me," he said. "I want to make sure you're listening, not tuning out like you usually do. I still feel the same way about you as I said before. However, simultaneously, you aggravate the shit out of me. You don't really know what love is. I don't think you have it in you. Your idea of love is a total error, three hundred and sixty degrees off."

"You mean a hundred and eighty," I said. I made a circle with my thumb and finger.

He dropped his cigarette on the ground. It lit some dry grass. The thatch puffed up and sent out a small smoke cloud, but the flame went out. We stared at the blackened bare patch left on the ground.

"I'm not the girl for you," I said.

"Yes, you are."

On the mud flat near the old bridge a Vietnamese family twenty strong was pulling a seine through chest-high water. The men dragged the end poles, and the floats swept out in a wide arc behind; on shore the women set green garbage cans in the mud to receive the catch. To my right curved the Mount Pleasant shoreline, coming into view again across a cove: verandahed houses, live oaks, boathouses, and rickety docks. And way in the distance the harbor, the city under the high bridges. In this light the city skyline was cream-colored again, the sky and water that hazy blue-pink.

"Look at that view," I said.

Wayne knew I was serious. He knew that a really good view had the power to draw me into it, so I seemed to float out along its curls and colors and receding planes. The world, I thought, was losing not only ozone and panthers but also views. Even this one was endangered: a condo complex, built in a Middle Eastern style, rose from a spit of marshland beyond the old bridge. I blocked it out by letting a lock of hair fall over it.

I have seen paintings that devote a whole canvas to vista, i.e., the long view outward from the viewer. Past trees, cascades, and mountains it goes, and humanity, if shown at all, is nothing but a blip of a canoe in the middle ground. Speaking from experience, I know of the human need for vista. Without it, I am in danger of losing myself behind my own eyes. Then, I *need* the Intracoastal Waterway shooting straight for Miami, high tide rising in the spartina, myrtle hummocks brown in the lavender haze. A person has to now and then break out of the head and heart, places that cannot, over any length of time, support life.

I went into a reverie. The Vietnamese picked up the flopping fish. A cormorant tried to tuck its wings back into position, and to my amazement, in spite of its precarious position on the burnt piling and the prodigious amount of wing to be folded, succeeded.

Wayne said, "I feel trapped by the oncoming day. It's going to get me." He gazed with me, as if we were an audience watching some show.

"Quit working so hard," I said. "You can't keep this up. They aren't even paying you."

"As my father is fond of pointing out. But listen who's talking responsibility. The girl who screwed up her exams. I noticed you weren't at the grand ceremony, but I didn't know why till this week."

"I did not screw up. I absented myself. Anyway, who told you about that?"

"Rhody."

"But how did Rhody know?"

"Rhody knows everything. I think she's weirding out. She got laid off from Palmetto Dunes, and you know what she's been doing?"

"Working at Fishbone's."

"I mean in the daytime. Dressing in disguise and going into the city."

"What?"

"She says she's doing research for a book. 'Observing.' She has it all planned out in her head, and she's observing for details."

"She told you this?"

"She called me about Evelyn, and I set her up for an evaluation. We got into a conversation."

"What's wrong with Evelyn?"

He looked at me with his exasperated look. Sometimes I pressed him to tell me the stories his clients called in with. My interest was purely for narrative entertainment, but he said everything he heard at the Center was confidential, and he would not reveal more than the bare bones of a tale. "There's nothing wrong with Evelyn," he said, "besides normal strangeness. She's better off than most of what I get. Jesus, am I sick of troubled youth. They call in with their sullen, dead voices and they think they are the center of the universe. They think if they let all their blood out into the shower stall, that's going to solve their problems. They won't listen to me when I tell them the real solutions. I have *got* solutions, too. I have a list. It's that easy! They can name any problem, and I've got the answer that will turn their life around, guaranteed. Abuse, drugs, acne, parents, money, sex, I don't care what, it can be cured. They won't *listen*."

"Sex can be cured?"

"You're a laugh riot, Lucille."

"Some of those people listen to you, I know they do."

"Some."

I knew for a fact that Wayne was responsible for getting Paula Govery off cocaine, and that he had talked several people out of doing themselves in. One afternoon I had barged into the phone room at the Center to find him hunched over the desk with the receiver hidden under his head and arms. He was cradling it, talking steady and low. He heard me come in, looked up, and pointed toward the door, meaning *get out*. But I was curious. I sat down and listened. I wanted to hear what he said, how he went about convincing somebody that life was worth living. He glared hard at me, then gave up and pretended I wasn't there.

"Listen, Philip," he said. He rested his forehead in one hand. I noticed that the morning paper was spread out flat on the desk under his elbows. "I got another one. 'Alfa Romeo,

1979 Limited Edition Sprint Veloce Millemiglia. Black coupe, sunroof, AC, special alloy wheels, wood steering wheel. 2000cc. electronic fuel injected 4cyl. This car is a rare beauty and a great performer. Needs some minor cosmetic work. Must sell at $4500.' *Give me a break.* 'Minor cosmetic work.' We know what that means, right? I think I saw this car getting towed on 17 South, garbaged. I wouldn't touch it. Now, here you go. '1984 300 ZX Turbo, Black, loaded, digital, t-top, low miles. Ex. condition, paid $20,000, sell $14,000. 883-3722, ask for Rick, nights and Sundays.' What do you think? I mean if it's really excellent condition. You think fourteen would be too much for a car like that?"

I frowned at Wayne and said out loud, "What are you doing?" I had assumed this was a Hot Line call, but he was getting advice on buying a car.

He mouthed "Shut up" to me, then went back to talking. "I don't know, Philip. Frankly, for me fourteen thousand dollars is too damn much money to put into an automobile. Maybe I ought to get a bike. Didn't you say you had one? . . . Is that right? Shit, everything in the paper is Japanese. Honda, Honda, Honda, Yamaha, Suzuki. One Harley, a '73 XLCH, but it's twenty-four hundred bucks. So you would recommend the British over both Japanese and American? Right. Well, I know this isn't what you called me about, but, ah, I'd really like to see that Triumph. What are the chances you might want to unload it? . . . Sure. Bring it by this afternoon. You have an appointment with Dr. Furman, don't you? Great, Phil."

When he hung up, he was white-faced. He looked at me. "Guy had his dad's twelve gauge and a coat-hanger."

"And you tried to *buy his motorcycle?*

"Get them interested in the affairs of the world," he said. "Whatever it may be, cars, food, making a buck. I find the newspaper helpful. Sometimes I read them the travel section, or what's doing in the malls. Merchandise for sale, that sort of thing. Puppies free to good home, that's the most effective."

My acquaintance with Wayne Frobiness had taught me that genius is not always measurable on the SAT. He hadn't scored so well on that; but here he was a brilliant strategist in the battle for human happiness. I thought his type of intelligence was more useful than the ability to figure the average speed of a locomotive or pick out a word that means the same or nearly the same as another word. Those pieces of measurable intelligence are so minuscule; a person could have them and still not understand the world. Wayne had a large intelligence, wide enough to take in the whole hodge-podge of trouble and joy in modern society. The Crisis Center had trained him to man the Hot Line: let the client know you're listening attentively, give supportive responses, facilitate the client's expression of the problem. But Wayne went beyond the guidelines, inventing his own techniques. He broke a lot of the rules—gave advice, told his own troubles, discussed religion and politics, showed disapproval. And then he'd do something like read the newspaper out loud. One time he sang a song over the phone, the one that says, "I can see clearly now the rain is gone." People called in to say they were considering a Valium overdose and Wayne would arrange to meet them at Cinema East to see a Molly Ringwald movie.

I was proud to know him. But I was not the girl for him. He needed somebody high-spirited, a lively, perky girl. I asked him, as we sat on the picnic table together, if he had been seeing Laura Migo.

"Christ," he said.

"Does that mean yes or no?"

"Okay, yes. On your instructions I took Laura Migo to a movie."

"How did it go?"

"It went great. The nerdy guy got the girl, after she realized he was the one she liked all along rather than the jock
she'd been trying to—"

"I mean you and Laura. After the movie. Did you and she
get along?"

"Sure."

"Well?"

"This is unhealthy. This conversation. But I'll tell you.
Laura wanted to go to her daddy's boathouse after the movie.
We went there. Laura wanted to get in the Whaler and take
off certain items of her clothing—"

"She didn't."

"She did," he said gloomily.

"Took them off?"

"No, wanted to. The whole situation was too much for
me. I thanked her politely, I said she was fantastic, I mean,
just so *great* and I felt like the luckiest fellow in the world,
but, um, no thanks. Listen, Lucille, I'm not interested in
Laura Migo. I want you."

I said, "We tried it and it didn't work."

"It would have gotten better," he said. "You would have
grown to like it."

"I don't think so. Please, let's not think about it any more."

"See, I *liked* it, that's the problem. I can't not think about
it. I'm thinking about it all the time. I'm thinking about it at
the moment," he said.

He looked at me. I smiled.

"You're too young," he said. "You're too young for me,
that's what it is. I ought to let you go for four, five years and
then come back for you. You're smart as a whip, I looked up
your I.Q. But you just aren't grown up yet."

"You looked up my I.Q.?"

"I had to go through some stuff at Wando for Dr. Furman,

and the folders were all right there. I didn't look *closely;* I didn't look at your subscores or anything."

"What was it?" I said.

"That's confidential."

"Tell me."

"I'll tell you if you'll go out with me."

"No."

He unwrapped his Whopper and ate it cold.

"I'm the same age as you," I said, "more or less."

"Less."

He shaded his eyes with a hand and looked to where the Vietnamese had drawn their long net out of the water and were culling their catch. They threw away the creek debris—plastic beer harnesses, Styrofoam cups, Baggies, picnic forks—whatever the yachtsmen had tossed overboard yesterday. They kept everything remotely edible: stingrays, mullet, crabs, the thin one-foot sharks called dogfish. Water was rising over the mudflats, a gray that glared to white under the high sun. Because the flats were wide, you could see the water rise, spreading over the green mud, seeping into the courses it had cut on the last run out. Two egrets were forced to move to higher ground. Behind the Vietnamese, up on the bridge, shrimpers readied their drop nets for the moment when the water would cover the mud underneath them, bringing in the little fat creek shrimp.

"And the solution to your problems is easy, too," Wayne said. "You're happy as long as you can see at least three hundred yards. That's when you're at your best. I think you're afraid something is going to sneak up on you."

"Maybe so."

"I have a favor to ask of you."

"Please. I don't want to keep going over this, I—"

"No, it's something else. I want you to go to the Yacht Club with me for lunch."

"We already ate." I didn't even mention the cheese and Snickers and cake I had downed earlier.

"The purpose of the lunch is not to eat. It's to have a little talk with my father."

"Well, I can't just show up. He's not expecting *me;* he wants you."

"Yeah, but I can't do it by myself."

"Hogwash," I said.

"If you're there, I'll behave. If you're not there, I can't take responsibility for what might happen, and it's the Yacht Club and all. One can't overturn one's table and throw soup in there. I need you to keep me in line."

"But I'm not dressed up. Neither are you. You can't go like that."

"We have time for you to change, and I've got a clean shirt and tie in the car. I'm not kidding," he said. "I need for you to go."

"All right."

My house was empty.

I put on one of Rae's dresses; she couldn't get into any of them nowadays. It had a lace collar and a brooch at the neck. I also put on a pair of her black flat shoes, because I owned only sandals and Nikes. When I got back out to the car, Wayne was wearing a yellow dress shirt and a clip-on bow tie.

"He won't like the tie," I said. "Let me get you one of Pop's."

"This is my lucky tie. It lives in the glove compartment and comes out when I need some luck. It works."

"He'll think you're wearing it on purpose."

"I am."

We drove across the bridge and into the city, down to the

Carolina Yacht Club. In the parking lot Wayne pulled right up to the steps and parked next to two Jaguars with cellular phones. "They're married," he said, standing between the cars and laying each hand on a Jaguar fender. "Guy practices with my father. He drives the car a year, then gives it to his wife. His is always a year newer than hers."

Dr. Frobiness was waiting in the lounge. He was puzzled to see me, and only vaguely remembered meeting me before, but it did not seem to bother him that I had come along. We went through the buffet line in the dining room. I helped myself to crab casserole, fried flounder, shrimp pie, rice, civvy beans and yellow squash. Wayne stared at my plate. His own contained a slice of watermelon, which he had sawed off the centerpiece, a watermelon cut in the shape of a basket and filled with fruitballs.

I shrugged. I couldn't help loading up, the food was so pretty, and my stomach was hurting. There was the long table and its thick dusky rose cloth, warm lights bathing the dishes in gold. I was adding a crab cleverly deviled in its own shell, when I saw that behind the buffet table was an eight-foot aquarium in which large gray bulldog-faced fish swam slowly from one end to another and around to the start again. I could not tell how it was that they achieved forward motion; they seemed never to flutter their tails or twist their thick bodies, but steadily drifted forward, making the circuit of the tank.

Ordinarily I loved the Yacht Club. From its porch you could see across the harbor to Mt. Pleasant, the very reverse of the view I had seen that morning. You could sit in the dark, cool dining room and eat old-fashioned food and look out into the dazzling sun where young Townsends and Pringles in sailing attire skippered their Sunfish back and forth, barely missing the dock. People eating there were always quiet and well-behaved. There was a high turnover in waiters, but often one of them was a Wando High black guy who would bring me double portions of charlotte russe. But today I didn't feel right in there. The aquarium was a new addition. It is hard to eat seafood while seafood swims in a tank before your eyes, especially when it swims glumly, the corners of its mouth downturned.

Dr. Frobiness started right in on Wayne once we were seated and had been served our iced tea. Wayne was ready to bolt. He had never liked the Yacht Club. I watched him squirm. Everything his father said or did annoyed him, down to the way Dr. Frobiness pronounced words and blinked his eyes. You know a relationship has deteriorated past the point of salvage when one person detests another's gestures.

"I understand your interest in the downtrodden," Dr. Frobiness said. "I like to think that as a young man I was drawn to medicine for similar humanitarian reasons. But look at yourself, son. *Look* at yourself. What's happening to you? Don't allow yourself to be pulled into their world. That's the danger. You've got to stay within your own world and help from there, not leap in with these people." He blotted his lips with the dusky rose napkin. Wayne's eyes were glued to the napkin: up to the mouth, blot blot, down to the lap. Wayne coughed.

"Now, I have a proposal to make." Dr. Frobiness paused for Wayne to respond, but Wayne was staring at something in the vicinity of his father's hand. "What I propose is this," his father said. "You take the remainder of the summer and do with it what you will. Continue at the Center if you like. Then in September you enroll at the College of Charleston. I know it's not Sewanee, but at this point I'll settle for any four-year accredited institution. I'll pick up the tab for tuition and rent. You get some sort of job, a *paying* job, to cover food and transportation. I'll expect you to maintain a decent average, but nothing spectacular. Just stay in, that's all I hope for. I've lowered my sights considerably." He smiled at me. "What do you think,

Lucille? A new bachelor apartment? Maybe you can help me get this young man on the right track."

"What is that on your finger?" Wayne said.

Dr. Frobiness looked at his hand. "It's a ring," he said.

Wayne was aghast. "What for?"

"Why, for nothing. A ring to wear."

"That's a diamond in it."

"Just a small one. It was a good investment. It's called a Man's Diamond. It was advertised in *The New Yorker*. A little less than two carats, but high quality. But, ah, look, son, if you don't mind, don't mention this to your mother. It might upset her."

"Dad, she said you were in debt because of setting up the new office and all the expenses of trying to build up the practice."

"I am, I am. She's absolutely correct. My God, the cost of secretarial equipment alone was over fifteen thousand, and I want you to guess how much I have to pay for liability insurance. Guess."

"I couldn't begin to."

"No, just take a wild guess. What do you think I have to cough up?"

"I don't know." Wayne was stubborn. I knew he wouldn't guess.

"Take a guess, son," Dr. Frobiness insisted.

"A million dollars," I said.

"Heh, no, little lady, not quite that much. No, I'm ponying up *twenty-one thousand* dollars a year for insurance." He pronounced the first syllable of "thousand" with a wide open mouth, and made his eyes big.

"Holy smoke," I said, to be polite. In truth, I thought that was a pretty good bargain. Suppose he botched a liposuction or misaligned an implant? If I were the insurance company, I would not have insured Dr. Frobiness for any amount.

He went on to say that some fathers, himself and Ronald Reagan included, had a lot at stake in the careers of their sons. It wasn't as if the sons of such fathers were free agents. "My heart aches for the President," he said.

"Excuse me," I said. I wanted seconds before they wheeled the roast beef away. It was already three o'clock, and the steamboat round was carved down like a saddle. The waiter in charge of slicing meat was standing over by the aquarium with two other waiters. I waited politely by the meat, plate in hand, but they were engaged in an argument, and a partially melted seahorse made of ice stood between me and them. They didn't notice me. One said, "Maître d' said, get that mother *out*." Another said, "Get him out how?" "I don't know, but get him out." "Shit, man, I ain't reaching my hand in there. It's crabs in there." "He ain't dead yet anyhow." "Sure he is." "Naw, he ain't. His gills is opening and closing, that's his breathing." "Any fish that is upside down is dead in my book." "Said get him out fast before a member sees him." "Get him out, James." "Go for it, James." "All *right, James*."

From behind the ice sculpture I watched as James took the roast beef fork and speared the ailing bulldog-fish. It was an expert move—not a splash, not a sound. The fish was spirited into the kitchen. James returned to the roast beef table where he carved me a slice of well-done gray beef. I thought I recognized him from school, maybe the basketball team; but I couldn't be sure, he was dressed in a waiter's black pants and coat, and he didn't let on that he saw anything recognizable in me. He only looked at the meat and sawed; he used a regular fork to hold it down, I was glad to see.

When I got back to my seat, I looked at my roast beef and realized I could not eat it. I put my napkin casually across the plate. Probably there was not a good filter system in the tank, not enough oxygen. The fish got sluggish, going round; lost whatever dim sort of consciousness fish possess; and bellied up.

"Wayne," I started to say, but he was gazing at his father, who was writing his club number on the check.

"We are all going to have to tighten our belts," Dr. Frobiness said. "For the time being. I can manage the college tuition and an apartment for you, but that's about it. Your mother's going to have to find an apartment as well and some kind of job. Has she discussed this with you?"

Wayne said nothing.

Dr. Frobiness said, "I spoke with a radiologist whose wife runs a dress shop. She has several gals helping her out part-time, and she needs somebody else in the afternoons."

"Lucille," Wayne said sharply to me. "Do you feel sick?"

"Mmmm."

"Lucille throws up at the drop of a hat," Wayne said.

Dr. Frobiness looked alarmed. He glanced around at the few remaining diners.

"Now?" Wayne said. I nodded. "Excuse us, Dad. We'll talk later." He ushered me out the door and onto the porch, down the steps and into the Ram Charger.

"Fantastic," Wayne said. "What a girl."

"I need air."

"Me, too. Me, too. God*damn*. I'm sorry you had to witness that."

"I need to get some fresh air or I'm going to be sick."

"Sick? I thought you were faking. I thought you were doing it to get me out of there."

"No. The fish in the aquarium made me dizzy."

"You look awful. Your skin is clammy. Here, let's get out and walk down on the dock." He ran around to my side, opened the door, and gave me a hand down. My knees wobbled.

"I never thought your father was the type for a diamond ring," I said.

"He's converting to tangibles. Hidable tangibles. Come

the day of reckoning, he turns over his financial records for a settlement, and there won't be as much on paper as she thought."

"I see."

A red Sunfish hit a green Sunfish, and the young sailors hollered blame at each other. They appeared to be no older than nine or ten. Rich people are careless with their children, I observed. A chill ran down my spine to think of letting a child go alone into the harbor on a small plank with a tiny sail. There were tankers and freighters out there. But the children seemed perfectly at ease, even when they wrecked or capsized, and they would be back at it again tomorrow.

"Lucille, give me another chance." He spoke without looking at me. He leaned on the railing and watched the children. "I'm desperate," he said.

Well, that broke me because I knew it was the truth. His bow tie was too small for his neck and had lost its grip on one side. His pain was bright, shining in his eyes and skin and shoulders. I made a mistake that girls commonly make. Out of a sense of honor (he was a good boy who deserved something from a good girl) I said yes. It was the generous and friendly thing to do, but it was a mistake. We agreed to meet the next night on the dock in front of my house. He looked happy.

CHAPTER 7

Do not think I didn't know what love was. The fact that somebody hasn't literally had it doesn't mean they don't know what it is. A person has certain understandings built in.

I had heard about a new theory that knowledge is shared within a species regardless of space and time, so when one rat learns a new maze, other rats have an easier time with it, even if they are in a different lab. This sounds like baloney at first, but when you think about it—why not? Many things happen invisibly and mysteriously. Creatures have links with their own kind. I knew what love was without the aid of empirical evidence, and furthermore, I believed that I did have it. It was in me. It had been accumulating silently over the years like equity in a house. I was rich in love, even though no one could see it.

But what I felt for Wayne was not love. What I felt for Wayne was what you feel towards Huck Finn. A kind of affection, because he is so good and American. But when you read that book, if you are a girl, you say to yourself *this kid has a long way to go.* He is so happy with his Jim, and his raft, and his old river. The light never dawns on him. Boys have that extended phase of innocence. I do not think girls have it at all. Imagine Becky Thatcher writing that book and you have an altogether different concept. You have something dark.

I couldn't decide whether to keep my word to Wayne and meet him on the dock. All day my mind went back and forth. For several hours I was firm in my resolve not to do it. I held my shoulders straight and went about fixing supper as if I were a virtuous woman. But then I imagined him waiting for me, showered and shaved, smelling like Dial, his two rubbers in his right front pocket. It went through me, how he would gradually sink from hope to disappointment. I decided I would meet him.

At supper Rae was cantankerous. The heat was getting to her, I concluded. All week record-breaking temperatures had put us on the national news. Hay was being trucked in from Indiana to feed cows because there had been so little rain, and crops were shriveling in the fields. The peach trees had produced little stones of fruit. Bulletins on TV advised the elderly and other high-risk groups to drink fluids and stay in air-conditioned rooms. Rae, of course, was in a high-risk group. I had tried to get her to stay in the living room, which had a window unit, but she had spent the day in her own room, lying on the bed in front of the rattly fan, watching the Sony. At supper she looked tired and drained.

"I'll tell you what my problem is," she said. "I've diagnosed it."

Billy glanced at her and shifted his weight. He didn't say anything; it was not clear who Rae meant her remarks for, because she was looking into her food.

So I said, "I didn't know you had a problem."

"Oh, I do," she said. "I was meant for a different decade. I was meant for the nineteen-forties."

Pop said, "That was a wonderful era."

"I would have loved the forties. The forties would have loved me," Rae said.

"The clothes were good," I said.

"Not just the clothes. It was a whole different world then.

It might as well have been another century. I long for the nineteen-forties."

"Personally, I'm fond of the eighties," Billy said. "I like TV and civil rights. The forties was Hitler and tires that blew out every time you went on a trip."

"Sometimes, honestly, I think to myself, what am I doing here," Rae said, not looking up. She continued to eat, methodically cleaning her plate, sipping tea between forkfuls of salad, the kind of steady eating you see in someone alone in a restaurant. Now and then one of the rest of us stole a look at her.

She frowned and looked up, as if something had occurred to her. "I'd have been a nurse in World War II. The whole decade was full of purpose and sense. Sometimes I just say to myself, what *is* this? You must have had this feeling, Lucille. You have those feelings that you can't quite describe. Do you know what I mean?"

"What is it like?" I was hedging. I doubted that I had had it; it didn't sound familiar. But when someone says, "Do you know what I mean," it is terrible to say no. It pulls the rug out from under them.

"It's like a nightmare," she said.

"Scary?"

"No, no: nonsensical. It has something to do with—well, I never felt it before. All of a sudden, there is not as much sense in the world as there was when I—when I was . . . single. I went to look at a new car yesterday, and I couldn't read the dashboard. It was more than I could handle. I took it out for a test drive, and I looked down and couldn't find the speedometer or the fuel gauge or even the radio. I about drove off the road."

"All that equipment is for the younger generation," Pop said. "I can't make head nor tail out of it. They say only the youngsters can operate today's machinery. Vera has to call in her neighbor's son to set up the VCR for anything other than playing a movie."

Rae looked at him. "Pop, I'm *in* the younger generation. I *think* I am, anyway. Aren't I in the younger generation, Billy?" She sounded worried.

"Of course you are," he said. "You're twenty-five years old. That is definitely the younger generation." He cleared his throat. "You went to look at a car?" he said.

"Yes."

"You want to buy a new car?"

"I did, but now I don't. I thought a new car might . . . Oh, I just remember when I first got my car, and I was really happy then. Pop went with me. When I saw the Impala, he went inside with the man and came out and put the keys in my hand. Didn't say a word, just put the keys in my hand." She smiled at Pop.

"I remember that," Pop said.

"I was so happy," Rae said. She looked around the table. Then she went back to eating her food. Because of the size of her belly she was sitting off center, easing her weight to one side. Suddenly she looked up.

"Let's get this out in the open," she said. She laid her fork down.

I had no idea what she was talking about. No one else did, either.

"What's that?" Billy said cautiously.

"This baby business."

"Okay," he said, nodding. "What about it?"

"I don't want to have it."

I said, "Excuse me," and got up.

"Hold it, Lucille. You're part of this," she said.

"No, I'm not."

"Of course you are. You'll want to get your two cents in. I want this settled aboveboard, nobody sits back high and mighty. The only reason I didn't have an abortion right away was I knew you would disapprove. I can't imagine why I cared, but I remember thinking, 'Lucille would not approve.' "

"That's not true," Billy said. "You thought it out carefully. You decided you wanted to keep the baby."

"Well, now I've decided I don't want to."

"But, ah, honey—you can't decide that, *now*," he said.

"Of course I can."

"You can't. It's too late, now. You're almost six months along. It's too late."

"I'm not talking about an abortion. Of course I can't get an abortion now. What I said was, I don't want to have a baby. I mean I don't want to *own* it. I intend to give it up for adoption. Yesterday there were twelve ads in the personals column. 'Loving couple desires white baby, incidental costs paid.' There are people out there who want a baby so bad. Some of them try for years to have one, and here I've got one accidentally. They deserve it more than I do. They'll love it more."

Billy and Pop stared. I had lost my breath temporarily and could not speak, which was just as well because I didn't yet know what I was going to say. Waiting for my lungs to recover, I got my words in order.

The time had come for me to do more than let life happen all around me. The time had come, because of my mother's abdication and my sister's carelessness, to take the reins of this family.

"That's out of the question, Rae," I said. "You're keeping this child. It's your child. You're keeping it and raising it."

"Am I?"

"You are. So get rid of any ideas to the contrary. Get used to all the things you don't want to get used to, like the thought of staying in one place, having somebody depend on you, living with the same man for a long time. You chose it. It's time for you to settle down.''

"It isn't as easy as you think to do all those things! You don't know, Lucille, because for Christ's sake, you're only seventeen. Something like this is not the way it looks. When it happens to you, it's different from watching it happen to someone else.''

"No, it's not different. It's a simple question. Do you grow up or do you not grow up? Those are your only choices.''

"Are you sure?'' She had tears in her eyes. "Are you sure, Lucille?''

"Yes.''

"Are you sure, Billy?'' she said.

"Rae, I—''

"No, he's not sure,'' I said. "But leave him aside. You're the one that counts. You have to decide now, for the rest of your life. You can't make a half-hearted decision, and sort of say, well, all right, I'll have the baby, I guess. You have to decide right now to *love* this baby, even if it's going to give you cavities and make you fat and tire you to the bone for years and years. You have to say, I *want* this baby. Otherwise you could give birth and raise a child and never know whether you wanted it or not. And the child will know you didn't know. Indifference is worse than dislike.''

"It's just that I don't think I'm really made for this. I don't think I can do a very good job of it, Lulu. I really don't.''

"Of course you can.''

"You think so?''

"I know so.'' I touched her cheek.

"Okay,'' she said, and she straightened herself in the chair and took a new breath, and for a minute her eyes were alert. But only for a minute. I thought, that's all right, it will take her some time. This is the first step, you can't expect somebody to do this instantaneously.

"We'll keep it then," she said. "Right, Billy?"

"Right."

"I don't know what it means when they cry. Some of them have milk allergies and crib death. But . . . sometimes I get the feeling that I've had a baby before. It's all kind of familiar. I have memories of objects. A loose-woven baby blanket with a satin ribbon running through it . . . a mobile with wooden animals of some sort, um, *lambs*, I think, hung on invisible wires . . . and a smell, peppery sweet-and-sour . . . I remember holding a baby, rocking it to sleep."

"That was me," I said.

"Oh. Do you think so?"

"I had that lamb mobile."

"You? God. I bet you're right." She said to Billy, "I took care of Lucille."

"And look, she turned out all right," he said.

"Yes, but you see, that was a game for me. That was only Lucille, and this is a real baby. I'm a little afraid. I'm a little, ha, *terrified*." She tried to laugh.

"Rae. Don't worry about it," Billy said. "Think how many people have had babies in the history of the world. It can't be too hard. Each of your female ancestors has done it, all the way back to the beginning of time."

She thought that over and smiled. "You're right," she said. "Thousands of generations. A family history of successful births."

"Nothing to it," he said.

"I am dying of the heat," she said. "Can we go to bed now?" She had been in bed all day, but nobody pointed that out.

I walked down to the dock just as the moon was rising. The land was still hot, even though the sun was gone. It was the greenhouse effect, of course. The water was higher than usual; it lay unmoving, like a gray floor. There was no wind. Rafts of marsh reeds that had been drifting in with the tide had come to a dead halt and dotted the harbor like islands. I didn't even see a bird. My heart was as flat as the world, and my T-shirt was damp with sweat.

Sitting on the edge of the dock I let my legs down into the water, which was warm and covered with a thin mud froth. The moon itself looked hot. We are going to scorch to death, I thought. We are all going to scorch to death before anybody gets a chance to have babies.

Behind me the lights in my own house went off, leaving it a gabled hulk against sky and trees.

Patience is a rare quality in human beings. People believe themselves to be patient, but most can't wait without entertainment for more than fifteen minutes. Dogs are more patient than most people. But I was unusually patient. One thing I could do was wait, even when I didn't know exactly what I was awaiting.

After a while I felt the tide turn and begin to move out. Against my legs, tiny particles of mud hit. I could feel the water itself slipping past my skin. I saw the reeds, now dark shadows on dark water, shift and make for the sea. I had almost forgotten that Wayne was coming, until I heard his footsteps behind me on the dock.

"Look at the moon," I called out. "It has broken into the water." Bits of it were bouncing in the small waves, as if the pieces had been scattered along a gold path. He came up behind me and stood still.

"I *love* the moon," I said. And I couldn't help starting to cry. It had been so long since I'd cried, it had probably backed up in me, a year or two of tears that needed to get out. He sat behind me and rubbed my back. But it wasn't Wayne, it was Billy.

"Lucille, don't worry," he said. "She's going to be okay."

I boo-hooed away like a child. I tried to stop, because I was embarrassed, but the sobs kept on coming out of me. "Oh," I said. "I'm trying to stop this, but I can't."

"You don't have to stop." He rubbed my back while I cried on. Pretty soon it was through, like a squall that sweeps over the harbor with full sun before and after it, gone in five minutes.

"Whew," I said.

"Yeah."

"What do you think is wrong with her?" I said. "She hasn't ever been like this." I reached into the water and splashed a handful of it onto my face.

"I don't know," he said.

"I'm sorry," I said. "I shouldn't have interfered in your personal business. I tried to stay out, but then she said not to leave, and then I felt like I had to say something. I had to say something strong. Maybe it was the wrong thing to do."

"It was definitely the right thing to do," he said. "She's much better. She's asleep now."

"Good."

"You were great," he said.

In that moment, with Billy behind me, the world in its night spin with only the moon to light what I saw, I decided that we would not be enemies. If I had harbored suspicions concerning his moral integrity, they vanished. I admit it had once crossed my mind that he had gotten Rae pregnant on purpose in order to marry her. But suddenly I could see that he was not that sort of person. I saw it only now because I had not been close enough to him before. Now with his face two feet from mine in the moonlight, I saw the planes of his cheeks, the wrinkle between his eyes, telling what kind of person he was: one that can lose himself to another. There are not many of that sort in the world. I was not one, Wayne was not one, nor were my parents; Rae was not one, for sure. I suddenly realized not only how much he loved her, but also what danger he was in.

He moved to the edge of the dock and took his boots off. He took his socks off and put them in the boots, rolled up his jeans, and set his feet down into the water. It looked as if our four legs had been cut just below the knee. "I think she'll get better as soon as the baby is born. I think she'll be her old self again."

"Let's hope so," I said.

"It's harder on her than I thought it would be."

"She isn't used to being two people. She is one strong self, *Rae*. She was raised that way. It is hard for that kind of person to have a baby, which is like splitting yourself."

"Yes, she is strong. That's what attracted me to her originally. She was sure of herself and really strong. You can tell it when you first look at her; do you know what I mean?"

"Most women are weak," I said.

"Well, I wouldn't say—"

"No, you have to say it. Compared to Rae, most women are weak. There is one trouble they all have."

"What's that?"

"They are afraid to be alone. Rae isn't."

"I found that out. In fact, it's her preferred condition."

"She's brave," I said. "Once she was in the newspaper for bravery. Did she tell you?"

"She hasn't told me anything. I'm married to her but she hasn't told me any of her past."

So I told him the famous and oft-repeated tale about the time Rae and Mother and I were driving down Long Point Road before it became Horizon Acres. We were headed for Rhody's house to deliver Christmas presents.

"We saw a knot of people standing on the side of the road," I told him. "It was cold. Mother thought the people were jumping and waving to stay warm, but Rae said something was wrong. When we stopped we saw a fire in the ditch, and looking close we saw a man at the heart of the fire. He was moving, but nobody could think of how to help him. A woman slapped at him with a sweater and cried, 'Heavenly days!' Rae didn't hesitate. She ran to the ditch and kicked dirt in on the man, then got whole armfuls and pushed them onto him, and yelled at the people to do the same. That's what she was like at ten years old. There was a newspaper story about her. 'Quick-thinking youngster saves man from flames.' That's what you're dealing with. That's the kind of strength."

He sat quiet for a minute, then said, "Then she'll be all right. Don't you think? If she has that in her?"

"Yes."

"I think so, too."

"Get her out in the car some," I said.

"Good idea."

"I think she needs some new clothes, a new nightgown or something."

"All right."

"Does she still smoke dope?" I said.

"Not that I know of," he said. "I told her not to."

"Do you?" I asked him point blank.

"Not really," he said. "I drink too much. I get drunk and carouse, and get myself into plenty of trouble without the use of further additives."

"How much trouble can historians get into?"

He laughed.

"No, I'm serious," I said. "What's the worst trouble you've ever been in?"

"The worst?" He looked at me sideways.

"Come on," I said. "Tell."

"I was arrested for running through a chamber music concert in my boxers. The Guarneri String Quartet. I zigzagged onto the stage, between the viola and the cello, and off."

"That is bad."

"The Guarneri were pissed."

"This was when?"

"Let's see. Ten years ago. Fraternity crap."

I nodded. "Ten years ago. And that's all you've done? You said 'carouse.' What sort of carousing do you do? I can see it now, the history people. They get together in the history department coffee lounge and carouse on Friday afternoons."

"Well—"

"No, wait, and then, I know, somebody suggests a bar downtown, and the history people pile into two Subarus, and they drink at Patrick's for an hour, and then half of them move on to the Italian restaurant, and you're home by ten P.M." His life before he joined us tantalized me. I had made up details for it.

"That's not far off," he said. "Not far off at all."

"Nickel-and-dime stuff. Academic carousing," I said.

"Okay, what's the worst trouble you've ever been in? I doubt you've ever even had a library book overdue."

"Me? I've been in big trouble," I said.

"Right. You can't even say four-letter words. How can you get in trouble?"

"I've shoplifted," I said.

He turned around and looked at me. I put my hand over my mouth. "I can't believe I told you that," I said. "Nobody knows."

"You can't stop now," he said.

"I was in Eckerd's four years ago with my mother; I saw a lipstick display and this color, apricot frost, struck me like thunder. I had to have it immediately, without going through the usual channels. It was a physical feeling. So I stole it."

"Well, but if you didn't get caught it doesn't count, you weren't in trouble for it—"

"I did get caught. When we were leaving, we had to walk

through some sort of sensor, these metal gates, and the alarm went off. It was horrible. The manager came over, a shiny little man, ugh. He said, 'Miss, I'm going to have to ask you to empty your purse onto the counter.' I dumped my stuff out. But the lipstick was in my shorts pocket. My heart was beating a thousand times a minute and I couldn't talk.''

"What happened?"

"My mother came over and stood behind me and reached into my pocket while he was going through my purse.''

"She knew you'd taken it?"

"Not till the siren went off. Then she figured it out. She sneaked the lipstick back to the shelf. The man said the machine was newly installed and maybe something was wrong with it. He apologized to me.''

"So you weren't in trouble."

I rolled my eyes at him.

"Oh, your mother," he said.

"I was grounded for a month."

"She really let you have it?"

I sighed. "No," I said. "She gave me a look, the kind of look that lets you know you're ruined and done for.''

"Well, you weren't, though. Weren't ruined.''

"No, I guess not."

"Because here you are."

I nodded.

"All teenagers shoplift," he said. "That's nothing. I thought you were going to come up with something juicy, but it looks like neither one of us has led a life of true misbehavior. Are we naturally good, or have we not had a good shot at badness?"

"There's no way to know," I said. "Until the good shot comes along."

"I like it here," he said, moving his feet in the water. "It's like Lake Michigan, but wilder. There are no sharks in Lake

Michigan, and the northern woods are squeaky clean compared to these. This place is crawling with critters."

"I love it here," I said.

We were becalmed. I heard barnacles ticking on the pilings under the dock. Yes, animal life was everywhere: snails, fiddlers, fish, blue crabs, jellyfish, dirt-daubers, bees, cicadas, mosquitoes, fire ants, snakes, lizards, toads, alligators. The water was moving. I was at home here. For the first time in a long while I felt some serenity in my heart. I realized that I was a patriot in the deep meaning of the word, which entails something more complex than loyalty to the U.S.A. Olympic team. It means loving the place as if it were your home, as if you were an animal and it your habitat.

"You are strange, Lucille," Billy said. He stood up and looked down at me, his pants still rolled to the knee, his calves dripping onto the dock.

"Well, I know that, I guess. But what aspect of my strangeness are you referring to?"

"You look so tough. You come across as a woman strong as Fort Sumter in its heyday, a bastion nobody in his right mind would try to take. But then half of your sentences start out with the words, 'I love.' You're saying, 'I love this,' 'I love that.' You love more things than anyone I've ever run into."

I swallowed down my surprise and tried to be casual. "I never noticed that," I lied.

"You have a lot of love in you."

"I guess I do."

In the stillness we could hear sounds coming across the water, music of other people's evenings. Somebody's white dog loped across the yard, one of those that belong in Alaska. I took that far-from-home dog into my breast, and all the moonlight, and the one, two, three, four shadowy docks like haphazard fences in the water. I sucked the whole night into me. I wanted it all.

He said, "You coming back up to the house?"

I said, "Not now. That is, I'm expecting someone. I'm not all that sure he's coming, but he said he was, and I guess he'll be here soon."

Billy looked towards the house. "I'm sorry. I thought you were down here alone. I'll get out of your way. You'll be all right, by yourself, until he comes?"

"Sure."

"Okay." He hesitated. "Well—who is it?" he said. "Who are you expecting?"

"Wayne."

"I thought you said that was over. Not even in the romance category."

"I did say that," I said.

"I don't know, Lucille. A moonlit night, nine-thirty, Bob Marley drifting out over the water." He winked.

"Go away," I said, slapping my hand against the water to send a splash in his direction.

"All right, all right."

I watched him go back towards the house, though by the time he was at the steps I wasn't sure whether it was Billy I saw or a tree or only night. I felt serene, but also thrilled. "You have a lot of love," he had said. That was me; that was *the* me. I had been recognized.

Sometimes you have to look through the eyes of a stranger in order to see anew the things you have been seeing in filmy old ways. I looked at myself through the eyes of Billy McQueen and felt as if I had made a lucky discovery. It reminded me of the time I had found my old safe in an upstairs closet. It had money in it, but I couldn't remember the combination. I took it with me into my room and fiddled with the dial, spinning it left then right then left, not even thinking about the particular numbers. All of a sudden it opened, and I let out a cry of pure surprise. Was it an accident? Or had something in me, deep inside, recalled the combination and sent it to my fingers?

"You have a lot of love in you." He had seen that.

I was breathing long deep breaths, to take in as much as I could of the salty, damp air. Without knowing it, I was making a noise similar to snoring, because when Wayne got there I didn't hear him until he said, "What in the world is that sound? Lucille? Are you having an asthma attack?"

"No," I said. "I'm breathing deeply."

"You sound like you're choking," he said.

He smelled the way I knew he would. I touched his hair, and it was damp from the shower. The touch shocked him; he drew back. Then he came forward again and kissed my mouth. His lips were cold; they felt good. Everything about him felt good and cool and clean. "Where'd you get the clean shirt?" I asked, but not too clearly, my mouth so close to the shirt itself the words were muffled.

"What?" he said. He was taking the clean shirt off.

Something was new here. Something was different. I had never felt exactly this feeling before. Usually at this point I began to feel dizzy, and I would wind down and start withdrawing, and Wayne would hurry and forge ahead in hopes of getting it done before I finally wrestled my way clear. I wasn't a tease; I wanted it to work as much as he did; but usually I simply couldn't hang in there. Most of the time, the feeling that I called "blinders" assailed me, and I had to get free; I had to see where I was and regain my balance.

This time, "blinders" did not come. This time I felt as if I were wrapped in a cottony blanket, and the blanket seemed to be Wayne Frobiness's skin. I had never given his skin much attention before, but now it was like magic. I touched his back with my whole palm, to make sure it was not my imagination. It was not. My hand itched with a pleasant tingle that spread all the way through me.

A wooden dock with three old boat cushions is not the best place in the world to lie down with your love, but neither of us objected. It was also not a very dark place, I noticed, once we had our clothes off. The moon was high now and its bright beams lit us like minnows in the shallows. I thought I was dancing, I thought I was swimming and burrowing and climbing the sky. I was amazed.

Wayne was taken aback, somewhat frightened; he was hesitant to move hard. Maybe he thought, who is this under me? What have I got here? The Greeks knew of female creatures taking animal forms, and maybe some of those came to his mind. I don't know. My own mind was quilted over with pleasure; nothing else was in it.

Afterwards, he was worried. He put his blue jeans on. Pushing his shirttail in at the waist and buttoning the fly, he said, "Are you going to get dressed?"

"I don't know," I said.

"I think it would be a good idea." He handed me a pile of clothes, and I put them on slowly. My arms and legs did not seem to be operating efficiently. He was watching me.

"Is something wrong with you?" he said. "Wait. Your sister gave you something. Am I right?"

"Gave me what?"

"Some dope or something."

"Don't be ridiculous."

"There was another time I thought you had been smoking something, and you denied it."

"So? You were wrong both times."

"What is this, then?" he said.

"What is what?"

"You know what I mean. What is going on here? How come all of a sudden you're . . . like this?"

"I thought that was what you wanted."

"Yes, but you—you enjoyed it."

"I'm not supposed to?"

He sighed and frowned. He was Huck Finn, naive, easy to deceive.

I certainly didn't set out to deceive him. I was after my own pleasure, drowsy and rolling and not thinking at all, never planning to do him harm. I suppose the woman never plans to do the man harm. Eve was not a calculating sort, not a premeditator. I didn't even figure out what was happening to me until later that night, so I can't be blamed for making that sort of love with Wayne. I didn't understand myself at the time.

"Lucille," he said, sitting next to me and helping me get my shirt on. "Are you sure you're all right?"

"Sure."

"I'm worried about you," he said.

"You were worried about me before for the opposite reason."

"I know, but I'm worried more now. You're not being yourself."

I didn't tell him, yes I was, that *was* me. All I really wanted to do was sleep. I lay back down on the dock, my cheek against the wood planks. Sleep overwhelmed me.

"Come on, I'll walk you back to the house," he said.

"Nnnn."

"Let's go." He lifted my arm. "You can't sleep down here. Don't fall asleep, Lucille. Goddammit. You did smoke something. I know the signs."

"Carry me," I said.

"No. No, I am not going to carry you. You weigh more than I do, for God's sake, Lucille. Here, I'll carry half of you. Get up, and lean on me." He helped me up, and he draped my arm behind his neck. I only had to use one leg. We hobbled down the long dock and into the wet grass and up the front steps. At the door to the screened porch, he said, "You'll have to get yourself into bed."

"I can't," I said. I went limp against him.

"Shit."

He opened the door and got me in. My room, as he knew, was right there—into the hall, then to the left. When he let go of me I went down face first onto my little bed and did not move. He stood there.

"You're going to sleep in your clothes?" he said.

I didn't answer.

"You can't sleep in your clothes." This is the kind of boy he was. Living in his car, with a sleeping bag in the back seat, a bow tie in the glove compartment, he believed it morally wrong to sleep in your clothes. He believed you had to brush your teeth every morning and every night. I think he said prayers. The children of divorced parents often turn out like that, their own stern guardians.

I sat up and began to take my clothes off. He turned away, then he turned back. "I'm going now," he said.

"No, stay," I said. I took my shirt off and folded it and set it on the bedside table. I took my bra off. I felt something as close to desire as I had ever felt, and this was firsthand, not in a movie.

"I can't stay," he said in a whisper.

"You can." I slid my shorts down, and my pants.

"Lucille."

"Wayne, I know you have another rubber in your pocket."

"This is crazy."

But he came to me. I wanted to do it again to see if the first time had been a fluke, but it wasn't. The second time was the same. I thought I must have broken through to some kind of new plateau. Maybe it had only been a matter of time, I had been too young before, and now I was ready.

He lay next to me for a while and I fell asleep; and then I felt him get out of bed. He said, "I don't know what's up with you. But something's wrong." Still I did not yet understand what had happened to me. I heard him leave by the front porch steps.

But later, past the middle of the night, at the lonely and sad hour when ordinarily I woke in a sweat, fearing for the welfare of the world, I had a love dream. It was strong and shook my blood, and woke me finally, sweating, my hand on my mouth. I understood then.

The man in the dream was never once Wayne, but was Billy, again and again and again. He was Billy McQueen, and had been, for some time.

Can I be blamed for a dream or for what was left after the dream was gone? In my bed that night, I sat up; the dream splashed over me in a warm wave, making me gasp, and then it receded, leaving something behind the way high tide leaves a shell. I recognized it. I knew its name: love, like a smooth whelk under my breastbone.

I never blamed myself. It came to me, and I decided to keep it. How many people harbor secret love, years or whole lives long? Everyone, was my guess. I can't say I was worried about any moral implications. Morality governs conduct, not feeling. As long as it stayed secret, what harm could it do? I could even see that it had certain advantages over a spoken love, in fact. No wear-and-tear. It would live in a frictionless environment, not ground down by the rub of the physical world. Yes, I could see plenty of reasons for keeping it. But mainly, the feeling was one I did not want to lose. It felt so good. Tears came to my eyes against my will; I regretted the waste, all that lost time, when I had not had it. I breathed so slowly I might have been a hibernating thing, wrapped up in love.

Billy in person had no role in this. He could have left the house forever, and I would have gone on feeling this feeling. "Walking on air" seemed like an accurate description, or "on cloud nine," or "sitting on top of the world." It affected my eyesight. When I looked out my window, after the night of the dream, I was shocked. Those houses clustered around the bay were as bright as houseboats, some dark green with white trim like ours, some gray with white, white with blue—thick and glossy coats of paint as eye-catching as candy. The colors seemed true. Porches and latticework and shutters gleamed. Silver roofs, dormer windows, flagpoles on the lawns, the thicket of sailboat masts where the little boats had been pulled up onto mud, trails cut behind them like turtle crawls from the water's edge.

I looked in the mirror and saw the usual Lucille, although maybe the eyes were different. People in love have dilated pupils. I looked close, but since I had never measured my pupils before, I couldn't tell whether they had grown bigger. I didn't think my condition would show. Nobody would have the slightest suspicion. It was a condition similar to what I thought the early months of pregnancy would feel like, when you have something the world does not know about.

When I saw him, of course, he looked different because of the dream. I had to remind myself that he didn't know about it. Even so, I blushed when my eyes met his. I talked too fast and made illogical statements. He was sitting in my favorite oak chair, circling ads in the newspaper. They needed a bed, I remembered. He was probably looking for a second-hand bed.

Sunlight hit his hair from the side, and I discovered red in it even though it was black hair. I watched his big hands. The thumbs were long as fingers, the nails wide and clipped straight. The black hair on the backs of his palms made the skin look almost blue.

"We get quite a few yard sales around here," I said. "I guess you'll need some furniture. But if you want the good stuff you have to go early. By eight A.M. everything's been picked over by dealers."

"You go to yard sales?"

"All the time."

"What do you buy?"

"Odd things. I bought that chair you're sitting in. Why buy a regular chair, when you can get one with history behind it?"

"You're a collector, then."

"Sort of. I got started when my bed broke, and for two months I slept with my feet eight inches lower than my head. Mother said she'd get it fixed sooner or later, but I got fed up, went to a yard sale and bought my bed. It's white iron with brass balls at the corners. I knew as soon as I saw it, it was for me." What was I saying? I blathered on. "So now when I buy something, I'm always looking for something special. Not necessarily an antique, but something I can take some interest in. Ordinary furniture isn't interesting. I'm not a decorator. But look at this." I stepped behind the chair and flipped the spring hitch a notch. He went flying backwards into a near-horizontal position.

"Whoa," he said, lifting his head.

I reached back under the chair and sent it forward again. "Sorry," I said. "It has eight positions and also goes up and down. I think it might have been an old barber's chair," I said, touching the arm, "even though it's wooden and has all this scrollwork."

"What else is yours?" he said, looking around the room. "That hall tree? The china cabinet?"

I nodded and watched him as he examined each piece. I wrapped my arms around my knees. I had gone through a major phase of my life without running into a single human being who understood me, and all of a sudden here was one who not only understood the general me but saw through to some of my top-secret qualities.

"We will need some furniture," he said, "but first I need a job. I'm reading the job ads."

"I thought you were a historian."

"Being a historian is like having dyslexia. It means you're going to see things differently, and normal life is going to be somewhat difficult. You do the best you can. Supposedly I am to finish a dissertation on Colonial traders in the next six months, and then I defend it, and then I get an advanced degree and a yellow velvet hood from George Washington University, and then I teach ninth-grade history somewhere the rest of my life."

"Teach?" I said, unable hide my horror.

"Pretty bad, eh?"

"What else is there? Let me see what you circled." I looked over his shoulder. "But you only circled 'Teacher wanted.' "

"There isn't anything else I can do. I'm not a bad teacher. I even sometimes like it."

"You won't like it here," I said. "The teachers are all unhappy. The school system is fiftieth on all the lists."

"See? They need me." He folded the paper and tucked it under one arm.

I grabbed it from him. "There's got to be something else. Look, there are some great jobs that you missed. 'Chiropractic assistant.' 'Tour guide.' 'Doughnut Maker.' Hey, 'Mixer Driver.' That's something with adventure. If you don't get there on time, the cement hardens in the vat."

"I'm not any of those things."

"But you don't go out and get a job that fits what you already are. That's what's so great about these ads. I read them all the time. They're little windows, and I look through into a possible new life. Listen: 'Hostess, top pay, good working conditions.' I could do that. 'Night auditor.' 'Care for elderly lady.' I could just go get one of these jobs, and my whole life would change overnight."

"Then why don't you do it?"

"Rhody says the ads are bogus," I said, giving the paper

back. "You go there and they want you to pay a fee, and they say they'll call you when something comes up."

"I couldn't do any of those jobs," he said. "I don't even know what some of them are. What the hell is a rodman? What's a golf ranger? No. I don't do well in the world of rodmen and golf rangers. I can't make it out there."

"But *teaching*? You have to do lunchroom duty, you have to patrol the parking lot. It kills you."

"I taught last semester. What's so bad about lunchroom duty? It took me back to New Trier High School. High school is the only American institution that hasn't changed. I can sit there and punch the food tickets and pretend I am back in tenth grade."

"You're really going to do it?"

"Don't look so grief-stricken."

The truth was I couldn't stand the picture of Billy McQueen as a teacher. It made my stomach sink. My teachers had always been morose because of their jobs. One reason I got straight A's in school was that I wanted to make these people happier. They were tired and hungry for love; and what's more, their cars broke down constantly. It hurt me to think of McQueen in a teacher's life. Grief-stricken was an exact description of how I felt.

But he winked and finished his coffee and left.

I watched him back the Impala into the street. He was wearing a blue shirt, sleeves rolled, collar open. He was a well-intentioned man, but teaching would ruin him. Men teachers are the sorriest spectacles in the world.

I had the ability to look into my own future unafraid. Nothing in it scared me personally, not the chance of poverty or ill health, not loneliness, not the black submarines. I was a brave person—as long as I thought only of myself. But looking into someone else's life was different. I was terrified of everything in McQueen's future. What if he took the teacher job? Or—

what if he applied and got turned down, and lost his confidence? I felt responsible for him. But what could I do?

"Rae?" I tapped my knuckles on her closed door. "Can I come in?" I heard her fan clattering in the window.

"Who is it?" she said.

There weren't a lot of possibilities. I could be me or I could be Pop. A new idiosyncrasy of hers was a disconnected politeness.

"It's Lucille." I waited, but she didn't say anything. I knocked again.

"Yes, yes, come in," she said. I opened the door. She was in her nightgown in the middle of the bed, sitting with her legs stretched, two pillows behind her back. She didn't even look up at me. Next to her on the bed was a cardboard box from which she was removing small objects wrapped in tissue paper.

"Did you know Billy's applying for a job as a teacher?" I said.

"Yeah, he mentioned it."

"Do you think that's the right thing for him?"

"This takes the cake," she said, holding up a peanut butter jar with a picture of Peter Pan in his green suit. Behind Peter, spirally arranged in a clear fluid, was a small thin snake. She shook the jar, and the snake rotated gently, its head lifted towards the lid in a lifelike pose, as if it were waiting to be delivered from the jar.

She pulled herself closer to the box, looked in, then looked back at the snake, the jar close to her face. I spotted a collapsible tin drinking cup and a hatchet next to her bare feet. It was eleven A.M.; already heat had collected in the corners and near the ceiling. The fan spun in the window, but it only seemed to be drawing in more warm air. Rae took more things from the box; she seemed to be looking for some particular object.

"What is all this?" I said.

"Billy's history. If you can believe it."

"Are you allowed to go through his things?"

She looked at me as if I were a lunatic. But I wasn't sure marriage gave a person the right to go through the other person's memorabilia.

"Lord, look at this," she said.

It was a leather billfold, its color aged to orange, the edges handsewn in rawhide. A bucking bronco had been punched into the leather with hundreds of little holes. "They make these at camp," she muttered. "Or maybe in Scouts, who knows." She opened the wallet wide and shook it. No money came out.

The short curls around her forehead were wet. When she leaned towards the box, I could see the back of her nightgown was soaked with sweat. She kept on lifting things out, setting them around her on the bed.

"Was he a Boy Scout?" I asked.

"Evidently." She held a metal kerchief clasp fashioned in the shape of a bear's head. "My God." she said. I was starting to disapprove of her attitude, her disrespectful and mocking air. She untied a roll of flannel, and some shiny tools slipped onto the bedspread.

"Boring," Rae said. "Tools." She stared at them.

"Ratchets and box-end wrenches," I said. Indenting the spread where they lay, the tools looked like chromium bones. I stared at them, too; I couldn't take my eyes away from them.

"There's got to be something good in here," she said, rooting in the box. She found a ball-peen hammer, a whittled animal, a cardboard folder with pennies inserted into crescent-shaped slots, a set of turtle shells in graduated sizes. I wanted to touch these items, these boy's things. My fingers itched.

The wallet looked so smooth, that bronco's mane flew out like flames.

I cleared my throat. "What sort of thing are you looking for?" I asked.

"Something personal."

"These things are personal."

"You don't understand," Rae said. She wanted something less innocent than these objects—a letter, or a photo of a naked woman. She wanted to open the Scout's wallet and find a rubber in it.

The window fan shook in its frame. Rae lay down and pushed her feet through the clutter. The whittled figure fell onto the floor, and I picked it up without looking to see exactly what species of animal it was. I couldn't help myself, the wood was almost pink, and I caught a glimpse of a sharp nose, the claws and nicked eyes. I pocketed it.

Late in the afternoon I coaxed her out of bed. "Let's be on the porch when he comes home," I said. "Let's have some hors d'oeuvres ready."

"What in the world for?"

"If he got the job, to celebrate. If he didn't—well, he'll be disappointed, and we'll need to cheer him up. Go on, take your shower. Put on your white dress."

"Lucille, please."

"You have to, Rae. I'll watch to see if he's coming."

I posted myself at the top of the back steps, just behind the screen door. Pop and Vera were, as usual, gone off together somewhere—to their cardiopulmonary resuscitation class or their soup kitchen shift. I supposed it was good for him to get involved in such activities, but we were seeing less and less of him. I worried about the influence of Vera Oxendine. I hoped he was not overexerting.

"Billy's here," I called out when I saw the car turn in. "He's not smiling. Looks gloomy." That was a good sign, to my mind, an indication that he hadn't gotten the job.

"That's his regular look," Rae said, coming onto the porch. "You can't tell from that."

He saw us standing there, and he stopped in the driveway.

"Did you get it?" I hollered. Rae was behind me; she slipped her arm around my waist. She had put on some perfume.

"The beer? Don't worry, Lucille," he yelled, "I got plenty. You're set for the night." He looked around toward the Lawtons' house next door, where Mrs. Lawton was pruning oleanders. Sometimes I babysat for her grandchild. Billy hailed her with a six-pack held high.

Rae chortled. "He got it," she said as he came through the door.

"Did you?" I asked.

"Wando Warriors, here I come," he said. "Ninth-grade history, junior varsity soccer, one section of Substance Awareness."

Rae still had her arm around me. She tilted her head toward me and, watching him, said, "The funny thing is, he's happy. All he wants is a history class and an old car and a little house."

"That's not true," he said, setting two six-packs on the table.

"What else, then?"

He inserted his hand between us and pried her away from me, pulling her to him by the waist. Her head swung back and her stomach touched his; he danced her around the kitchen. "You guess," he said. "You just guess." He bent to kiss her neck, and she looked at me over his shoulder.

"There's nothing else," Rae said to me from the embrace.

"He's easily pleased. He wants a normal life; that's all in the world he wants."

What was wrong with that, I wondered.

We ate crab claws on the front porch while the sun went down, Rae slouching in the swing, bare brown legs stretching out from under her white dress, while Billy talked about my school as if it were a place I had never seen before, a place worth being in. Now and then his eyes went to where she sat, listening. At least, she seemed to be listening. You couldn't always tell.

I stuck my hand in my pocket and found the carved animal, and, without taking it out, I rolled it between my fingers. Its body was smooth. It fit well into the cupped palm of my hand. I began to see how a life can divide in two, and the daily, visible portion move further and further away from the secret, invisible part. Ideally, you want to live a unified existence; but what if you can't? I didn't want to become a split personality. But I could see how it might happen to someone whose interior life got out of hand. Like a little fox in the dark, with sharp teeth and claws, the secret life will gnaw and gnaw.

CHAPTER

9

*P*oor Vera thought she could just step in. She didn't know the power of a twenty-seven-year-long love. He couldn't give it up, was still on the trail of it, even though Vera cooked exotic food for him, tried to interest him in community affairs, and occasionally stayed the night. He had not given up the search. He still waited for Mother to call.

It occurred to him that Mother might have gone to Parnell for money. He wanted to check that out, so we drove into Charleston.

I always found it exhilarating to go into the city, now that it was spiffed up. Everything was freshly painted. I recalled an earlier stage when the place was close to run-down, but in the last ten years, money had come in. Where from, I didn't know.

Pop didn't know either. When I asked him, he said, "I've wondered that myself." We were driving over the bridge and had a bird's-eye view of the city. Most people don't notice it, but the colors of the Atlantic seaboard are peculiar. They are not the clear, vivid colors of the Pacific coast. Our water is gray-blue, our marshes yellow-green, and everything seems to have a wash of pink over it. I had seen paintings of the city of Venice that reminded me of Charleston. A creamy city emerging from a haze of pinks and grays and blues.

The new money might have come from industry (German pharmaceuticals, French tires, Belgian chemicals), or it could have come from tourists (millions every year). But personally I thought the money had come from drugs. Not that these Broad Street lawyers were dealing cocaine; it was more complex than that. My theory was that Florida was the first to fill up with drug money, until Florida got saturated and had to spill over. Money had gradually worked its way up the coast, just like armadillos and fire ants. I couldn't think of any other explanation for the wealth that I saw everywhere around me. Every third car was a German luxury sedan. I appreciated the gleam and precision of such cars, those cold silvers and greens that appear nowhere in nature. But they made me nervous. I never stepped off the curb when one was near, especially if the windows were tinted dark. These cars and their mysteriously rich drivers were not signs of prosperity in the land— only of money in certain hands.

My father's office had always been a place I loved. It smelled pure, probably from a pine oil cleaner the maids used when they came in at night. The office also seemed emotionally clean, no sadness or grudges or personal disappointment in the corners. I felt very logical in there, with the electronic typewriters humming, the complicated telephones jingling and flashing.

So I was glad when Pop said he needed to talk to Parnell, and I willingly drove him into town. The office was downtown, on Broad Street. The city was shaped like Manhattan, and where Wall Street would have been, we had Broad, with lawyers and banks and insurance agents, and a view east to the old Exchange Building. New buildings in town did a good job of imitating the old ones; I could not always tell which ones had been built in 1800 and which ones in 1985. But some buildings were easy to spot as new. They were among my favorites, the massive cubes with long holes running the width of the building: parking garages. I liked pulling my car into a parking garage, the arm automatically lifting to let us into the echoing cavern. I parked in one of the delineated spaces.

We walked down the street, and Pop looked in all the windows. Sometimes people who have gained weight don't know the extent of it until they catch sight of themselves by accident. Pop did a double-take at the first window. He pulled his stomach in when we passed the next one. "Do I look okay, Lucille?"

"You look fine," I said.

"Parnell puts a lot of store in appearance."

"What do you care?"

Parnell Meade had never been high on my list. He was blank in the eyes like a weakling. I sensed that there was nothing to him, not even evil. He was harmless; nevertheless he made my flesh crawl. Why Pop had gone into business with him was a puzzle to me, except that Parnell was my mother's third cousin.

"I'll wait in the reception room," I said.

That was a mistake. I had forgotten about Sharon. She came out from behind her desk when we entered the room, one hand on her skinny hip.

"Somebody's been out on the golf course," she sang, wagging her finger at Pop, "or under the sunlamp, one. And eating naughties." She tapped his stomach.

"Lucille, this is, ah—"

"Sharon," I said, holding out my hand and nodding. "We've met."

Parnell had an interest in this girl, I had heard. But she was not much older than I was! Parnell was natty but no Adonis, fifty years old at least and all fifty had taken their toll. Sharon was a category of girl that I did not understand. Pop was obviously embarrassed when she teased him and poked him in the stomach. But some men don't mind that sort of thing.

They never seem to realize how silly they look. Whenever I saw one in a restaurant with the girl dolled up and batting her lashes, I had to laugh. "Roll your trousers!" I wanted to holler across to him. "Get a cane! You're a geezer and a codger!" But I held my tongue. What did I care about old men's foibles: let them make fools of themselves if they want to. But the girls were another matter. I always felt sorry for them. I felt sorry for Sharon.

Parnell came out of his office. He was dressed like a male model, even though he had a paunch and a bald spot. The sleeves of his linen jacket were pushed up to the elbow, the shirt was pink. His shoes looked like bedroom slippers. Thank goodness Pop had retired and was no longer partners with Parnell.

"It's about goddamn time," Parnell said, clapping Pop on the shoulder. "Every morning when I get to the office, I look around and have the feeling something's missing. It's just not the same without the old man, everyone says that."

"Looks like you got things under control," Pop said.

"And I see you brought the lovely Lucille along with you. Come in, come in."

He didn't know how close he was to bodily injury. The lovely Lucille! "I'll just wait out here," I said.

"Sharon, take good care of this girl. She's a precious commodity."

I sat on the sofa near Sharon's desk and picked up a magazine. Sharon clamped a Dictaphone earpiece over her head and turned toward the typewriter. I wondered if she could hear as clearly as I could the conversation from the next room. I could hear every word, but then, my hearing was abnormally acute.

Pop said he only wanted to ask one question.

"Sure," Parnell said. "Shoot."

"Do you know where Helen is?" Pop said.

"Come again?"

"She's left, and I don't know where she is. I thought she might have contacted you. I've ascertained that no banks have given her any money, so I wondered if she might have come to you. For a personal loan."

"Come to me? Why would Helen come to me? Helen never liked me."

"You didn't lend her anything, then?"

"Of course not."

Pop was quiet for a few seconds. I hoped he was studying Parnell's face. "Oh, well," he said. "I thought I had figured it out. I had narrowed it down to you. Helen, you know, didn't have many friends. I can't think of anyone she would have gone to besides you."

Sharon began typing whatever was coming into her ear. Did she love that jerk? I looked at her desk, bare of clutter. No photographs. She probably thought of herself as a good girl, tithed to the Baptist church, sent her mother a monthly check, and took in stray animals. She actually was a good girl, in every respect but one, and maybe that one was not her fault. Still, I could not visualize Sharon and Parnell together without clothes on.

Parnell said, "Well, to put the best face on it, old man, you're restored to the joys of bachelorhood, right? Christ, I wish Mary Nell would take it into her head to strike out on her own. Of course it's hopeless now. I should have sprung for freedom years ago, because after they get slack and gray it's just too cruel to put them out in the street. What would Buzzy say? He tells me that I make her miserable. Is that what a son is for, to berate me to the end of my days?"

Sharon adjusted her earpiece and lifted up off the chair to smooth the skirt under her behind and settle its folds. She was still looking at the typewriter, and I had no way of telling whether she was listening to the conversation in the next office.

"I'll let you in on a recent discovery," Parnell said. "Although I guess you don't need it now. I ought to market this one, it's so good. See, my main problem is Mary Nell is on me like a tick. It's like I'm under surveillance. She drops by the office, she calls at odd hours to make sure I'm here. I thought once that she had a detective following me, I noticed this guy shadowing me on Broad Street. So I'm thinking, how do I get out from under this? I figured it out. You are going to appreciate the beauty of this setup."

Sharon rolled her eyes. Not as a signal to me, but privately, to herself.

"I worked out a deal with the health club, the one just across the bridge. I pay them an extra forty a month. They have three-way calling. Three-way calling. Do you get my direction yet?"

"I'm afraid I'm not quite following it—"

"Okay, I tell Mary Nell I'm at the health club. Maybe she's not buying it, but what can she say? I know she's going to call and check up on me later. When she does, Pete says, 'Yeah, he's here, hold on. I'll go get him off the rowing machine.' Puts Mary Nell on hold, calls me at the number I've left him, patches me through to Mary Nell. It's foolproof. It's beautiful."

Sharon was an amazing typist. I figured her rate must be up around ninety per minute. It got faster as Parnell talked on, her wrists stationary in midair like a hummingbird's body, while the fingers flew.

"Well? Is that a setup or not?" Parnell said. "Maybe you can file it for future reference. You're a temporarily free man, but it won't last long. Marriage is like a goddamn pit bull. He don't let go of you." When Parnell felt like he was waxing eloquent, he tried to talk like a black man, but all he could do was imitate the grammar. The flow eluded him.

"You think she'll be back, then," Pop said.

"Who?"

"Helen. You said marriage will hold on—"

"*Marriage,* yes. You are a man who'll always be married. Who to is another question. And what difference does it make? Marriage is like the old paper bag. This one, that one, it don't make a whole hell of a lot of difference. I can tell you that. That's my piece of wisdom for the day. I love the ladies, everyone knows that, but the surprise of them is the degree of similarity. Not taking anything away from Helen, but you wonder sometimes, where are the individual women? Sometimes I swear to God, I couldn't tell you the name of one I last year thought I couldn't live without, because the new one's just as good."

"I can't agree with you there."

"Hell, I can prove it. You saw Sharon out front? Let me do you a favor. Sharon can make you forget your troubles, I guaran-damn-tee you, in a matter of twenty minutes."

"No, thanks, I couldn't handle it."

"Couldn't handle it!" Parnell laughed. "Don't worry about it, she'll handle it. This girl does a thing she got the idea for in a Chinese manual, you won't believe it—"

The lids came halfway down over Sharon's eyes but she didn't miss a key. At the end of the line, the carriage returned, and she dug right in again, but halfway through that line she looked at me and stopped typing. "Your mother was here," she said.

"What?"

"She was here," she whispered.

I heard Pop say, "One more thing, Parnell."

"What's that?

"How do I look? How do you think I look?"

"You look terrific. Hell, what does she care how you look? You look super, a damn sight better than I do, and she never complained about how I look."

"That's not what I mean," Pop said. "I meant how do I look as compared to a couple of months ago?"

"You look great. Same old Warren Odom. I mean it. You decide you want to get back into action, nobody's more welcome. You were the founding father here, hell, it's your damn company. Always will be. You could walk in and sit down at your desk tomorrow morning."

"I don't see my desk."

"Figuratively, I mean. We moved payroll into your old room, and the payroll gal wanted a new desk like the data-processing gal has. You know how that goes. But I mean it. Tomorrow. You walk right in, it's like you never left."

"I appreciate that," Pop said. I saw him edge towards the door but Parnell stopped him, laying a hand on his forearm.

"Jupiter Fitness Center," Parnell said. "That's the one. You want the other, ah, contact"—they were fully visible to us now in the doorway—"you change your mind on that score, just give me a call, I'll set it up. Deal?"

"Deal."

Sharon said quietly to me, "He offered her money, but she wouldn't take it."

"What did she want, then?" I said.

"A job. Not here; she wanted him to give her some leads."

"Do you remember what they were?"

"He said he couldn't think of any. He made her an offer of another sort, and she laughed at him."

"She always laughed at him," I recalled.

"Yeah. I loved it every time."

I bet she did. I also bet that Parnell was in for trouble.

Sharon had been working here for four years. Too long: he had kept her too long, and sooner or later she'd lash out. Paternity suit, maybe. Photographs.

"Good luck, Sharon," I said.

I didn't know exactly how to break the news to Pop. I was only a daughter. In ordinary circumstances, I would have held my tongue; but I said, "Pop, Parnell was lying. I heard what he said, and it's not true. He did see Mother."

"I know it," he said, buckling his seat belt.

"How do you know?"

"I was in with him for thirty years, Lucille. You get to know a man in that time. Thirty years with Parnell Meade! How did I do it? There must be some sort of reward for that kind of endurance. Or maybe it was stupidity. Thirty years, and I never thought about getting out. I might have gone right up to death's door without realizing the waste! I killed those years. At least I've salvaged the last stage. Ten years, that's what I have according to the Bible. Ten years. I can see all ten of them gathered in front of me in a beautiful bunch. Let's go, Lucille."

"But why didn't you ask him then, if he knows where she is?"

"He doesn't know where she is. She hates his guts. Maybe she went to him for money, but she would never confide in him."

"She didn't ask for money. She wanted him to help her get a job. But he wouldn't, because she laughed at him."

"Oh, Lord, again? He hates to be laughed at. A man like Parnell can take any amount of criticism, it shows somebody is taking him seriously. But laugh at him, and he falls apart. She did it before, several times! Where did you get this information, anyway? Intuition?"

"Sharon told me."

"Hmp. I imagine Parnell has dug himself a deep hole there. Sharon is no dummy. A girl like Sharon could very easily gain the upper hand."

"I wish her all the luck in the world," I said, knowing she didn't need it. Anyone that fast on a typewriter doesn't need luck; she is *skilled*. And it's not mere manual dexterity, either. Those are words, going in her ear, coming out her hands. That is linguistics. Parnell was dumb as a bus and no match for Sharon. I trusted in justice.

"Where to now?" I said.

He looked tired.

"Don't you want to go on home and take a nap?" I said.

"Your mother used to like to walk along the Battery. She sometimes said, 'Let's go for a stroll.' I'm thinking, now that she's on her own, maybe she'll be doing the things she always liked to do."

"You want to go look for her at the Battery?"

"That's a good idea."

My father, I realized, was an addict, no different from a drug-user or an overeater. He was addicted to the memory of her, to the idea of her. He could not give her up.

"You need a new car, Pop," I said, as we pulled over next to the Battery wall. "When you get your license back, let's buy one. It will give you a new lease on life."

Men in their youth grow accustomed to periodic changes marked by new cars: "That was when I had the '53 Ford," I had heard Pop say. If they hang onto one car too long, they start to feel as if their life isn't moving along.

"I'm too old to face a car salesman," Pop said.

"What do you mean? You could go into the ring with the best of them. We'll do it together, you and me. We'd make a great car-buying team."

"You've never bought a car, Lucille."

"So what? I know what it's like. I know what everything's

like. Just because I haven't done something, doesn't mean that I—oh, well." He wasn't listening, he was carefully watching the faces of the people passing us.

A tour bus pulled in front of us, but the occupants did not get out right away; the guide stood up and gave her spiel about Fort Sumter, and the bus ran its engine to keep the tourists cool. The smell of bus fuel had become the dominant smell of the city. I had an urge to commandeer the bus and take the tourists on a different kind of tour, run them up Highway 17 to the new Builderama, Osceola Pointe, Palmetto Villas, Rhody's house, Fishbone's. I'd roll down all the windows of the bus and let people hang their heads out and really see something worth seeing, the transformation of the world. "Look what's *happening*," I'd say into the microphone.

I tried to keep my eyes on their faces as they climbed down off the bus, but all the faces had a deadly sameness that made it hard to look one in the eyes. I could tell what the trouble was: they had been to Epcot. After Epcot, Charleston is hardly worth seeing; no dinosaurs are going to lunge at you on the Battery, no music comes out of the azaleas. After Epcot, a real place is boring. There's something very thrilling about the fake.

I closed my eyes. Unbidden, the face of Billy McQueen materialized. I didn't try to conjure it up or anything; it came to me. Perhaps the right thing to do would have been to open my eyes, but for a while I kept them closed.

"Lucille, if your eyes are shut how are you going to be able to spot anyone?" Pop said.

"Okay, okay."

"You watch that side where they're walking along the wall, and I'll watch the benches."

They came towards me in a steady stream. A feeling was growing again inside me, and I tried to keep it down by studying faces, a game that Rae and Rhody and I had played long ago, based on the hypothesis that a person's whole life is traceable in the facial features. You clear your head, and let the face sink into your subconscious, and you have that person's life story. But I found that I couldn't do it any more. At one time, I had been the best. I could get not only the characters and histories of the people, but *names*. Whether I actually got them right or not didn't matter. All I had to do was convince Rhody and Rae. Always, they liked my guesses; they liked the complexity of the stories I told.

Behind these faces, I saw nothing. And it wasn't the fault of the faces; there were some good ones. There were several Oriental ones, some old ones, and one that was intricately scarred, maybe burned, and I touched my lip when I saw it, but no story came to mind. There were only the faces. I couldn't see into the lives because one imagined face blocked my view, one dark-eyed face. I tried to shake it out of my head, the way people shake themselves awake, squeezing my eyes shut and tossing my head. I would have given my cheek a little slap if I'd been alone. Billy McQueen was consuming my inner attention, and I couldn't see things I'd seen before. I had to banish him.

When I opened my eyes, one tourist was in focus, an old black woman. Black tourists were unusual, but we did get them. Since *Roots*, black people sometimes came looking for their heritage. They liked to go to Boone Hall Plantation to see the slave cabins, and they liked the Old Slave Mart Museum. This one was looking right and left as fast as she could take things in. Funny—she seemed to be looking not at the fort or the cannons and cannonballs, but at the faces of the other tourists. She seemed to be looking my way, into the car, into my eyes; and then she turned her head quickly away. She must have put her life's savings into the trip, I thought. Maybe she had come from Detroit. Had moved away as a child, and was coming home now. She had on a pink pantsuit, its trousers too short, and she walked with a cane. I could tell she had once been very tall, but now was bent and knobby. Maybe she had once been beautiful. I turned to watch her as she passed, and I frowned.

"Wait a minute," I said out loud to myself. "Who is that?" I straightened up in the seat and leaned out the window. "Isn't that—"

"Where?" Pop said, slipping over in the seat to look out my window.

"In the pink suit, behind the Japanese man. It is! I'd know that walk anywhere! She's *in disguise!*"

"Pink suit? But that's a black person, Lucille. You don't mean she's in blackface?"

"No, it's Rhody!"

"Oh," Pop said.

"Let's see where she's going," I said, opening my door but keeping an eye on the woman who was now climbing onto the bus, steadying herself with one hand on the cane and her other on the bus driver's outstretched arm, as if she were ninety years old.

"You go on," he said. "I need to stay here."

"Rhody!" I called out, but she was already inside the bus.

I ran alongside the bus and saw her take a window seat. I grinned up at her and tapped on the black glass. She looked down at me once, and then drew away from the window, and I couldn't make her out. Could I have been mistaken? Maybe it was not Rhody at all, but a real old lady. I started back to the car. Then I thought, wait just a minute. I knew that was Rhody, and I wasn't going to let her get away with pretending not to know me. I stuck my head in the car and told Pop I'd meet him back at home.

"Take a cab home, okay, Pop? There's a stand across the park. I'm going to follow Rhody."

"Wait, Lucille, just give me the car key. I'll drive myself home."

"Nothing doing," I said.

"I refuse to get into a cab. If you don't give me the key, I'm going to call Mrs. Oxendine to come pick me up."

"Fine," I said. "Go right ahead."

The bus was about to pull out, but I beat on the rubber panels of the door, and they opened. "I want to join the tour," I said to the guide. "I'll pay the whole amount."

"Fifteen dollars," she said, which seemed exorbitant, but I paid. While she made change, I looked back down the aisle. Rhody was not to be seen. I began to worry. Maybe she had slipped off while I was talking to Pop. Then I saw a bit of pink polyester sticking out from behind a seat, and I made for it.

She was pretending to stuff something into the pocket on the seat back in front of her, bending over so her head was down and her face averted. I still knew it was Rhody. I slipped into the seat next to hers.

"What are you doing?" I said.

"Don't talk to me," she hissed. "You're going to give me away."

"Who to?"

"Are you deaf, Lucille? Turn around and look straight."

I did. More tourists got on the bus. One man nodded to Rhody as he passed our seats. I spoke without moving my lips or looking at her. "Why are you dressed like that?" I said.

The bus pulled out into the street, and the noise of its engine gave us more privacy. Rhody narrowed her eyes at me. "How come you take it on yourself to butt into my business?" she said. "Don't tell me. I get it. Your boyfriend Wayne told you."

"He's not my—"

"Whatever he is. He told you and you decided to sneak up on me, find out what Rhody is onto, right?"

"No. Pop and I were sitting in the car looking for my mother. He thought he might see her on the Battery, since she used to like to walk here."

She looked down her long nose at me. "Okay, maybe so. I have seen you and your daddy just about everywhere I go, and you are always looking off in the distance. That's what you're doing, then, still looking for her? I saw you in the mall and in the Calhoun Park."

"You were there?"

"You didn't see the old colored woman sitting on a rain-coat? Writing in a notebook? That was me." She snickered.

"But what is this for, Rhody?"

"I am writing a book. I am doing the research for my book."

"What kind of book?"

"Like that story of the white man who dressed up black and wrote what it was like to be black. Only I'll be a black person telling what it's like to be black. I think that will be an improvement, don't you? Evelyn's helping me with the writing. I've got it all thought out in my head, and she's helping me get it down on paper. At first I thought Evelyn would write it, she's the smart one. But I come to find out, to my surprise—I am smarter! Evelyn has a high I.Q., but still I am smarter in the ways of the world. We're collaborating."

"Why the disguise?"

"To get a different viewpoint. It is hard to see out of your own head. You get in your way."

That made sense to me. I settled back into the seat. We were so high we could see down into cars as they passed, and into the first-floor windows of houses. I saw a piano in one, a desk cluttered with papers in another. This was worth the fifteen dollars. I saw a family eating at a long dining table.

"You were always an easy girl to talk to," Rhody was

saying. "Easier to talk to than your sister, the way you just sat quiet and listened with your eyes. I appreciated that."

"Thank you," I said.

"So now I'll give you some advice." She scrutinized me. "I think you are a girl who can accept advice."

"I am."

"First, your sister is a sick person. She is not reacting properly. Mamma had a cousin once that the same thing happened to. It isn't craziness, it's hormonal change, but you have to do something about it."

"What can I do?"

"Why, take her to the doctor."

"She won't go, Rhody, I tried! She won't go."

"Tie her up then and carry her bodily."

"I don't see how I can do that, I—"

"Let me tell you about this girl, Mamma's cousin. Finally the baby was born, and she came home from the hospital. Young girl, no husband, home to her mother's house, and she sat there a long time looking at the baby and then she dropped it into the creek. Up to that time, I mean during her girlhood, she had been a normal person. It's a disease. Get Rae to the doctor, today is not too soon. I've been saying something was wrong from the beginning, but no one believes me, because how could something be going wrong in the Odoms?"

"But who did you tell?"

"Well, I'm telling you, see? *Do* something, Lucille. If you don't, you could be responsible for the consequences. You're not just a bystander, you know. I mean, you are a good listener, a good observer, two fine talents, but you can't go through life that way. There is a time when you've got to *move*."

"All right."

"Second, about your mother. You have to let that one go. You understand me?"

"No."

"Your father is leaving no stone unturned, am I right?"

"Right."

"Put an end to that. Get him distracted to something else, get his mind off her."

"What do you think I have been doing?" I cried. "I've bought him a TV and all sorts of other things, I try to interest him in activities—"

"Ain't but one thing going to work, Lucille."

"What?"

"Got to get him interested in another woman."

"Oh." That took me aback. I'd been willing to try anything, but now the image of Vera Oxendine popped into my head, and I balked.

"You don't want him interested in another woman," she said.

"Of course I do, I want him back to normal, whatever it takes."

"No, you want *them* back to normal. You want both parents back, everything the way it was before. But it isn't going back that way, darling. It isn't ever going back that way. Some marriages drift back, but . . ." She shook her head.

"How do you know?" I said.

"I know these things. I am single, but a marital expert. I could set up with Wayne Frobiness and make a fortune on marriage counseling. Trouble with your mother is, she is an adventuress. She always was. She married your father in a spirit of adventure."

I knew the truth of that as soon as Rhody said it. As a girl, Mother had been marooned in old Charleston, looking at a sea of debutante parties, Yacht Club dinners, Junior League placement; and along had come a man representing the whole world of chance and risk. He had no money, he worked in the midst of danger, he flew an airplane. Those were the things she had married him for. Those were the things he had eventually worked himself away from, back towards the safety of feet on the ground and money in the bank.

"If he finds her," Rhody said, "it will do her in. Because she loves him and she will go back with him if once he gets to her."

"So I should prevent him from looking for her?"

"If you can."

"I wish I hadn't seen you back there."

"It's a load on you, no doubt about it. And coming at the time in your life when you ought to be fancy-free, ought to be out there dancing, living it up, familiarizing yourself with men. That was point number three, loosen up yourself. This time of your life you need to be, pardon me, humping your eyes out. No, I am serious, girl. Nobody ever told you that, did they? But it's true. I don't care what they say about what you can catch and the forty-eleven different ways that sex can ruin your young life. There are preventives. The main thing is, you need the practice for later. Now is the time. That's all there is to it. Even if Wayne Frobiness is not what you consider your boyfriend, still there's worse candidates in the field, and if I was you—"

"Rhody, wait. It isn't like that. I mean, I've tried it."

"You tried it. And?"

"Uh, I didn't do so well. I didn't exactly like it."

"Hmm," she said. "You may be one of the ones who needs love with it."

"Is that weird?"

"Most definitely. I was one myself."

"You?"

"That is hard to believe, isn't it. But yes. Matter of fact, I only have had one old man, from the time I was twelve years old. I was lucky. The one I practiced on turned out to be the one I was practicing *for*."

"But you never married him," I said.

"No."

"Why not?"

"You do ask questions, don't you? 'Why not?' Because I am like your mother. Marriage does not agree with me. One reason your mother befriended me all these years—and it was her that did it, not Rae—was we are two peas in a pod. You could believe we were sisters if not for the skin color. I even look like her, I think." She lifted her chin and turned her head.

I had never thought about it before, but there was a resemblance.

"I saw what happened to her," she said. "Over the years. And I said it wouldn't happen to me."

"I see," I said. I rubbed my lip and thought. "But, um . . . what did happen to her?"

"You were there, Lucille. You tell me."

"I don't know."

"You know."

"I don't."

"Maybe you ought to ask her," she said. There was a soft tone to her voice that made me stop and think. I had given up quizzing my mother. When we spoke on the phone now, I stuck to the details of housekeeping—where the fitted sheets were, how to make the oven cook a chicken in your absence, which dentist Pop should see for a new crown.

"I will," I said.

The tour guide stood up at the front of the bus and began telling the facts about certain houses along Meeting Street. One was where a television mini-series had been filmed. Everyone was impressed. Rhody pulled out her notebook and wrote in it.

"You're going to put that in the book?" I said.

"I'm putting everything in this book, honey. When I get through, the truth will be *known*."

I believed her.

"It's going to be a good book, Rhody," I said.

"Yes," she said. "It really is." She reached into her bag and withdrew a beer. "Let's sit back and enjoy this tour," she said. "You wouldn't want a beer, would you?"

"Sure," I said.

She got out another can. We popped the tops at the same time; only one person looked around, but the cans were out of sight.

"I could get arrested for this," she said. "But if anybody ever needed a beer it was you, God knows." She watched me take a sip. I didn't like the bitter edge of it, but it was cold.

"Insulated," she said, holding up the bag. "You like the taste?"

"It's okay."

"I'll go to my grave knowing I did one good deed. Gave Lucille Odom her first beer. That's something."

"Where does this bus go?" I asked, settling into my seat.

She read from a brochure. " 'Historic downtown Charleston, where descendants of the original lowcountry planters preserve the traditions of their forefathers.' "

The guide pointed out sights and lectured on their history. Rhody amended and corrected where necessary. "Bull *dog*," she said, when the guide said slaves jumped over a broom to get married.

"Here is where they hung the pirates," Rhody said to the people in front of us. A little farther on she said, "Here is where they hung the Negroes."

"Is that really true?" the lady in front of us said, turning around in her seat.

"Twenty-two all at once, 1822," Rhody said. "But they were troublemakers."

. . .

I liked touring my own city. It was a new perspective. I saw many things I'd never seen before, and I gained an appreciation for architecture and beer. Rhody's insulated bag exactly accommodated a six-pack, which we split evenly. As the bus pulled up in front of the Slave Mart Museum, Rhody said, "Here's where we get off. My car's there." We swung down off the bus like long-distance travelers.

"You want to go back to where your daddy is, or you want to come someplace with me?" she said, watching the white people file into the Slave Mart.

"Where are you going?" I said, but I already knew it didn't matter. I was going with Rhody. She took off her old-lady turban, and put her big gold hoops back in her ears.

"You don't look so good," she said, fastening the gold post behind her left earlobe.

"That's what Rae always says."

"You feel okay? You had too many beers for a beginner."

"No, I didn't. I wish we had more." I laid my head down onto my knees.

"I take you home in this condition and I'm in trouble," she said.

"I'll just go with you. Can I?" When I raised my head, the world took half a spin.

She thought hard, pursing her lips.

"You are older than I thought you were," she said.

"How old did you think I was?"

"I thought you were a child. I didn't give you any credit."

"Maybe you were right," I said.

"No. I see now. Come on."

"Okey-doke," I said.

"Hold onto me. Good Lord, Lucille, you only had three! You're drunk as a coot."

"That's why I don't, or didn't, drink it, it has this effect on me, I thought it did like this to everybody. Oops. Sorry."

"Hold on. No, it doesn't do like this to everybody. I thought the reason you didn't drink was, you were part of the new generation that doesn't do anything, from sex to sugar. The New Puritans."

"No, it's because I get so dizzy."

She loaded me into the car. People on Chalmers Street were staring, so I waved to let them know I was okay. The truth was, I had never felt better. A new day was dawning on me, now that Rhody had given me answers to questions that had long held a cloud over my head. Of course Rae needed professional help; a doctor would give her an injection of hormones and she'd be all right. I'd get her to the doctor tomorrow morning. And I'd speak openly with Mother at the earliest opportunity. I'd take the direct approach. "Why did you leave? What was the real reason?"

"You ever think about getting a place of your own?" Rhody said, her earrings swinging.

"Why would I want to do that?" I said.

"That's what I was afraid you'd say." She shook her head. In her Tercel we headed out of the city. I set my head back and let myself be carried away. I couldn't think exactly what a Tercel was in real life, but I had the idea it was a bird. I had read true accounts of what is called avian rapture, and the notion had always appealed to me: birds snatching humans away. I wouldn't put up a fight, I tell you, if one came for me.

"You want to read our first chapter?" Rhody said. I looked blank. "It's written. We're mailing it off to a New York publisher," she said.

"Sure."

"If they like the first chapter, then we'll talk about a deal, paperback rights, movie possibilities."

"Ah, Rhody, you know a lot of books get submitted to publishers."

"Three hundred thousand a year."

"Okay. Just so you know."

"None of them is like this book. I told you, Lucille. It is a book that reveals the truth. You didn't hear me?"

She had her jaw thrown to one side; when it was like that I knew she was capable of saying anything. Rhody had a habit of switching back and forth between strict truth and imagined truth, and I could tell which mode she was in by the position of her lower jaw. I wasn't worried about her.

She was the only person I wasn't worried about.

"Where are we going?" I said. "Don't take me home yet." We were on the road towards Mount Pleasant. She said nothing, but drove on as if she hadn't heard me. And it felt so good to be in the passenger's seat, I could have ridden forever. We passed the turnoff to my house. Good. I closed my eyes. *Good.* We were going somewhere else, not home, not home; and my relief was audible, a sort of whistling sigh that escaped from me without warning.

"I'm keeping my eyes closed," I said, "till we get there. Wherever it is. I'll open them when we stop."

She said nothing.

"Will it be a nice surprise?" I said.

"No."

That aroused my curiosity so I did open my eyes for a second, but I allowed myself only an upward view. I was low in the seat, my knees on the dashboard, and I caught sight of the sky, the utility poles, and a turkey vulture, before oaks closed over us and the road got darker. I ought to be able to figure out where we were. I'd ridden all these back roads. But the beers had destroyed my sense of direction, and I hadn't been able to follow the course in my mind. It seemed to me that we ought to be somewhere near Rhody's house, but probably not on her road, which had more traffic. We'd be

behind Wakendaw Lakes subdivision, but still south of the
highway, and heading toward the Wando River.

I felt a bump, meaning the paved road had run out. We
were on a soft dirt road, ungraded; I could hear weeds snap
against the side of the car and grass brush underneath us. I
thought hard. We could be on the old Keeler place. The title
wasn't clear, so it hadn't been developed, though the Keeler
family had long since quit farming it. All it was doing now
was keeping many lawyers busy.

"Okay," Rhody said, and the car stopped. The sound of
cars was still there, but it was distant, and muffled by the
woods all around. We were in what had once been a clearing,
maybe three years before. Weeds and bushes had sprung up,
and grass several feet high; honey locusts were already taller
than a man. There was a house sixty feet in front of us.

Or the exoskeleton of a house, a dream house. It was
concrete block, with doors and windows and a roof, but the
builder had abandoned it before it actually became a full-
fledged house. Vines had started up the back wall and hung
down in a matted curtain over the roof. I loved it.

"How'd you find this?" I said jealously.

"Daddy built it. He thought he owned this piece, between
the Keeler farm and our house, but come to find out halfway
through construction that he didn't. Our house is down that
path." What looked like a deer trail led back through the
woods. "We drove up the back road."

"But it looks nearly finished. There's a roof, screens in the
windows."

"No electricity, no finishing inside. But somebody who
had to, could live in it."

She was getting at something. "Not me," I said. "I need
creature comforts."

"Lucille, sometimes I swear you are dense as a phone pole."

She strode towards the house, and I followed. We stepped over the threshold into a cool, damp room. I expected to see cobwebs and dirt-dauber nests, but the place was swept clean. In one corner were a cot and a table, kerosene lamp, water pitcher, and three dresses on wire hangers hooked over a nail. They were Rhody's dresses. In another corner was a propane tank and a two-burner camp stove.

"*You're* living here," I said, swinging around on her.

"Now why would I do that?"

"I don't know."

"Think again, Lucille."

Then I saw a picture on the table, a snapshot in a red frame I recognized, of two children. Rae and me.

"Mother's living here," I said matter-of-factly. That was the only tone I could speak in because my heart was so thrown out, its pace went wild.

"Finally you got it," she said. "I thought you were one of the Genius Odoms."

"Where is she?"

"She's at our house. She'll be here in a minute. Daddy brings her home from work and she walks back through the woods."

"Where's she working?"

"That place near the waterslide where they sell sharks' teeth and ice cream."

"But that's only half a mile from our house! We've been looking everywhere for her."

"Didn't look there."

"No." I turned and surveyed the room again. "You don't mean she's been here for three months," I said.

"One night she was at our house, the first night; then she moved over here. Daddy had this old army cot."

"You should have told me."

"Why?"

"Because we were looking for her."

"That wasn't a good enough reason," she said.

"But, Rhody," I said, losing patience, "Mother can't stay here."

"Why not?"

"Because it's not a place for her. There isn't even a bath-room."

Rhody got up and opened a small door in the corner, and I saw a toilet and a shower stall, a mirror, a toothbrush holder on the wall and one red brush hung in it. "Daddy put this in for her," she said, standing back so I could see the whole room.

"Who paid for it?"

"She did, but it wasn't much. He had all the fixtures, and the basic plumbing was already in. I think it's a pretty good job. I think it's a pretty nice place to live, myself. You, Lucille—you're spoiled."

"I don't think it's spoiled to want a roof over your head."

"Nothing at all wrong with this roof. One minor leak maybe."

"Rhody, you wouldn't live in this house. Would you?"

"No, I wouldn't unless I had to, but if I had to I could."

"She doesn't have to," I said.

"Ask her about that." She nodded towards the door. Mother was making her way through the weeds up the path to the house.

I had forgotten her looks. Her loveliness had slipped out of my mind. It was different from Rae's, softer and not so strik-ing immediately. You might not notice at first that she was a beautiful woman, because there were none of the usual sig-nals, no eye makeup or blush-on. Her thick hair was coiled at the back of her neck like bread dough. She had on a dress of Rhody's, and it fit her exactly in size if not in spirit—a flow-ered sarong skirt with a matching low-necked blouse, and high-heeled sandals. *Oh, she has gone crazy*, I thought, while she passed from the sunlight into the dark house. I had never been so glad to see anyone in my life, but I couldn't move or speak. I stood in the dark and tried to think of what I ought to say.

"Who is that?" she said, squinting towards me.

I said, "Lucille."

"My Lucille?" she said, her eyes lighting up. When she hugged me I smelled her cigarettes, her sweet hair, and it was too much for me. "Baby, don't cry," she said. "No, no, no." She held me tight and swung me back and forth in her arms. I couldn't stop. "Rhody," Mother wailed, "she's heartbroken. I didn't know! I thought she was all right, all this time. You said she was all right! Lulu, stop, please. She never cries, Rhody, this is serious. What's wrong with her?" She was holding me and rocking me and calling to Rhody over my shoulder.

"Homesick," Rhody said. "Homesick and drunk on three beers." She lit the kerosene lamp, and one corner of the room glowed bright.

"Oh, Lucille," Mother said. "You can't drink. You can't handle it."

"I know," I cried.

"Okay, sit down, I'll make you some coffee." She guided me to the cot. She poured water from the pitcher into a pan and lit the camp stove. Stopping in front of it, she adjusted the flame to pure gold, and it lit her face.

"I owe you an explanation," she said.

I didn't protest.

"It didn't occur to me that you would be hurt, Lucille."

"Then why didn't you let me know where you were?" I said.

"I was going on the theory, out of sight, out of mind," she said. "I knew it was going to be a hard time and I figured it would be easier if your father and I just didn't see each other. I thought it would ease the pain. Sometimes just seeing a face can bring back too many memories."

"Well, it didn't work. He had the memories anyway, and the pain."

"*He* did? I'm talking about me. I was afraid if I saw him I'd go running back. I tried to keep my mind off of him. It was like self-hypnosis. But you're right. It didn't work, not completely. Sometimes I couldn't stand it, a wave would hit me. Some little thing would set me off, a song on the radio, or a smell, or once a little airplane high in the sky, and I couldn't help myself, I'd get to a phone and call him." She took a deep breath. "Well, it's still not over, look at me." She held out the cup of coffee, and her hand trembled. "Just talking like this does it."

I was dumbfounded. "I thought you didn't want to see him," I said.

"I *didn't!* I don't."

"But if it's so difficult—"

"Of course it's difficult, but it's necessary. Marriage was killing me. I managed all right until he retired, but then—he—*it*—was always there, and I couldn't just be. And then the driving. . . . He wasn't to blame, I wasn't to blame. In fact, we did the best two people can do, that's what I don't understand! I can't help wondering what we were supposed to do, different from what we did. . . . But anyway. Here we are now, you and me." She sniffed and cleared her throat and sat next to me, putting the coffee to my mouth. "I have to admit, Lucille. You were the last one I was worried about. It was so hard, all that time. It was so sad. I was just trying to stay afloat."

Then I was the one comforting her, as her gray eyes watered over, but she tried to laugh a little and stiffened her mouth.

"I assumed you'd be fine," she said, "because you haven't needed me for anything since the sixth grade."

"But I have," I said.

"No, not you. You wanted to take care of yourself, and you succeeded, too." She touched my hair. "But I always worried a little bit about you, for being so tough so young. I still worry."

"Don't worry about me. There are people who could use it more than me. There's Rae, for example, who has gone off the deep end."

"I know about Rae. Rae and I got together a few times. We met and had some talks, and I think she'll be okay, she's just going through a transition. . . ."

"You met? Where? She didn't tell me. Why did you see her and not me?"

"Because I knew you would try to persuade me to come back, and I knew Rae wouldn't. She'd let me go."

"Why did you leave?" I said. "What was wrong with the way it was?"

"It was permanent."

The word she chose was one that hit me like the rumbly shock of an electrical current, because I understood it. *Per*, throughout, plus *manere*, to remain. Staying the same, through and through, on and on.

"People say that as you get older time passes faster," she said. "But in our house it wasn't even moving. Nothing was ever new. Nothing! I don't mean it was his fault, his fears were not his fault, they came from the Depression and his mother and father—but he wanted to protect everything. That was his goal. To protect me, the children, the house, even the dogs. And from what, I wanted to know! From the world. But people should not be protected from the world, Lucille, it cripples them. Look at me. I am unfit for the world, and I always loved the world. I loved travel and politics and art;

you never even knew that about me, did you? I was crazy for the world, at one time."

"But you love him."

She laughed at me, her long high laugh. "I knew you wouldn't understand," she said. "Let me put it this way. We carried love to its conclusion."

After awhile she turned down the wick on the lamp, and we went outside to sit on a board between two stumps. There were a lot of stars but no moon, so the night was black. I could see nothing at all, sitting there between Mother and Rhody. I was respectful and quiet because I realized the two of them knew things I didn't know. Mosquitoes bit my legs, and I slapped at them even though I couldn't see them.

"They won't bite you if you got a clear conscience," Rhody said.

I laughed, and she said it was really so, having to do with chemicals in the skin and body heat. "You can see they ain't biting me, can't you?"

"I can't see anything."

"You're the only one they're going for."

"Let's get her inside," Mother said. "You can sleep here, Lucille."

I was so tired I was almost passed out; it was a mental state similar to the drugged reverie of wisdom-tooth extraction. They took me back inside and lowered me onto the cot, which was lumpy but clean and cool. I smelled the brown wool of an army blanket and the musty ticking of an old pillow, and did not even have time to wonder, before I fell asleep, where Mother would sleep if I was taking her bed. I heard them talking but I heard only the tones, not the words; I fell asleep to that low music of women talking seriously.

And later, at my accustomed hour of three A.M., I woke up, my eyes expecting the familiar outline of my dresser, my three windows, my orbed bedposts, but instead I was blind. I saw no shapes. Night thoughts of the worst variety assailed me, those that say *You will be no more,* as if this great truth were not one that could be told in the light of day.

I put my feet on the concrete floor and stood up carefully; in absolute darkness it was hard to walk because I had nothing by which to gauge the vertical and could only hope my internal notion of it approximated reality. I felt along the concrete block wall about eight or ten feet, and my toe came up against something furry. I froze and pulled back.

"Lulu?" Mother said. "Don't step on my head. I'm on the floor."

I knelt down and found her, wrapped in a sleeping bag on the hard floor. She patted my hand.

"Are you okay?" I said.

"I'm just fine. Rhody brought me the sleeping bag she took to Camp Kanuga. There's a roll of foam rubber under it. I'm fine."

"I don't mean that."

"Oh. Well, I'm fine in every other way, too. Or will be."

I made my way back to the cot. I believed her. For a long time I stared up where I believed the ceiling was, and listened to a screech owl's spiralling-down call, and waited in hopes that she might, through the darkness, say my name and ask me the same question I had asked her. I would have said, "Oh, Mother, no, I am in grave danger; I feel it near me." We could have been the mother and daughter of a true-love ballad, telling what we knew.

When I heard her breathing the long sighs of sleep, I turned on my side. There seemed to be little reason to close my eyes, it was dark as sleep anyway, and the owl had hushed. I slept for awhile, I'm absolutely sure, with my eyes wide open.

C H A P T E R

10

*A*fter that night I often paid visits to my mother in her cinderblock house. My own house was more than I could deal with. I would burst out of it, grab my bike from under the steps, and ride with my head lowered all the way to Rhody's, through the Pooles' junk-strewn yard, and down the path into the woods. Then I felt calmer: a path into woods is one of the best inventions of man, tempting at the start and mysterious all the way in. This one was not easy to ride, slippery with pine straw and threaded with knobby roots. I bumped along, ducking under branches and the looping woody vines of wild grapes. In one place a summer fire had burnt the undergrowth, and the black ground had sprouted a cover of cinnamon fern, green in August but now dried to copper. Grape leaves dropped down; birds as small as moths moved through the woods in loose flocks.

I stopped in there awhile and watched the pine trees move, limber in the wind. This was an accidental and temporary forest, a mere patch of woods between the shipping terminal and the highway. As soon as the title was cleared, it would disappear—woods, path, little block house.

Mother knew that. Nevertheless, every time I visited, I saw something new in the house. She was adding improvements— a screen door, a braided rug, an orange cat. She had bought a set of handyman's tools. This morning I arrived while she was putting up curtains.

"What do you think?" she said, standing on a chair and holding the rod over her head.

"You don't own this place, you know. You could get kicked out tomorrow. Don't put too much into it."

"Hold this rod while I screw in the hooks, please."

I took the curtain and steadied the chair she was standing on.

"I don't own this place, no," she said. "Wait, are you talking about this house or the planet Earth?"

"This house. Nobody owns the planet Earth."

"Well, in either case, I don't care about getting kicked out tomorrow. In fact, the possibility makes this place all the more valuable to me right now. I'm putting everything I have into it."

"Don't fall on that screwdriver," I said. "You'll put your eye out."

She laughed at me. Laughing at people was a bad habit of hers. She didn't do it maliciously; she couldn't help herself. "Where did you learn to be such a good mother, Lucille? Not from me. Lord knows, I *should* have said 'You'll put your eye out,' but I don't think I ever did. You didn't get it from me. I have a feeling the maternal language comes natural to you. You'll make a terrific mother some day."

She stepped off the chair and backed away from the window to appraise the curtain. "Not bad," she said. "The yellow looks cheerful, doesn't it? I used to read those decorating magazines and go into a tailspin. I bet half the cases of clinical depression in women are caused by *House Beautiful*. I'd read it and say, hey, I can make those slipcovers. Remember those chintz ones I made for the living room chairs? I got so excited about the fabric I dreamed about it. There was a blue bird of paradise on peach-colored flowers. Dreamed about slipcovers! Oh, well. Then when I got them on the chairs, they were all wrong, didn't look anything like I'd envisioned, because there was so much I hadn't taken into account—all the other things in the room, the bureaus and tables and sofas, the geometric pattern in the rug, the flowers in the curtains. My slipcovers got swallowed up. Now I see that the secret is to start with an empty room. Your father and I bought that house furnished, and it just attracted more and more junk, all those so-called antiques." She looked at me. "Oh, I didn't mean that your things are junk, I meant—everything taken together."

"It's all right," I said. The orange cat rubbed its scarred triangular head against my leg. "I know it's junk."

She didn't contradict me. She nodded toward the cat. "He likes you," she said.

"No, they do that for a reason. They have glands near their whiskers."

"You see, at my age, you just can't take too much furniture. It is one of many things from which value drops away. Whereas at your age you love furniture, you can see possibilities in every chair. You can see furniture fitting smoothly into your life, a pie safe and umbrella stand and gateleg table. But to my mind it is all nothing but a headache. I want a room, bed, table, maybe a yellow gingham curtain, one rug. Old people pare things down."

"Mother, you're forty-nine."

"Oh, my God, no, Lucille. I'm much older than forty-nine, at the moment. Maybe I'll return to forty-nine before the year is over, if I can stay here. I'm recovering myself. Some people go to spas and ashrams, but I'm in this ruined house of Sam Poole's on Long Point Road, a ghost house on a piece of no-man's-land; and it's working. I'm recuperating."

"You don't plan on coming home, then."

She turned toward the window and tied the curtain back with a strip of gingham, flouncing the bottom part out like a skirt, poofing the top. "I don't think so," she said.

"We could redo the house," I ventured. "You still have the architect's plans."

"It isn't a matter of the house."

"Pop would change, too. I know he would. He would change to whatever you want, if you came back."

"I wouldn't want him changed. I love him as he is. How can I put this, Lucille? It sounds horrible however I say it, but what I want to get away from is the whole package, the house, everything. The family. Let me get away from it, I've been in it so long, Lucille. We did it for so long!"

"I didn't know you felt that way," I said coldly.

"Yes, you did know. You and your father and Rae all know that things will be vastly better for all of us this way. Your father is already improving. He was in a rut, and now I can hear in his voice on the phone that he's excited about new things. He's taking up new interests."

"One of them is a woman," I said, watching her face.

"Oh, really? Well, wonderful, that's good. I thought he sounded happy, and I asked what it was, but he said he was reading a lot of books and going for walks and—but, good. Someone he met recently, or someone he knew? No, don't tell me. Don't say anything about it, not yet." She wet her lips and lifted her head. "Okay, let's do the other window, and then I've got to get over to Rhody's house to catch a ride to work."

There was still one unanswered question. I asked it.

"How much money are you making?"

"Don't ask me that, Lucille. You and your father keep asking me how much money I've got. The truth is, a human being doesn't need as much money as you and your father think. I'm earning a tiny little bit of money. So far, it's more than enough for me. I don't want a car, I don't want any electronic equipment. Money makes me feel anxious."

"Promise me that if you need anything you'll call me," I said.

"I will. Oh, I don't want to be a worry to you, sweetheart. I can tell you're worried about something, look at the circles under your eyes." She held me by the shoulders and examined my face. I hoped she would see. I hoped it would come through to her what was wrong with me.

"Nothing is worth worrying about too much, you know," she said. "The world is not that dangerous a place. It is where we are meant to be. I am going to be all right, I promise you. And Poppy's going to be all right, too. Or is it Rae you're worried about? Lucille, what are these tears for?"

"I don't know," I said.

"Something else is bothering you. Tell me what it is." She sat me down on the cot and put her arm around me, and I wanted to tell her. For a moment I considered it; her arm was tight, she held me as if she wanted to know. I looked her in the eye and opened my mouth—and then briefly, but not so briefly that I didn't notice, her eyes wandered, the way a person's eyes wander when they are not seriously listening to you. Her eyes left my face and went, for a split second, to her yellow curtains.

I caught myself just in time.

"Tell me, darling," she said, coming back to me.

"It's school," I said. "I'm taking my make-up exams next week, and I've forgotten everything I ever learned." Which was true, but not something I cared about.

"I'll help," she said. "I'll call out vocabulary."

"No," I said. "I just need to hit the books."

But I couldn't open a book. Until now I had loved books with an almost physical love, had taken one to bed with me every night and heard its voice speaking low to me alone.

Even a textbook could seem intimate, a tutor telling me important things. But now, books were stupid. When I thought of studying Latin, I laughed.

All I wanted to do with my life was watch Billy McQueen. I would be content being his sister-in-law, even though it sounded like a hawk-beaked thing. I would watch him eat, watch him swim, watch him write his Ph.D. dissertation.

He had taken his typewriter downstairs into the little room under the house. It was not an integral part of the house, but an addition nailed in between the pilings that held the house above floodwaters. There was an air-conditioner down there, so it was a good place to work: cool, quiet, removed from the troubles upstairs. Rae was hard to be around. I had used the little room myself as a hideaway when I wanted to be alone. Pop's workbench took up one corner, but there was also an old oak desk, a couple of reject chairs, and a sagging couch covered by a brown ribbed spread worn soft as a rabbitskin. I liked the idea of Billy in that room. I could think of examples of women kept in rooms (Rapunzel, Colette, the Lady of Shalott), but none of men, and I found the idea of it . . . well, *delicious*. Every afternoon when he got home from work, he went down, worked for a couple of hours, came up for supper, then disappeared again. On weekends he was closeted in there all day long, and I took him his lunch. Sometimes I hung around and watched him eat, then carried the tray back up, unable to think of an excuse to stay longer.

It was September, a month I'd always liked. But something was wrong with this one. For the first September in memory, I was not going to school. I ought to have been pleased with the freedom, but instead I was at loose ends. There must be an innate need for school, a seasonal urge similar to the migration instinct. As summer eased into autumn, I got hungry for pencils and a new loose-leaf notebook. No matter how boring school is, at least it gives you fresh starts on an annual basis. Without school, the future can look as dense and uninviting as a book without paragraphs.

On Saturday morning when I took Billy his lunch, he pushed his chair back and took off his glasses, peeling them from around one ear, across his nose, and off the other side. He was old-fashioned; nobody wore glasses like those any more. He also carried a handkerchief and pocket knives.

Rae was right: this was one of those men who truly want a normal life, the routine of meals, mail delivery, evening television, bedtime at ten. From his looks you could have mistaken him for the other kind of man, and maybe Rae had. But he had little interest in adventure. He ate his turkey sandwich happily.

"What's that?" he said, still chewing.

"This?" I looked at the book in my hand as if I'd never seen it before. "Oh, this is my history book. I have to take these dumb exams next week." I tucked the book under my elbow.

"Want some help?"

"Oh, no." I shook my head. "I'm fine. You're busy." I nodded.

"Tell you what. I'll give you some hints, just to get you started." He reached to the sofa and swept Pop's old magazines onto the floor. "Sit right there. Let me see this book. How much does the test cover?"

"Up to Eisenhower."

"Do you do SQ3R?"

"What?"

" 'Survey, question, read, review, remember.' Even if you're as smart as Rae says you are, you have to develop good study skills. What's so funny?"

"You sound like a teacher."

He put his feet up on the desk. "And a good one. I can teach even hard cases like you, the stubborn, scared ones."

"What do you mean, scared? I'm not scared. Hah, that's crazy. Scared of what?"

"Sit down, then, and read that book."

"I don't have time to read the whole book. I've got the teacher psyched out. Most of the time she makes her tests from captions and headings."

"Read the book," he said. "Look, it's only America. What if it were China? Anybody can do America in two days."

"But I have three other subjects, and only one week! How can I do all this in a week? I haven't looked at it since May. It's impossible. I should just answer a classified ad and spend my life earning an hourly wage."

"It's not impossible," he said. "Look me in the eye. It is not impossible. Nothing's impossible for you." He tapped my forehead. "You've got what it takes. Don't forget that."

I opened the book and looked at the table of contents, and my insides hurt. "Rae said I was smart?" I said.

"She used the phrase 'steel trap.' Now. You've got eight hours a day. You can use this room; I won't be back until four. At night we'll work some more and then discuss the material you've covered." He was serious. "Go on," he said. "Might as well get started now." He pulled his chair back up to the desk, put his glasses on, and shuffled his notecards. In minutes he was sunk in thought. I took long, deep breaths. A man sunk in thought is an inspiring sight.

The air-conditioner was on high cool, and its mechanical drone kept out every sound. Through the one small window I could see only white sky. We might have been in a tower or a cell or a bunker. Upstairs my sister was stewing in the craziness of pregnancy, thinking, I supposed, of her precious lost youth.

Lost youth is no tragedy. Personally, I longed to lose mine.

"You're not reading," Billy said. "Maybe you aren't so smart, after all."

I dug in.

I spent every morning for a week in the little room. During the day, I read, read, read. I hurt from so much reading; my eyes ached and itched. But when he came in at four, I was able to say I had read three hundred pages of history. The evening discussions were mostly his but sometimes mine, out on the screened porch with a view of moving lights in the black harbor.

He was, as he had claimed, a good teacher. When he quoted Thomas Paine—" 'Danger and deliverance make their advances together' "—I heard excitement in his voice. "There is more than meets the eye, see, Lucille? There are underground streams." Even in subjects that were not his field he got wound up, leaning forward in his chair toward the starry night, speculating on how life could have sparked up from mud, why Othello is such a fool, what makes the ablative absolute a particularly wonderful grammatical construction. He knew a lot. "Everything is history," he confided. We were alone those nights, and I was happy. Listen, I said to a small insistent questioner inside me: I'm better off with a teacher than with a romantic partner. I'm *lucky*.

And the teaching worked. I saw three hundred years of American history collapse into two days. Then four books of the *Aeneid;* a medley of William Shakespeare, Emily Dickinson, Ernest Hemingway, and Alice Walker; and a general survey of all life forms on the face of the earth, including internal details on the shark and the fetal pig. At the end of the week I was stuffed with knowledge.

Not only did I pass the make-up exams with all A's, but I found myself feeling smart, walking around with an overview. Parallels occurred to me that I had not thought of before, ways the world repeats itself in theme and form.

How could I stop now? Even after I was through with the exams and had been promised a diploma by mail, I asked

Billy to let me keep on reading downstairs while he wrote. "I won't bother you," I promised, "but I need to make up for lost time. If I can work on my own this fall, I might get into second-semester classes at the college and not be behind."

"Sure, all right," he said. "You've never bothered me; it's great to have you there, in fact. Keeps me going. Sometimes I have dark moments when I think maybe I should just give up."

I must have looked horrified.

"On the dissertation, I mean," he said.

I did make certain that Rae was well taken care of. I unplugged the phone so it wouldn't bother her, and also because I wasn't sure whether she would follow the directions I'd given everyone in case of a call from Wayne: to say I wasn't home. I checked in on her. "You want anything?" I asked. It was Saturday, and I guarded my Saturdays. "If so, let me get it now. I'm going to be downstairs all morning." Outside, Pop was mowing the grass again, while Vera, incredibly arrayed in halter top and shorts, lay in a plastic lounge chair and smiled his way.

Rae looked at me from her bed and said, "I want air."

"I'll turn the fan up for you. But it's pretty cool outside today." I was well aware that she meant something deeper, but I didn't want to go into anything with her. She was reading the Sierra Club magazine. She lowered it and spoke quietly to me.

"I'm going to die, Lucille."

"Right." I turned the fan up to high and tried to quiet its rattle. Someday I would strangle this fan. Kick its face in and stop its noise for good. The air outside was chilly. "You're going to die of pneumonia," I said.

"You don't believe me."

"Rae, if you need anything, don't yell for it, okay? I'll

come back in an hour and see if there's anything you want."

"I regret that I never joined the Sierra Club. Where did we get this magazine?"

"It's Pop's."

"I wish I had subscribed. It's a good publication. The only magazine I ever subscribed to was *Newsweek*. My obituary will say, 'Miss Odom was a lifelong *Newsweek* subscriber.' "

"Mrs. McQueen," I said.

She stared at me.

"You're Mrs. McQueen," I said. "And you can join the Sierra Club when your baby is born, and take the baby on hikes in a backpack."

She didn't acknowledge anything. I might as well have kept my mouth shut. Her eyes had an empty look; something crucial was missing—the welter of daily emotions.

I went downstairs, where Billy was already at work; I took my place without speaking and opened my Virgil. Aeneas had by then abandoned Dido, journeyed to the underworld, and made his way finally to the banks of the Tiber. The story at this point was starting to drag: preparations for war, intervention of the gods, and so forth. But the words still held me, the perfect sentences so much more precise than English. Latin tried to pin things down. English, I realized, didn't even have a subjunctive mood, for use "in matters of supposal, desire, possibility," according to the grammar note.

Wait . . . I read that again. Matters of supposal, desire, possibility? My moods, the feelings that came upon me without warning and seemed to have no name—that's what they were. Subjunctive moods, somewhere between what's real and what's not. Maybe they were nameless in English, but in Latin they were well recognized and given grammatical status. I looked up to tell Billy, but he was hunched over the desk, his hand propping his head, his eyes closed.

Rae had lit into him the night before; what for, I couldn't

tell, even though I had stood close to my wall and laid my ear against the wood. No doubt her temper came as a surprise to him, since it was the type that lies low for months between eruptions. I felt so sorry for him: this was no honeymoon.

At noon, he pushed his chair back and stacked his papers. But he didn't say, as usual, "Let's eat." He looked tired. He stared into the plywood wall behind the desk, where filled knotholes resembled boats in the stream of the woodgrain. Something was bothering him, and it wasn't the deerskin trade.

I tried to think of something cheerful. "Why don't we all go out for a picnic?" I said. "Pick up some hamburgers, find a place with a good view . . ."

"Rae's feeling bad," he said.

"Oh."

"But . . ." He looked up. "We could bring her back some food."

"Sure."

"Good idea. Let's go."

We took her car. He turned on the radio, and we arrived at Burger King with music playing so loud, I was a little embarrassed. I looked into the restaurant to see if there was anyone I knew inside, but all I saw was kids in gold cardboard crowns crawling all over the booths. We waited in the drive-through line. He was solemn.

"Where's a good place to picnic?" he said.

"We could just go on home, and take Rae—"

"No," he said. "I need an outdoor eating opportunity."

"Well, I know one place, down by the water."

"Perfect."

We pulled up to the microphone, and he ordered. "Nine Whoppers, two large Cokes, two fries," he said.

"Nine!" I said. "I only want one, and Rae probably won't even finish a whole one."

"We're celebrating," he said. "You have to eat three."

"What are we celebrating?"

"The future." But he was only trying to convince himself. "I have a job, I'm progressing toward the doctorate, and I'm reproducing. In a matter of weeks I will have successfully perpetuated my genetic material. And you—the straight-A girl— you're clear for the future, too. What better cause for celebration? Two futures." He passed me the food and drinks.

I looked into the paper bags. "Nine is a lot of Whoppers."

"You don't think we can pull it off. Hell, Lucille, I told you. Have more confidence." He looked better now, his arm spread across the back of the seat, his face lifted to catch the sun. "Forge ahead," he said into the sky. "That's my motto. Even when things look bad."

" *'Forsan et haec olim meminisse iuvabit,'* " I said.

"Christ, Lucille. I don't have the energy—Okay, I'm sorry. . . *'Forsan et haec . . .'* Perhaps and this?"

" 'Perhaps someday we'll recall with joy even these things.' Aeneas encouraging his men?"

"Yeah. Perhaps. But also, perhaps not. Ah, fuck it. Sorry. Where's your picnic place?"

The Episcopalians had improved the picnic area. The broken lightbulbs had been replaced, there were new tables, and the oyster oven had been cleaned up. We tried all three tables, to get the one with the best view. I felt a slight tug of guilt, this being Wayne's picnic spot. But he didn't own it, did he? A place where Indians have lived, where blind people congregate and believers roast oysters—a place like that I considered to be open to the public.

"Do you mind if I smoke this?" Billy said. "I've had it in my wallet for four months." He held a flattened joint between his fingers and tried to pinch it into shape.

"I don't mind," I said.

"You won't turn me in."

I gave him a look of dismay.

He hurried to say, "When I first met you, I could have believed you'd turn in a family member. You were a little shit that first night we came."

"Well, if I was, I still am. I haven't changed," I said.

"You have," he said. "We all have. It hasn't exactly been an easy time, but I think—I hope—it will get better soon."

We ate without talking. I said to myself there was not much more in the world that I wanted, other than improvement in Rae's attitude; and that would come, as Billy said, soon. *Soon.* Time alone can sometimes be the simple cure nobody thinks of until it has done its quiet work. I believed that. Over us, bees flew as crazily as electrons; but from the start of the world, time has converted random motion into sweet, solid things.

"You know, there are ways to cheer Rae up," I said.

He didn't respond.

"Like, buy her something," I went on. "There's a new shopping plaza near the bridge; we could go there and get her a present."

"Okay. Just wait a few minutes. You have another hamburger to eat." He lit the bedraggled joint and inhaled, then automatically passed it my way without looking at me. I had it in my mouth before he realized what he had done—before he realized, I guess, who I was. He reached to get it back just as I drew in the smoke, and I was stunned, not by marijuana but by his finger on my top lip. He had touched the scar; he was looking at it.

"Don't," I said, covering my mouth and losing all my smoke.

"Don't what?"

"Stare at my scar."

"Move your hand." He took my wrist and guided it away from my mouth. "What scar?"

"I had a harelip. Didn't Rae tell you that?"

"No. You mean this tiny thread? Mine is better. Gouged out a hunk of my skull fifteen years ago falling into the bleachers in a basketball game. I always hoped it would fade away, but I think it grows. I hide it with hair." He lifted his hair and I saw his white forehead. I almost couldn't speak.

"I, uh, don't see a scar. Whereabouts is it?" I said.

He searched the skin with his finger. "Here. I can feel the hole."

"No," I said. "Nothing."

"You're not looking close."

I leaned forward for an instant. "A pinprick," I said. "It'd take a magnifying glass to see it. You can cut your hair."

He rubbed his forehead and let the hair fall back onto it. "I guess we're suffering from imaginary injuries," he said. "We're not nearly so marred as we thought."

"Look again," I said. "Don't joke, okay? Tell me the truth."

He bent close to me this time, and said, "If you hadn't pointed it out, I'd have seen nothing. I see something close to invisible. I can tell that maybe it lifted your lip a fraction higher than where it might have been. But it's quite lovely. The way it goes up like that." He backed off. "So. No scars. I promise, there's nothing there."

We stashed the burger bags in the All Saints' trash barrel and started towards the car. "Wait," I said. "I thought of something." At the edge of the water I let myself down onto the mudbank near the twisted oak and reached back up under the lip of the bank. I probed, feeling nothing but the cold roots at first. But then my finger found one small piece of pottery the size of a playing card. I tossed it up to him and waited to see what he'd say.

"But this is—where'd you get this? It's 500 B.C., Woodland period."

"I know! And there's more all along the bank, hidden in roots and mud." I thought if he could get his mind off his troubles and back onto the mystery of life, his outlook would improve. Indian pottery had often helped me that way.

And it almost worked. He turned the shard over and over in his hands as we walked back to the car. "During the Woodland period, there was a pottery boom," he said. "Suddenly, a great burst of pots, all over the Southeast. Why do you think that was?" He had the Socratic gleam in his eye.

"Um, they learned how to do it?"

"Technology is never a cause, Lucille. The only cause is need. Men were giving up the rambling life, so they needed a lot of new things. Garden tools, pots, houses, burial mounds. That's what happens when you decide to stay in one place. You accumulate. And where are you going to keep your acorns, your bear fat and seeds? You've got to have a lot of pots. Think about those cupboards in your kitchen. Same thing."

His face clouded again.

We drove home. "We forgot to buy Rae a present," I said in the car, but I don't think he heard me. He was thinking about the origins of domestic life. "Pots were the beginning of the end," he said.

I was surprised at how easy it was to conceal something as large and flashy as love. Nobody knew. It was as if I had deposited a gem in a Swiss bank. I shared it with no one, paid no taxes.

I took opportunities where I found them: drove him to Wando in the mornings and picked him up at three; fixed his food and washed his laundry; stood nearby when he polished his shoes, breathing in as much as I could of the smell while a shine rose across the leather toes. In the evenings we worked together: I read parts of the *Aeneid* that no one has read for centuries, deep in Books XI and XII. I was happy. But always I bore in mind the need for secrecy. Every day I saw how Vera wore her heart on her sleeve, and I knew it would be her ruin. There are some loves that can't survive revelation. I would never let mine out. I didn't even like to put it into words within my own head: *in love with your sister's husband.* To me the phrase seemed distorted and mean, and I tried to think of other words to express the concept; but I couldn't.

Loyalty to my sister was in my heart. I saw to it that she got the right foods; I stayed polite in spite of her grouchiness; and as soon as we could get an appointment, I took her to the doctor as Rhody had advised. I went in with her. She had washed her hair and put on makeup, so she did not look as bad as usual. Makeup will often fool doctors. She hardly spoke, but she gave the doctor her beautiful smile, and he found nothing wrong with her. Privately, I told him that she seemed depressed, and he recommended exercise.

"Rae, honey," I said at home, "try the exercycle. Vera has lost twelve pounds riding it. She goes twenty miles a day."

"I'm staying put," she said. When I tried to return her car keys, she said, "Keep them. Consider yourself the owner of a once-beautiful automobile."

On Saturday morning, I went down to read more battle accounts, and I saw a pillow and sheet on the sofa. "Did you spend the night down here?" I said.

"Rae can't sleep if I'm in the room. Anyway, I'm working late at night now."

"Okay, we've got to do something," I said. "Don't you see, she's always had people giving her things, awards, medals for bravery, attendance pins, Miss Wando. Now there's nothing. No attention. Let's go get her a new nightgown."

"She doesn't want attention from me."

"Sure she does. Let's go now."

"Now? I'm in the middle of a paragraph."

I tried to be patient, but found it difficult. I looped my bag over my shoulder and thought of going without him, but he was the one who ought to be doing this. "What's more important?" I said finally. "Rae or a paragraph?"

"All right, all right."

Oddly enough, I could get piqued with him. Some of his habits bothered me, but I was in no position to correct them. Sometimes I found myself on the verge of blurting out an inappropriate remark that would have revealed everything— like "Don't wear that shirt," or "You shouldn't eat sour cream"—comments a person makes only to a loved one.

"Billy—" I said, impatience driving me to the use of his name, which I usually had trouble saying directly to his face.

"Okay." He rolled the paper out of the typewriter. "I'm yours."

Every day I had to endure these ironic instants, but each new one packed as much wallop as the last. "*I'm yours.*" My heart was being pummeled! I could only hope that as time went on, I would grow hardened to the onslaught.

People were forsaking the malls, I had noticed. One or two malls were dead already, empty even on Saturdays. The new thing was plazas, smaller and more emotional places designed to make you feel festive. The plaza at the foot of the bridge had a courtyard and a fountain, tables with umbrellas, and specialty shops.

We went into Sweet Nothings, where underwear floated in the air. Bikini pants and bras and camisoles hovered just above my head, and Billy's eyes were on a level with the garter belts.

He batted at a slip that touched his hair, then tangled with a length of monofilament holding up a Christian Dior teddy. The plastic popped, dropping the little silk suit to the floor. A salesgirl picked it up.

"Can I help you, sir?"

He looked lost.

"We want a nightgown," I said.

"On the left, back here." We followed her.

"Fancy items," Billy said, lifting price tags along the way.

"Did you have a color or a style in mind?" the girl said.

"We want something beautiful," I said. "Something white. I'll just look through these, thanks." I slid the hangers one by one along the rack, looking at every gown. They were all either too glamorous or too matronly.

"Here you go," Billy said, holding up a pink negligee with fur on it.

"No fur," I said.

"No fur," he said to the salesgirl.

"This one," I said, coming to a white silk. It stopped me cold, its plain bodice cut like a slip, with thin rolled straps. It was soft and wispy, and just the thing to make Rae feel beautiful again.

"That one," he said, "is not going to go around her."

I spread the hips of the nightgown. "I guess not," I said. I had a strange habit of forgetting Rae's girth; in my mind she was still her old unpregnant self.

"We need something big," Billy said to the salesgirl. "Something really big." He measured a space with his hands.

I still held the silk between my fingers.

"Get that one for you," he said.

"For me?"

"Yes, why not?" He took the hanger off the rack and gave it to the salesgirl. I could have said no, but I thought of my old dingy nightgown with square sleeves and a ripped hem. The white gown looked like a wedding dress. I followed the salesgirl to the dressing room, where she left me alone.

I hated dressing rooms because I didn't like to watch myself undress; it was unnerving. In addition, I didn't really like the look of myself once I got undressed, awkwardly standing there in the cubicle. So turning my back to the mirror, I took off my shirt and bra, then slipped the nightgown over my head. Then under the gown I unzipped my jeans and let them drop in a stiff heap to the floor. I turned around and faced the mirror.

The sight was almost too much for me. I stood there ogling myself. I even wiggled my hips some, regretting it immediately, but then I did it again. I stood sideways to my own reflection and tried to keep from smiling.

The salesgirl pushed the curtain aside and said, "Wow. That sure looks good on."

"Do you think so?"

"You've got the figure for it. Everyone else that has tried it on looked flat as a pancake."

I turned and looked at my rear. The gown was cut on the bias, Jean-Harlow style. I could have worn it to a party if I'd wanted to, if I'd been a party-goer.

"There's a three-way mirror out here," the girl said. I stepped past the curtain and into a mirrored alcove in which I saw myself from multiple angles.

"The shoes don't do much," I said, lifting a Nike into the air. But salesgirls rarely have a sense of humor, or even congeniality. She stayed poker-faced.

"You might want to take the shoulders up some," she said, standing next to me and pinching up the strap. "But I don't know. Maybe not. It looks good low."

I turned once more to see myself, and in the mirror I saw Billy watching me. Instantly I reddened and looked away, shamed by my own vanity. I hurried back to the dressing

room, and a chill made me shake my neck. I dressed fast and
handed the nightgown back over to the salesgirl. "It's not
what I was looking for," I said.

"That's a shame." She looked sorrowful.

"Aren't you getting it?" Billy said.

"It doesn't fit," I said.

The pouting salesgirl said, "*I* thought it fit great."

"I don't want it," I said. The store was making me dizzy,
with all that flying lingerie. It gave me the feeling that invisible girls were cavorting up there, skimpily clad. "Did you
find something for Rae?" I said to Billy.

"This one. What do you think?" He held up a nice yellow
cotton gown cut full enough to accommodate all of Rae but
still pretty, with lace at the neck.

"Great," I said. "I'll wait outside."

Stepping onto the sidewalk, I felt better. The shop had
been full of perfume, and I welcomed the open air and the old
familiar smell of marsh mud and gasoline from the river. I
made my way to the Impala and relaxed in its wide front seat.
Sun had heated the seatcovers. I sat facing the door and leaned
my cheek against the warm vinyl, my back to the steering
wheel. Insane affection for the car swelled in my throat, and
I closed my eyes.

I heard the car door open. A package hit me in the small of
the back and dropped, rustling, to the seat.

"Perk up, Lucille. I don't like depressed women. One depressed woman is the absolute limit."

"I'm not depressed."

I righted myself and ignored the bag next to me. Billy
drove out of the parking lot and onto the highway home.
With his right hand he reached over and picked up the bag
and laid it in my lap. He glanced at me once, then turned his
eyes back to the road.

I knew what was in there. I didn't know what to do,

whether to look in or not. My heart in all its vanity and cunning was nevertheless trembling like the heart of an innocent creature. I looked straight ahead and kept my eyes wide open, my eyebrows slightly raised, as if I knew nothing.

We were getting closer to home. We were passing the television station.

"Look in there," he said, nodding toward the bag.

I opened it and lifted out the white gown.

"You tend to deny yourself, Lucille. You shouldn't."

I held the bodice up to my front. "Thank you," I said. "I love it."

"I could tell." He didn't look at me, just kept his eyes on the road and his hands on the wheel, but I saw him swallow.

That night I took a bath in my paw-footed tub, the water so hot it made me queasy. With a new razor I shaved my legs and my underarms and the tops of my thighs. I shaved the thin gold hairs off my big toes.

History says the Puritans wrongly accused young girls of witchery. But I thought of a New England house in winter, the long skirts, the stern family bunched together in the kitchen, and I had a pretty good idea of what a girl would feel like in that situation, the let-me-out-of-here feeling, the stomachache, the eye on the locked door. Why not call it witchery? The important thing is to understand that it is an involuntary condition.

I got out of the tub and dripped a trail of water across the floor to the towel rack and dried myself; but when I put on the white gown I was still partly damp, and the material clung to my skin like a webbed and sticky gauze spun by insects.

In the faculty parking lot I hunched behind the wheel, wearing my father's fishing cap, one with an abnormally long bill and a backflap for sun protection. I didn't want anybody at school to recognize me. I enjoyed seeing the place *incognito;* it didn't look half bad. What could I have had against these happy-go-lucky people streaming out of the gym and the auditorium and the classroom building? What struck me immediately about them was their health. Health glowed in the air around them like an aura. Healthy hair and skin, healthy limbs, brains, hearts. I watched cute Laura Migo duck her chin and set her books on a hip and laugh endearingly, flirting with a teacher. I moved my head forward to get a better view from under my cap. The teacher was Billy. I honked the horn.

He got in on the passenger side.

"There's something I don't know," I said.

"What's that?" he said.

"I don't know. That's what I said, there's something I don't know."

I started the car and eased out of the lot onto the access road.

"I'll buy you an ice-cream bar, how about that?" he said. "You aren't in the best mood."

There were not very many places that I could go with him. The range was limited to stores and fast food establishments and the Wando parking lot. Much as I disliked the shopping plaza, it was somewhere I could legitimately walk around with him in the out-of-doors. I'd like to have taken him to spots I knew off the beaten track, where you could still see what I thought of as the original landscape. But we were stuck with the plaza.

We bought a couple of two-dollar ice-cream bars and sat on a bench near the fountain. The chocolate exterior of my bar cracked off in large sheets and fell onto my shirt; I salvaged what I could of it and got chocolate all over my hands. Billy wiped my face with his handkerchief. We weren't talking much. The handkerchief, like any possession of his, mesmerized me, and I kept my eyes on it. He tracked them and looked at it, too.

"My father's," he said. He set it on his knee. He glanced at me. "And—pocketwatch." He drew a round flat gold watch from his pocket and let it swing from its chain. I reached for it, but he moved it out of my grasp.

"What you don't know won't hurt you," he said, looking away.

"That's not true. There is something, isn't there?" I said.

"Pocketknives. Tada." In a row on his thigh lay the handkerchief, the watch, and three small knives. "My inheritance," he said. "After they had removed my father from his hospital room, I snuck back into it and saw a plastic bag on the table. Contents of his pajama pockets at the instant of death. I took the bag, knowing it was due me. Okay, first is Blackie."

He opened two blades of the black knife downward and flicked out a bottle opener at the end. He stuck the blades into the wood of the bench seat between us, and the knife became a little horse, blades for legs, the bottle-opener an open-jawed head.

"Then Hans, the roan." Into the wood went the blades of a red Swiss Army knife, fat, with an inlaid silver cross at the shoulder, hind legs longer than forelegs, a spoon for the head, nail file for tail.

"And finally, Pearl. Beautiful Pearl, for special occasions. Old Blackie will sharpen a pencil and Hans strip a sapling, but Pearl will be saved for special occasions. Yes, Pearl will be saved. To peel a peach, perform a tracheotomy. . . Look at the thoroughbred legs, the narrow neck and head."

"Pearl did the whittling," I said.

"How did you know that? Actually, Blackie did the rough jobs, but the intricate work was Pearl's. Here, she's yours." He laid the beautiful knife in my palm.

Quickly I handed it back. "Don't be crazy."

"Better take it. Rae says the whole herd has got to go."

"What do you mean? She can't make you get rid of your childhood souvenirs."

"No—" He raised his eyebrows and rubbed the wrinkle in his forehead. "She means me included. After the baby is born. She—wants me to go."

I answered immediately. "That's impossible."

"I know she isn't thinking straight right now. I know that, and maybe she'll change her mind—"

"Of course she will."

"But I don't think so. It's complicated. It's more than you think. She hates me. She's never going to forgive me."

"Forgive you for what? Love isn't exactly something you inflicted on her."

"Well, you see, it sort of is." He breathed in and raised his shoulders. "It definitely is. To be honest—she's got a point. I did it on purpose. Jesus, I can't believe it now, but actually that is what I did. I admit it." He sighed and threw his arm across the top slat of the back of the bench. "I was insane. But I had never come across anyone whom—anyone I loved so much and wanted so much, and she was not that desperate for me. Not like I was for her."

"What are you saying?"

"I got her pregnant on purpose. It was the only way I could get her to even consider marrying me."

"How?"

"Excuse me?"

"How did you do it?" I said.

"Shit, Lucille."

"I'm sorry, I just don't get the picture. You took away her pills and substituted a placebo? Or you stole her diaphragm, or you raped her—"

"For Christ's sake. Okay. I—punched a hole—" he grimaced, "in the, ah, condom."

I stared at him. "Once?" I said.

"No."

"How many times?"

"Every time. For a month." He pushed the hair off his forehead and stared at the tiers of water falling in the fountain. "It wasn't a sure thing. I left something to destiny. I mean, it was a smallish hole. My God."

"I knew it," I said.

"I'm sorry. I shouldn't have done it. But there's nothing I can do about it now except go away like she says."

"You ruined her," I said, looking straight into his eyes.

"I know." We sat still. He moved the mother-of-pearl pony forward six paces until it came to the edge of the bench. "Looking into the great abyss, the little pony tosses her head and whinnies, sensing the danger of the rocks below."

"You ought to hate yourself," I said.

"Yes, but how can you hate yourself for an act of love? It was for love. Do you believe that?" He took my hand in his. "Please, believe me," he said.

"I do." I withdrew my hand.

"If I had known then how it was all going to turn out, I'd never have done it. How she would grow to hate the sight of me." He laughed and slumped. "She wants me to go now, but I can't. I have to see her through this, of course. But Lucille, I didn't want you to know." He turned my way. "I didn't want to involve you. For one thing, I didn't want you to hate me, too. You've been the only bright spot; you don't know how much good you've done me."

I closed my eyes. Horror is built in, I told myself. I should have known. And then I suddenly panicked. "You're not going to leave town, though, if she makes you go? You'll have to stay in this area."

"Yes," he said. "I'll have to stay."

. . .

Luck gave me my start in this life. I never thanked any higher force for my conception and birth: the luck of my parents' meeting, the luck of the Lucille sperm reaching the Lucille egg, the luck of the vacuum cleaner failing to search me out. And luck is nothing; luck is the absence of power.

But love, luck's opposite, pulled me into the world. Without it I'd have stayed ensconced. Even much later when I could look back for the retrospective view, I didn't wish it had never happened that way. I will never wish it had never happened.

I saw Wayne once, as he crossed the faculty parking lot at school. He recognized me in spite of my cap, and came over to the car. I had nothing to say to him; I found it difficult to look at his face.

"You have something up your sleeve, Lucille," he said.

"I don't—"

"But, hey, I'm not prying. I'm only saying take care."

I nodded. He had a new tie. "Where's the lucky tie?" I said.

He smiled and said, "Inoperative. I heard you aced your exams."

"How'd you know?" But he was on his way already toward the office, where he did peer counseling in the afternoons. I had liked Wayne. I really had.

CHAPTER
11

*R*ummaging in my mother's closet on Halloween, I found what I was looking for, in a plastic clothes bag jam-packed with folded woolens we would never wear again: there was the tell-tale striped fur, sticking out from under a mohair scarf. Memories hit me; I grabbed a corner of the fur and pulled. Mothballs scattered across the floor like beads of poisoned white ice, releasing their sad futile smell. I had carefully packed these things away—cardigans and pullovers of bygone cold seasons, out-of-fashion Scottish kilts held in place by giant safety pins, feebly small gloves—and mothballed them in case the day came when they might be needed. Mother had scoffed at the effort; but now I had been proved right. I needed her old Halloween costume.

I sat there on the floor trying to locate the tail, finally spotting it under Rae's old green crew neck. I bent the kinks out and gave it a smooth arc. The head was a problem. I couldn't find it anywhere, and doubted it had survived. It had been made from a paper bag; it had probably been thrown away. But I recalled its every feature, the large mad eyes, the smile, whiskers, ears; and I knew I could replicate it.

"Look here," I said to Rae. "Can you give me a hand?"
She was on the sofa in the next room, watching television, smoking. She didn't answer.

"All the materials have been assembled," I said, standing by the dining table with my hands on my hips, fingertips towards my back in the posture of a kindergarten teacher. "Glue, scissors, paper, Magic Markers. First we have to locate the eye-holes. Can you come here for a sec and draw a spot where I put my finger?"

She took a drag, lifted her chin, and blew out the smoke in a long thin stream.

I put the bag over my head and pointed to where the eyes should be. "Right here, see? Just make two marks, here and here." I waited about a minute. A long time. It was hard to breathe in the bag, but the interior of it was a beautiful golden-red, and it smelled good. The forests of the Southeast had been clear-cut to provide American shoppers with such high-quality paper bags as this one. Pine was the origin of the color and the smell. I breathed it in.

After a while, I marked my own eyes and took the bag off.

"The grin goes like a crescent moon flopped onto its back, wide, with lots and *lots* of teeth," I said, drawing the face in. I actually whistled briefly, a made-up tune that she, as a singer, would automatically recognize as a sham. "Gee," I said, shaking my head, "nobody enjoyed Halloween like Mother did. She loved it, didn't she?"

Rae turned her eyes in my direction, but her face was stone-cold, the skin above her cheekbones puffy.

"It's her cat costume," I said, holding up the suit and the tail. "I'm remaking the head. I have a good idea of what it looked like, but I'm a little worried about the ears. You wouldn't happen to remember how they were done, I don't guess."

She looked through me, and I was shamed by my own voice, that teacher's fake conviviality, the ruse of arts-and-crafts. Rae's eyes said, *You don't know anything.* She was sick. I knew that, I knew that, I ought to have called her doctor, but at the same time I was thinking everything would be okay soon. A few more weeks, and she would be delivered. She would get her chemistry back and be her old self again.

For the last week, we had been literally tiptoeing through our own rooms, afraid that any little creak or scrape would disturb her. We never mentioned pregnancy. We brought her soft drinks, tea, magazines. I tried to think up activities besides television, anything that might pique her interest.

"This is how the whiskers went, I think. Cut long strips of paper—I'm just using a second paper bag here—and run the flat edge of the scissors down the strip to make it curl. Voilà. Then glue each whisker, like so, next to the nose, four on a side." She was watching. I glued quickly so I wouldn't lose her. Maybe I ought to be a kindergarten teacher. They have to be sneaky.

"For ears, let's try a small triangle cut from a double thickness and cupped, earlike. A flap bent at the bottom can be glued down to hold it on, for a perfectly adequate ear. Rabbity, maybe, but fine for a temporary cat, in my opinion."

"Excuse me," she said, getting up with difficulty.

"Oh, don't go, Rae." I dropped the bag onto the table. "I didn't mean to annoy you."

"Nothing annoys me," she said. "I feel bad."

"Do you want me to call Dr. Ellis?"

"What for? It's nothing serious. I must have eaten something that didn't agree with me."

"Well, he might be able to do something to make you feel better."

As usual, she paused a good three seconds, as if it took that long for language to make its way into her understanding.

"I don't think so," she said. "But thank you." It was the first time she had said anything polite to me in days.

· · ·

I finished the mask myself, and it looked beautiful. I took off my shirt and skirt and got into the suit, zipped it up the front, and lifted the bag carefully over my head. It settled down onto my shoulders perfectly. Minor adjustments were needed on the eyes, a slight enlargement of the holes, but otherwise I couldn't have done better. I looked at myself in the mirror. I had never been fanatically interested in any kind of clothes or makeup, but looking in the mirror now, I felt the sudden liberation of spirit that a full costume can provide. I understood clowns and transvestites and mummers. I was no longer Lucille. I danced and sang in front of the hall mirror, twirled my tail, pranced with my paws held high in front of my chest, wrists loose. I pounced at my own reflection. I meowed.

Then I knew what I wanted to do. Sometimes purpose does not insert itself into a given thought or action until near the end, and a person can busy himself mindlessly for quite some time before realizing the aim of the business. I went down to the workshop and knocked on the door.

"Come in," Billy said, but he didn't look up when I entered. I stumbled over the threshold, because I had a limited range of vision, about forty-five degrees at eye level; and I ran into his chair.

"My God, Lucille. I knew you were crazy," he said.

"How did you know it was me?"

"I have a sixth sense."

"Want to go trick-or-treating?" My voice inside the bag came back upon me rich and undissipated.

"Where did you get that?"

"Mother made the costume years ago, and I just now made the mask."

"Good whiskers. Cheshire Cat, eh? I guess that means I have to be Alice."

"No, you could be a pirate or a bum or a vampire. That's what my Dixie League ballplayers always are, things you can be without buying a costume."

"You're serious about this," he said.

"It's Halloween! I have to go out to take candy to the neighborhood kids. The house is so far back off the road, nobody ever comes to ring our bell."

"Let me finish this paragraph."

I sat on Pop's workbench. Billy squinted at the paper, then closed his eyes and started typing. It was a different kind of typing from Sharon's at the office. Hers was smooth as a train, his was stop-and-start. He made little noises in his throat the way musicians sometimes do.

When he finished he threw himself backwards, and the oak chair slid on its wheels to where I sat. The curved back touched my knees.

"Do I have droplets of blood on my forehead?" he said, snapping his neck back and looking at me upside down. I was shocked that the face I loved and saw in dreams was unrecognizable upside down. I didn't have the same feeling for it from this angle.

"No. Let's go."

"Give me ten minutes," he said.

I waited on the porch. The sun was setting and the smallest children were starting out with their shopping bags, mothers following half a block behind. The wind blustered. Clouds of yellow butterflies blew past the porch like bits of trash; I understood they headed for Peru this time of year, to a single mountain home. A cold front was coming through tonight; this wind was its leading edge. Hundreds of migrating birds would be killed by the new television tower, but by mid-morning the corpses would be gone, thanks to ants and beetles, horned owls that sat on the guy wires in wait, raccoons, hawks, and vultures. Fall is the season of movement and hunger and panic.

When Billy presented himself, I had to laugh. "You make a great bum," I said.

"My true self." With a charcoal briquette he had given himself a bum's stubble, and he had stuck a square of black paper over his front teeth. He offered me his arm. I rested my right hand in his bent elbow and carried my basket of candy in my left. We stepped out into the last of the day, passing Mr. Lawton's pile of burning leaves, passing a long streak of sunset through the pines, passing the Igleharts' snaggle-tooth picket fence. I smelled singed pumpkin flesh. We met up with a frightened band of ballerinas and robots, who hesitated to take my candy.

"They're afraid of you," Billy said. "They think you're a real cat."

"No, it's you. They think you're a real bum. You are the person their mother has warned them about." I dropped cellophane-wrapped mints into their bags, and we moved on. It was an orange, yellow, gold evening. At the foot of each street we could see an unusual color on the harbor, a bright aquamarine that lasted several minutes; and all objects in it were aflame on the western side: channel marker, two dinghies, a lone trawler. I could only see them one at a time, by moving my whole head.

"I think you can take the bag off, Lucille."

"No, I can't."

"It disconcerts me. The grin. I walk along thinking I'm with you, then I glance up and see that thing."

"I can't take it off. Here come some more: what are these?"

"One punk, one ghost, one TV set." He doled out the candies.

We made the rounds of the whole neighborhood. I heard a

noise that sounded like sweeping, and traced it to the blowing popcorn trees along the drainage ditch, wide leaves shivering in the wind. Goldenrod bloomed, rattlebox and camphorweed, and lantana in great collapsing humps. All their flowers, coincidentally, were gold. The sky was the same color; and the golder it got, the darker the street, the wilder the goblins who dodged in and out of azaleas, cracking branches, snagging their capes and tails, shrieking. Two strange figures came striding towards us, and I thought, troopers? giants?—but I recognized them as local mothers doing the evening fast walk, swinging their strong arms, stretching their long thighs. A man jogged by, with a pain-stricken face; two girls on a lawn tried to light their grill but failed in the wind. Through all this goldenness I walked easily, as if I were one of the townspeople and as if the two of us, me and Billy, were quite at home.

But deep in me was a feeling that comes sometimes with autumn, the farewell feeling, when whatever is most beautiful around me seems also saddest. Good-bye, good-bye, I said to myself.

At St. Anne's we stopped to observe the remnants of a carnival—three boys dunking one another's heads in a galvanized tub of icy water; black and orange crepe-paper streamers waving from the string of electric lights; two mothers with hammers knocking apart the plywood booths. The boys' faces came up white with cold. While we stood there, the lights came on. I had never seen them on. They gave the place a new air, festive and yet simultaneously melancholy. The boys carried the washtub into the parish house.

"Sit down?" the bum said.

"Thank you," the cat said. He helped her up onto the picnic table.

"It's a beautiful place you got here," the bum said. In the black water, boat lights moved quietly past; someone was out for a sail.

The cat pulled her knees up under her chin and wrapped her long tail around her Nikes.

For a few minutes there was a dreamy, low hum in her head that was like nothing so much as purring. Her shoulder touched his.

Then he said, "I'm thinking about going away, Lucille. I'm thinking about going back to Washington."

There was not enough air for the cat. Her lungs hurt.

"I don't know, though," he said. "I won't know for a while."

In autumn the world darkens fast after the last sliver of the red sun goes down. It's not like summer, when daylight lingers and shimmers. It's wham-bam, *dark*. The cat could not see much anyway, and was virtually blind after a few minutes on the picnic table. The yellow overhead lights illuminated only themselves.

"If you go to Washington, I'd—like very much to go with you."

"Lucille, take that goddamn thing off your head, I can't hear you." He reached toward the mask.

"No!" I held it on.

"Okay, okay. Talk louder then."

"I said, I'll go with you."

His face revealed nothing, not surprise or puzzlement or displeasure. He had been looking down. Now he raised his face towards me. I could see nothing. I, who could read minds and handwriting and every nuance of a stranger's face, could not tell anything when it mattered, when I needed to know.

The strung-up lights went off, and the moms loaded the boys and the plywood into a van, slid the door shut with a heavy clunk, and drove off.

I said, "I can't tell what you're thinking." So I took the mask off. Cold air billowed at me, eddied around my ears, and froze my neck. I took hold of his forearms and said, "Can I go with you?"

"You don't mean that."

"I do," I said. "It's the only thing I want." I released his arms, and they fell to his sides. I began to feel like someone who is in the middle of a very bad mistake and can't easily escape. "I wouldn't have said anything if things were working out . . . between you and her . . . I'd never have said a word. I was going to keep it a total secret."

He was looking at me, and I couldn't keep my mouth shut, as I should have. "It isn't something I planned," I said. "Believe me." I touched my lip; but I couldn't find my little scar, I couldn't find comfort.

"So what do you think?" I said, trying to sound nonchalant. "I wouldn't press you except that I . . . I really sort of need to know." I was out on a limb. The moment was so horrible I closed my eyes and tried not to think of the risks and the implications and the consequences. "If it's just me, I need to know. Is it just me? If so, I can try to—"

"Lucille, stop. You know it's impossible."

"Oh. Impossible? Okay. Yes, I see what you mean. Oh. I'm sorry. I've made a terrible mistake, and I apologize."

"There's no need to apologize." He caught my arm as I was sliding off the table. "Don't go."

"I have to go now," I said. Looking down at myself, I recoiled at my own stupidity and childishness, my self-importance, my striped fur hide.

"No, you can't go yet. Listen to me." He stood up next to me, and I could smell him, and I shivered.

"Please let go," I said.

"Come on, Lucille. Don't get mad. Here's what we're going to do. We're going to walk home." He hooked my arm through his left elbow and bent it tight. "This is how old people walk. Take a deep breath. Look at me." He pulled his father's handkerchief from his pocket. "Don't cry," he said, dabbing at my eyes.

"I don't need that, thanks."

"You do."

"Let go." I jerked myself away from him and ran, through the streets where the mothers on the porches were calling children inside now, and fathers were blowing out the candle-stumps in jack-o'-lanterns. The Lawtons' arctic dog rushed out of his yard and barked at me, blocking my way when I was almost to my own yard. As if it wasn't enough that my parents had abandoned me and my family had fallen apart and I had made a fool of myself for love—the neighborhood dog was against me. Then I remembered that I was not my famil-iar self; who knows what a dog sees, but I certainly had a tail, and that may have been the problem. I spoke to him by name—"Ranger, hey Ranger"—and he fell back in puzzle-ment to let me pass. But the delay had cost me my lead. Billy caught up with me.

"Stop, Lucille," he said, reaching out for my arm.

"Don't grab me," I said, lurching forward. He stayed at-tached, and we swung through the yard like a clumsy dance couple.

"I said *stop*," he said.

"Don't *yell*," I said, trying to shake him off. But he had me. He made me stand still. He looked away and then back at me as if I were a problem he could not think how to dispose of. But what he said surprised me.

"What can we do?"

"I don't know what you're talking about."

"You and me," he said.

"There is no you and me. You said so. You said, impos-sible."

"I think I was wrong," he said with some difficulty.

"You think."

But I was caught. He had me. We fell on each other. There were no preliminaries, there was only desire, mine so long pent-up that it broke loose in a roar through my brain. And it was not just me. Not just me. I knew instantly what I had not been able to see in his face: that although this man did not love me, I had won him. For someone different from me, that might not have been enough. For me it was, at the moment. I wanted physical comfort so much, how could I quibble about what was in his heart.

We were next to the cedar tree in the middle of the back yard. We had nowhere to go. I began to shake, a little shiver at first and then an enormous trembling until even my teeth were chattering.

"Come with me," he said. We ducked under the cross-beams that reinforced the pilings under the house, and he unlocked the workshop door.

"Lie down," he said. "You're hysterical."

I stretched out on the couch, and he patted my arms until I had control of my lungs, and then he lay down next to me. We had to be on our sides, and I was against the couch back, which gave me stability and a sense of safety. And I had, at last, what I wanted. I had everything I wanted.

"This presents a problem," he said. "This fur."

"It unzips."

I was the girl then who flies through the air, letting go and somersaulting across space in the sure knowledge that at the end of the spin someone will catch her wrists and swing her back. And he did that. In the middle of the lovemaking I lost myself, but he caught me up again and we went on for a long time. It was unlike anything I had ever felt before, and maybe unlike anything I will ever feel again. Once, he got up to turn on an electric heater in the corner.

"Don't go," I said.

"I'll be back."

"You look happy," he said. "Can't say I've ever seen that before."

"You look sad," I said.

"Well, you must admit. There is a potential for sadness."

If so, it was all his. I lay back and drowsed. The glow of the heating element was nothing compared to me, the light and warmth in me enough to get me through whatever cold spells would come.

Later, we got dressed—me in a workshirt of Pop's that was hanging on a hook on the wall—and ran through the cold, up the steps and into the kitchen. His mood was somber, mine the opposite. In the dark I groped for the light string over the table, but I couldn't find it. Billy's leg hit mine, and I pitched forward. He held me, and said, "I want to know what's going to happen to us."

"Nothing," I said.

"You said you'd come with me."

"You said that was impossible," I reminded him again.

"Well, maybe it isn't. I just don't know, Lucille. How can I know?" He rubbed his forehead.

"You can't. Nobody can know," I said. But I didn't mean that. I knew. Not that I foresaw the one huge thing I ought to have seen; but I did see, from the way he moved, from the way he massaged his temple, that I did not figure centrally in his future. I got two beers and unscrewed the caps and set the bottles on the table. I felt pretty good.

"You're all right?" he said.

"I'm only sleepy."

I heard a cat crying outside, and I shivered. It was cold already out there, colder than the weatherman had predicted. The beer bottles sat untouched on the table, bubbles rising behind the green glass.

"I'm not going to give you up, Lucille," he said in an even voice.

"Give me up! You don't have me to give up. We don't have each other. We are only in the same kitchen, drinking the same brand of beer. That is the extent of our connection."

"No, it isn't. Not now," he said.

"We'll see," I said, picking up a beer. I held it but drank none. We stared at each other across the table with a strange antagonism, and I said, "I'll bet you a million dollars that I don't even cross your mind this time next year."

He held out his right hand. I shook it, but he didn't let go. "I don't know anyone else like you," he said. "I don't know what's going to happen, but I know I won't let you go."

The cat cried again, just beyond the window, sounding hurt.

"What the hell is that?" Billy said.

"A cat."

I was watching his face and, as I recall, thinking he looked different to me now, when we heard the cat a third time. I went to the window, where cold air was standing just outside but not coming in. The sound was coming from under Rae's window, where her room angled out from the house. Then I thought, no, it's coming from . . . her *room.*

Carefully, I set my bottle down and said, "Excuse me a minute." I walked down the hall to her door, which was open, and I looked in. Even though it was dark, I could see that the bed was empty. It was a white square. There was no sleeping form in its wide expanse.

"Rae?" I stepped into the room. I heard nothing. There was her white bed, white dresser and mirror, the oak armoire. No noise. The bathroom door was closed, and no light came from underneath it. But I crossed the bedroom, my eyes adjusting to the dark. I knocked on the door.

"Rae?" I said, and opened it without waiting for an answer.

She was on the toilet. She looked up at me and her face scared me to death. Her new nightgown was soiled in big blotches, and there were more blotches on the floor, and a smell.

"Are you sick?" I said.

"Yes," she whispered.

"Here, come back to bed. I'll help you."

I put my arms under hers and lifted her. "Can you walk?" I said. "Can you stand up by yourself and—wait—Rae— what is that— Rae, what is that in the bowl?"

"I don't know," she said, terrified, clinging to me. "I don't know, I don't know!"

I let her go, and she slumped to the floor.

"Billy!" I screamed. "Billy!" I lunged for the baby, grabbed its slick leg and turned it right side up.

"What is it?" Billy said.

"Turn on the light," I said, crouching next to Rae. He switched on the light and saw us.

"What is that?" he said.

"Call 911," I said.

"Oh, God. Let me have it," he said.

"No, don't, it's still connected. Rae, lie down here, just, okay, put your head against the door. Call 911, Billy."

But he wasn't moving. His eyes were horrified. "Here," I said, pulling him down. I shoved the baby into his arms. "Don't stand up. Stay here." I ran for the phone on Rae's bedside table. The whole time I was talking, I watched the bathroom, where they were huddled on the white and red floor. Then I ran back to them.

"Let's get her in bed. They said keep her warm, don't cut the cord, don't do anything except take her gown off so we can put the baby on her stomach."

Billy raised her up from the floor and I carried the baby, still tied on. It was a solid, chunky baby, breathing fine as far as I could tell, and staring me down with pinpoint eyes. Its skin was hot and slippery.

"I can't get the nightgown off," he said. "Rae, sit up. She's too limp, Lucille."

"Well, you have to. Can't you tear it?"

With two hands he started at the neck of the gown and tried to tear the cotton, but it wouldn't tear. I picked up the hem and ripped it with my teeth, and he tore it the rest of the way, and we got the baby onto her stomach. I put a towel under Rae. Still the child did not make a noise, and I wondered if the sounds we had heard had come from it or from its mother.

"How soon will they be here?" he said.

I made up an answer. "Five minutes."

He sat by her head and touched her hair, touched her chin and neck. He looked at the baby. "It's breathing. It looks okay. I think the baby's okay. But this—" He picked up the towel and his eyes widened. "This towel is already soaked. Lucille, it's soaked all the way through!"

I ran to the bathroom for more towels.

"This is wrong," he said. "It's just too much blood."

I rolled the towels tight and then pushed Rae's legs together on them. And I sat there next to her with my eyes closed, saying to the ambulance driver to get fucked, lazy son-of-a-bitch asshole, over and over again until in the distance I heard the whining siren.

"She's bleeding to death," he said.

"No, that's normal," I said, but I didn't think it was. Blood was all over the bed, all over the floor, smeared bright on the white porcelain in the bathroom.

"Rae, do you hear me?" I said. "You've had a baby girl. The ambulance is here now, and someone will take care of you."

Her eyes flew open, and she said, "Good."

CHAPTER
12

*T*ragedy, well-known for its convoluted methods, reunited the family. Mother came home to care for the baby. "I have wanted another one of these for years," she said, cuddling it so close I was afraid it wouldn't have enough breathing space. She moved into her old room upstairs, with a PortaCrib next to her bed. For a few days Rhody moved in, too, sleeping in the workshop. Why she came I don't know, but she spent all her time with me, telling me jokes, watching more television than I had ever been able to take in before.

Billy moved back into Rae's room.

When I saw him, it was always among a crowd of people, so many people it seemed like a party with guests, and I paused to identify them all; but it was only us. We ate our meals in the dining room, as if every day were Thanksgiving. At first nobody talked much about Rae, but gradually the air of hushed gravity cleared to a normal atmosphere, and her name could be mentioned.

"She denied her pregnancy," Mother explained to me. "Or that is Dr. Ellis's theory. He's seen it before, usually in college girls."

"But she'll be home in a couple of weeks," Pop said, looking at me. "She'll be all right." They were sitting at their usual ends of the table as if nothing had happened between them, as if these last six months were like a television serial that had gotten so complicated the plot could only be resolved by calling itself a dream, backing up, and starting over again. I was dazed not only by the ease of their reconciliation, but also by the instant harmony that had fallen down over us all. You can't be really surprised when everything suddenly goes *bad:* the tendency toward disaster is speedy. But can things go good overnight? I thought goodness progressed only slowly, uphill all the way.

At the dining table, all the voices seemed muffled and distant, the logistics of the meal clumsy and interminable ("Pass the rice, Lucille," "Is there more meat?" "Helen, I don't seem to have a fork. Does anyone have an extra fork?"). The clink of utensils and dinnerware seemed to go on, on, on. I had the feeling of "Sunday Morning," one of my oldest and least favorite sensations. Now and then I'd look up and find everyone at the table looking at me. They dropped their eyes and went on with their conversations. I felt asleep.

But I knew it had not been a dream. There was the baby, and a baby is the best proof in the world that something has happened. At first I wanted to ignore it; I lowered my head when it was carried into the room, I could not bring myself to call it by name. Mother unwrapped it and I averted my eyes from the naked sight of it, the dried bulb of cord, the bare female cleft. "Look, Lucille," she said. "Look at the fingernails." So I took a quick glance and saw the tiny square translucent scales at the tips of the fingers, and then my eyes met the baby's eyes, for the second time.

And I woke up. "Phoebe," I said, forcing out the unappealing name Rae had given her out of the blue. Her eyes returned me a stare of meanness, the look of a girl who is going to be hard to handle; and I smiled. Her face reddened and tensed and then turned all mouth and noise.

I clutched Mother's shoulder. "*What's that on her lip?*" I said.

"That? Oh, a little blister from sucking. She's a vigorous eater, like you were. In fact, she reminds me of you. She has a mean streak."

"I never had a mean streak!"

"You did. You bossed us all around. Your father used to say you were mean as a bird. But that is what happens to the baby of the family, and your case was even worse because you were a surprise baby, and you were all the more special. We spoiled you. You ruled the roost."

Well, I knew exactly how much of a surprise I had been to her, but it had never occurred to me that I had been a welcome surprise. Maybe she had had regrets! Maybe she'd had nightmares, and wished she had not done it, and then, of course—the news of my presence would have been more than welcome. It would have been a miracle. But I didn't tell her I knew the whole story. I only watched her dandle Phoebe, working her arms and legs, kissing her skin, whispering into her ear.

"What are you telling her?" I said.

"Same things I told you and Rae. However, you were a head-strong child, paid no attention, and forgot it all. But maybe it will come back to you. I told you all the important things."

"All right, Lucille," Rhody said. "Monopoly." She opened the board on the coffee table in front of me. Folding her long legs under her, she sat on the floor and got out all the game pieces.

"No, I can't play," I said.

"You can be the shoe. Your favorite."

"Rhody, why are you treating me like I'm emotionally disturbed?"

"Because I believe that is what you are. I don't know

exactly what happened; nobody seems to have the full story here. But I do know that of the two, you and Rae, you were worse off."

"I was sedated, the day you got here."

"Yes, and you know why. You went hysterical in the night, so they had to dope you. Now you seem okay, but who can tell, maybe you are just as off in the head as your sister."

"Well, I'm not. She didn't even know she was pregnant. She forgot she was eight and a half months pregnant! You have to be pretty crazy to do that."

Rhody stopped dealing out the money and looked at me. "You forgot it, too, I believe. Think about that. You denied it as much as she did."

Tears came to my eyes.

"Take up your money," she said. "It's blowing away."

She called everyone else in and gave them their bankrolls, and we played Monopoly. Mother landed on Pop's Boardwalk and went bankrupt, but he gave her a loan; Billy monopolized the utilities; and I spent long periods in jail to avoid getting in trouble out on the streets. The game came to its usual unresolved end without any winners, and everyone drifted away, deathly tired of money and real estate but pleased with the overall outcome, the general survival of all. Mother and Phoebe, the inseparable pair, went up to her room to bed. Billy made a quick exit. Pop and Rhody packed up the game while I carried beer bottles into the kitchen. It was only nine-thirty, but it felt like the wee hours. I was still on a drug at night that put me into a sleep as dense as rock, and during the day I was fuzzy-headed.

I heard a tap on the kitchen door and opened it. There in the cold was Vera Oxendine.

"I've brought a chicken," she said, putting into my hands a warm foil package. "It's the kind your dad likes, from Pick-a-Chick."

"Thank you," I said.

"I can't come in," she said. "I left the car running." She pointed down into the yard.

"Well, thanks, Vera. We appreciate it."

"Let me ask you—I really have to run on, but tell me, Lucille—has she come home?"

"No. She'll be in the hospital a while longer. They moved her to Whispering Pines for evaluation, but she's okay now."

"Rae, you mean. Good, I'm glad to hear that. But actually, I was asking about your mother. Has she come back? I haven't heard from Warren in some time . . . and I was hesitant to call, not knowing, you see."

"Yes, she came back."

"Okay, well, do give him the chicken for me, will you? And the baby's fine?"

"The baby's fine, yes."

"Wonderful. Bye-bye, then." She hurried down the steps and into her car. She looked almost pretty, I thought. Watching her car move on down the street, I knew what she had in store, and I hoped she would be all right. She had been fond of saying, "I'm a survivor," and I expected she was one. But I knew how hard it was going to be.

"Where did this come from?" Pop said behind me, his loud voice making me jump.

"What, the chicken?"

"Vera was here. Where is she?"

"She's gone. She just left."

"Well, but . . . what did she say? What did you tell her? Why didn't you ask her in?" His voice was rising. He had his hand on the chicken bag as if it were a treasure. "Lucille, you didn't tell her—that your mother is here—you didn't say that, did you?"

"Of course I said that."

"Okay. Let's go. Drive me over to her house. Let me get my jacket, and I'll meet you outside."

The whole thing was starting over again, but I was not going to let it repeat itself. This time I would hold things together around here. "No, Pop," I said. "You can't leave. Everything is finally back to normal, and you can't go on with this."

"Vera is important to me. If you won't drive me, I'll drive myself."

"I'm sorry. I can't let you do that."

He saw my pocketbook hanging on the doorknob, and he emptied it onto the table. "Where are the keys?' he said, spreading my things out with a swoop of his hand. I had the keys to all the cars, safely in my backpack under my bed.

"Lucille, I demand that you give me the keys to my own car."

"If you go over there, I'll die," I said. "Look at me! You're sixty years old! It's too late to be starting life all over again. You're married, you have children. Oh, Pop, at least wait until tomorrow. Don't rush out tonight and do something you'll regret. Just do this favor for me, okay? If you love me, please don't go tonight."

He sat down and sighed.

"We are all so tired," I said.

"You're right about that."

"Why don't you have a glass of milk and go to bed?" I said. I poured the milk and watched him drink it and watched him climb the stairs to his room.

Whether I had done the right thing or not I couldn't be sure. At the time, I believed I was right. But as I watched him go up, his hand on the bannister, doubts hit me. How could I be sure that Mother was going to stay?

I drank a beer alone. The lights in Rae's room were off. I sat by myself and looked at my hands on the bottle.

When I went to bed, I lay on my back wearing the most useless nightgown in the world. With my feet making a vee down at the end of the white stretch of silk, I certainly re-

sembled a corpse. Alive people ordinarily curl up in sleep, or
snuggle next to one another. Sleeping like an embalmed body
has got to be a bad sign; yet I couldn't take the more comfortable, relaxed positions.

And after a while, the old balloons came on—Pop, Mother,
Rae, Billy . . . Wayne's ghost, Rhody watching me . . . and
the dark-eyed Phoebe McQueen . . . and then a mowing machine, cutting a swath of grass, like a boat through green
water, laying low grass and flowers, crickets, frogs, snakelets
in its flat wake; and I recognized the mower, I saw him the
way you can see him at night, as if he were real. Grasses fell,
creatures stopped. *And you will stop,* the mower said to me,
and you will be as if you never were.

I sat bolt upright. I didn't mind death. What I minded was
being left out, being unable to see the activities of the world.
I won't mind not participating, I said to him. But for goodness' sake, let me watch it all! I looked at my real dresser,
with its wooden drawer pulls carved in the design of sunrises,
and at the matching oval mirror set in a tiltable frame, and the
soft rag rug on the floor. I was awake. Yet I heard the mower.
I shook my head, and I heard the mower still.

Jumping from bed I unhooked the window screen, letting it
drop with a scrape onto the bushes under the window. I leaned
out and got a partial view, through the shrubbery, of the road
under moonlight, and I could see my father. "Pop!" I yelled.
I saw him nearing the corner streetlamp, then taking the turn
at full speed, in the direction of Vera Oxendine's house. He sat
tall, almost noble, riding his Snapper lawn mower into the dark
of the oaks along Bennett Street. The sound of the motor faded
gradually, and was replaced by the shush of winds in the myrtles and oleanders along the water's edge.

He was gone. I sat by the window a long time looking
down the line of trees, but that was all I saw. The oaks under
the moon. The street disappearing.

13

*I*n the end, what I saw was a girl waiting in a car. I saw it mentally, clear and in 3-D. Girl in a car.

At the same time I felt it. The car heater was on, yet some cold was seeping through the loose rubber at the top of the window, so there was the smothery feeling of heat pumping vigorously out of the vent, cut now and then by a paper-thin sheet of cold. There was a hot and dusty smell, and a sweet smell, too, not the sweetness of flowers, not food, not quite animals. . . . I had once smelled pigs, and this was not pigs, but something in the same category, sweeter and sadder than pigs. It was also—I concentrated—soapy. Yes. The girl in the car had a baby in her lap. Heat had stunned the baby into partial sleep; its eyes were half-shut. It smelled like a well-washed piglet, which is, I guess, the human smell.

Phoebe was the baby and I was the girl in the car. I both saw and was the girl. I was waiting while Billy, who had said, "Wait in the car," climbed the small hill to the hospital. We had had a talk on the way over, our first private talk in two weeks, and he had told me what I did not need to be told: that Rae had changed her mind. He could stay. "Great," I said. "I'm glad."

But he looked worried.

"I'm not going to tell her," I said, "if you're worried about that."

"I'm worried about you, Lucille."

"What, my well-being?"

"Well, yes."

"I'm fine. I'm getting a job at the library full-time until January, and then I'm starting school. I'm fine."

"I know you'll do all that. I just—I hate to think that I, somehow, harmed you—you've been so quiet, and I just wondered—"

"I've been quiet! You've been quiet. You left the room every time I came in."

"I had to. It was crazy, what we did. We let ourselves go crazy for a while, you know? I had to straighten myself out and let you get straightened out. Now we're on solid ground, we can think better, we can see clearly. Under other circumstances, everything could have been different, but there's Rae, there's the baby . . . it's impossible. You see that. When I think about it—what might have happened—anyway, we are lucky. We got out unscathed. We can go back to how we were before, and everything is pretty much okay, as far as I can tell, with Rae. But you. I don't know how you will be affected, that's what worries me. You are so . . . goddamned impressionable. You don't forget things."

"I forget everything."

"You've forgotten—"

"I have forgotten it all."

"You promise?"

I promised him that I had forgotten what we did. He looked relieved. We were on our way to get Rae and take her home, and I had Phoebe in my lap. The hospital was just off the Interstate; we exited and spiralled down the ramp, and I held Phoebe tight, and he went in for Rae.

Waiting, I felt entirely simple, that is, all of a piece, one-parted. A month earlier, I had considered myself complicated, tangled as hopelessly as someone can get in the course of a young life. But now, here I was, period. A girl. I felt an unplanned sigh of relief escape my lungs from way down deep, and Phoebe stirred in my lap. Maybe we had both been briefly asleep. Sleep can strike in a flash and be gone before you even close your eyes, a millisecond of sleep. I knew not much time had passed. Billy was still climbing the hill.

I had thought that love might leave its mark the way thinking puts new wrinkles on your brain. Love is supposed to deepen and complicate a person. But all this troubled love I had been through, not just with the man but with them all, had in a way not even touched me. You could even say that it had missed me. To my surprise, I was nothing but myself, I was simple and . . . unscathed, yes. But I would not forget.

The hospital was low and gray, on a rise of unnaturally green grass. Maybe they thought these patients might get cheered up by green grass, but to me it was depressing, a chemically elicited green. I preferred the gray sky, the gray river and brown marsh behind the building. It hardly looked like a place where Rae could have been made better; it looked like the regional office of an insurance company. In olden days, places like this were hidden in the country so the people could be helped along by nature. They had wooden lawn chairs and afghans and a view of the Smokies.

My feet were as neatly and solidly placed on the floor as the feet of a paraplegic. I could not make the toes move inside the shoes, and that worried me. I couldn't make the heels rise from the floor. Then Phoebe kicked one of my thighs, and though she was only three weeks old she had a powerful kick. My thigh sent out stars of pain so sharp and distinct they were nearly visible, like pain in a cartoon strip, a sparkler of pain. That's what was wrong. My legs had gone to sleep, their blood supply cut off by Phoebe's weight. I hoisted her up and the blood rushed in again.

I watched a line of puffball clouds that hung low and

changed shape but did not move on. I saw Phoebe's future. Trouble in school, for sure. Teachers writing notes: "Phoebe is not considerate of the needs of others"; "Phoebe is head-strong and uncooperative"; "Erratic work habits." Also trouble at home: doors slamming, tears, sulking; a long and bitter adolescence. But with luck she would be the kind of girl who gives herself away to ballet or horses or some boy, maybe even to a religious cult, goes deep into that love and then comes back. Phoebe. I kissed her chin and neck.

On the other side of the parking lot, up the green hill, the glass door opened. A nurse in white held it while Billy and Rae came through. Rae was thinner. Somebody had done her hair wrong. Otherwise she looked good. She walked with a sure step, touching his elbow but not leaning on him. She looked cured.

"Here she comes," I said to Phoebe.

I held the baby up to the window for Rae to see. I waved the baby's hand.

She ran down the hill to us, leaving Billy behind. He watched, walking slowly with his hands in his pockets; then he took them out and folded his arms across his chest, then unfolded them and put his hands back in his pockets. I see him that way now, I see him walking to the car, worried, trying already to forget me, and maybe already succeeding. I don't know. It is possible to forget anything. It is also possible to remember everything, which is what I try to do.

Now I ride into old Mount Pleasant, with Phoebe in a molded plastic seat on the back of the bike, and we are silent all the way; she leans with the curves and watches the trees pass overhead; and there is our house at the end of the road, prominent now with a triple coat of new white paint, bushes chopped back, yard sprigged with zoysia. The new owners have parked sleek automobiles in the recently paved driveway.

"You were born here," I tell her, stopping to let her see.

The place looks eligible for a feature article in *Southern Living,* and I am as happy for it as I would be for a friend who has met with sudden success after hard times; its good fortune relieves me. We sold it furnished, and I worried briefly about the fate of my pie safe and barber chair and bed; I didn't want to keep them, but I didn't want them to be thrown out. Luckily the lady of the house remodeled in the country look, with calico curtains and straw brooms and stuffed-cat doorstops, and my furniture fit right in. And though I once believed I could not live without that house, the ease with which I gave it up was almost frightening. I miss it now only on occasion, when I smell an old smell or hear the wind in the screens in Mother's new cinderblock house, and I tell myself it is the "Old House" feeling that is giving me goose bumps.

I like all the new places we have settled into: Rae and Billy and Phoebe in a carriage house on Legare Street; me and Mother in the replica of her original dream house, built for her by Sam Poole out in the country, in a field, behind pines; Pop and Vera in the wavy-shingled bungalow with the stork and the goose. Rhody and Evelyn found an apartment, once Rhody landed a reservations-clerk position in the new convention center, a perfect place to study human foibles, she says; and Wayne emptied the contents of his Ram Charger into a dormitory room at the college. Our family is not what it was, but we are all gravitating back into family lives of one sort and another; it is a drift that people cannot seem to help, in spite of lessons learned the hard way. Mrs. Frobiness has married a golf pro; Sharon has married a lawyer. I think often of the ancient times, long before Latin, when words were new and had no connotations. Pure words stood for single things: "Family" meant people in a house together. But that was in a language so far back that all its words are gone, a language we can only imagine.

"I don't think I will marry," I say out loud to Phoebe, who is kicking her heavy white shoes into my thighs. "I'm not afraid to live alone." But I am honest with Phoebe, at least for the time being, and I say, "But who knows what will happen? We'll have to wait and see."

What I want her to know is the strength and fragility of things, the love and the luck hidden together in the world. How to say so is hard. We ride farther and farther to get a view; we forget more and more what ought to be remembered. But she is like me, and she will know.